THE LOVE OF MY YOUTH

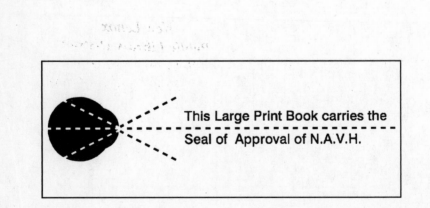

This Large Print Book carries the
Seal of Approval of N.A.V.H.

THE LOVE OF MY YOUTH

MARY GORDON

THORNDIKE PRESS
A part of Gale, Cengage Learning

New Lenox
Public Library District
120 Veterans Parkway
New Lenox, Illinois 60451

GALE
CENGAGE Learning

Detroit • New York • San Francisco • New Haven, Conn • Waterville, Maine • London

GALE
CENGAGE Learning

Copyright © 2011 by Mary Gordon.
Thorndike Press, a part of Gale, Cengage Learning.

ALL RIGHTS RESERVED
This is a work of fiction. Names, characters, places, and incidents either are the product of the author's imagination or are used fictitiously. Any resemblance to actual persons, living or dead, events, or locales is entirely coincidental.
Thorndike Press® Large Print Basic.
The text of this Large Print edition is unabridged.
Other aspects of the book may vary from the original edition.
Set in 16 pt. Plantin.

LIBRARY OF CONGRESS CATALOGING-IN-PUBLICATION DATA

Gordon, Mary, 1949–
    The love of my youth / by Mary Gordon.
      p. cm. — (Thorndike Press large print basic)
    ISBN-13: 978-1-4104-3766-2 (hardcover)
    ISBN-10: 1-4104-3766-3 (hardcover)
    1. First loves—Fiction. 2. Middle-aged persons—Fiction. 3. Rome (Italy)—Fiction. 4. Large type books. I. Title.
    PS3557.O669L68 2011b
    813'.54—dc22   2011008966

Published in 2011 by arrangement with Pantheon Books, a division of Random House, Inc.

3 1984 00295 7007

120 Veterans Parkway
New Lenox, Illinois 60451

Printed in the United States of America
1 2 3 4 5 6 7 15 14 13 12 11

For Penny Ferrer

We have come this far
This is given to us, to touch
each other in this way.
— Rainer Maria Rilke,
from the Second Duino Elegy

ACKNOWLEDGMENTS

I would like to thank Gail Archer and Richard Goode for advising me on matters musical. Also I would like to thank everyone who has opened to me the joys of Rome.

My time in Rome was made possible by research funds provided by the Millicent C. McIntosh Chair in English at Barnard College.

OCTOBER 7, 2007

"I hope it won't be strange or awkward. I mean, what seemed strange to me, or would seem strange, is not to do it. Because in a way it is strange, isn't it, really, the two of you in Rome at the same time, the both of you phoning me the same day?"

Irritation bubbles up in Miranda. Had Valerie always been so garrulous? So vague? Had she, Miranda, always found her so annoying — the qualifications, the emendations, laid down, thrown out like straw on a road to muffle the noise of passing carriages when there'd been a death in the house? Where did that come from? Some novel of the nineteenth century. The early twentieth. And now it is the twenty-first, the first decade nearly done for. There's no point in thinking this way, focusing on Valerie's habits of speech and diction. As if that were the point. The point is simply: she must decide whether or not to go.

It has been nearly forty years since she has seen him. Or to be exact — and it is one of the things she values in herself, her ability to be exact — thirty-six years and four months. She saw him last on June 23, 1971. The day had changed her.

Adam tries to remember if he had ever been genuinely fond of Valerie. What he can recall is that, of Miranda's many friends, Valerie was the one who seemed most interested in him. The one who asked him questions and then listened to his answers, who assumed he had a life whose details might be worthy of her attention. 1966, '67, '68, '69, '70, '71. A time when he spent his days trying to determine the perfect fingering, the ideal tempo, for a Beethoven sonata, a Bach partita. A way of spending time that Miranda's friends considered almost criminally beside the point. The point was stopping the war. Stopping racism. Stopping poverty. Diminishing the injustice of the world.

In those days, he couldn't speak to anyone about his pain over the fact that Miranda seemed entirely taken up by the problems of the world. The things that absorbed him no longer captured her attention. Not that he ever wanted to *capture* her attention; her attention was not a bird he was trying to snare, a fish he was netting. For that was what he loved most about Miranda: her mind's speed, but not only her mind, her quickness in everything. Darting, swooping, leaping, thrilling to him, who moved so slowly, whose every gesture was considered. Those who criticized his playing of the piano accused him of being incapable of lightness. She was a bright thing, a shimmering thing, a kingfisher, a dragonfly. Thirty-six years later she would be no longer young. Had she kept her quickness? Her lightness? Which would he have preferred, that she had kept or lost them?

Is that why he's agreed to it, to seeing her after all these years, at this dinner Valerie has arranged? Out of simple curiosity? Along with lacking lightness, he has been charged with lacking curiosity. But perhaps both had always been untrue. That curiosity has in this instance triumphed over shame: this must be a sign of strength. For if his soul is, as he'd learned in Sunday school, a clear vessel that could be blackened by his sins, what he did to Miranda was among the blackest. When he told himself he couldn't have helped it, that he had done the best, the only thing he could have done under the circumstances, the words rang

13

false. He would be tempted to say that to her now, but he would never say it. He is hoping there will be no need. That they will see each other once again, no longer young but healthy, prosperous, intact. That he will see the proof: that he did not destroy her.

She stands before the spotted mirror. A dime-sized pool of expensive moisturizer — rose scented, ordered especially from a Romanian cosmetician in New York — spreads in the heat of her palm. Miranda wonders what Adam looks like. She tries on a long black skirt, throws it impatiently on the bed, then Nile green silk pants with wide legs. She tries on the black skirt again. Then a violet knit top, which she rejects because it emphasizes her breasts. Once a vexation to her on account of their small-ness, her breasts had done all right with age. She's glad he won't be seeing her naked. Or in a bathing suit. Well, she is nearly sixty now, and her body shows the marks of bear-ing two strong healthy sons. Her legs, which, he had said, caused him a desire that was painful in its intensity when he saw them in her first miniskirt — September 1965 — but which she'd always thought too thick, too straight, these had gone flabby. She's tried — swimming, running, yoga —

but nothing really helps. Most of the time she doesn't think of it, she doesn't really care. It's one of the benefits of age: such things have lost their power to scald.

She's blonde now; he would not be accustomed to thinking of her as a blonde, and her hair is short, boyish. In the time they knew each other her hair had hung down her back at one point almost to her waist. Her hair was brown then, a light brown; he'd called it honey colored. She'd parted it in the middle or braided it into a single plait. Then she remembers: he did see her, briefly, with boyish hair. She doesn't like to think about that time.

She looks at the lines around her eyes, her mouth. Her face has not ceased to please her, but it could never be the face that he had loved.

He has read about her. An article he found in a doctor's office. "Does Your Office Make You Sick?" Sick buildings. She is an epidemiologist specializing in environmental threats. Her subspecialty: molds.

He thought that such work seemed ill suited to her. Quiet, painstaking work. Requiring patience, which she'd always lacked. But then he remembered: it was only with people that she was impatient. With the physical world, she held her quickness in check; she could spend hours looking, sorting.

He wonders how she does her work. Does she go around old buildings, masked, accompanied by young acolytes collecting things in closed containers, tiny bits of plaster prized from the walls with tweezers? He can imagine her sitting at a microscope, one eye glued to a lens, silent, looking. Or perhaps no one uses microscopes anymore. He knows nothing. Valerie told him — he was grateful that he didn't have to ask — that she is married. A doctor, an Israeli; he is, Valerie said, something important in the California Department of Public Health. He learned this only days ago. Before that, if anyone asked, he wouldn't have been able to answer the question, *What has become of her?*

She would know nothing of what has become of him. She would never have read anything about him; he has done nothing that would have placed his name before the public. A music teacher in a private school. Director of the chorus. One day, he might be known as the father of his daughter, if she continues her early promise on the violin. But up to now, it would be accurate to say he's done nothing worthy of note.

16

■ ■ ■ ■

Miranda has heard something, vaguely, some tragedy about Adam's wife. A suicide. She was not, to her shame, sorry. She would not ask details of Valerie. Even to say the woman's name, even after all these years, would be an offense against her pride, and this, too, had seemed to her excessive. But it was an impulse she could not give up.

Bitterness.

Pride.

Grievance.

Of course it would be better to be free of them. Of course.

Ridiculous to feel it still all these years later. A sense of betrayal. A sense of abandonment. Two-thirds of her life. Sixty-six and two-thirds percent. She had had a thorough training in statistics; numbers are her friend, they have often made her point, they've told the truth, they've uncovered poisonous equivocations. How many years has it been since she'd even thought of Adam? And — what was her name. HER. She looks in the mirror and castigates herself for her own falseness, a falseness all the more ridiculous because it is for no one's benefit but her

17

own. She would never forget the name. That name. Beverly. Bev.

She tries the black skirt on again. Perhaps the white shirt would make her face too pale. Above all she must appear to have, over the years, flourished. A rose-pink camisole, then, and a jacket: small pink and white flowers against a background of black silk. Yes, that's right. As a young woman she would never have worn pink, disliking what the shade suggested: weakness, girlishness. But she has grown to like pink. No one, she is certain now, would think of her as weak. Or take her for a girl.

Adam stands before the mirror that attaches to the front of his *armadio,* a looming and reproachful piece, reminding him of its glorious pedigree, hinting reproachfully of his current status (American and not wellborn), an interloper, taking the place of his betters because of Yankee dollars and the slow steady erosion of the values of the lovely past. The people who own the apartment can only afford to keep it because they rent it out most of the year. They live somewhere cheaper. Adam had asked Valerie not to tell him the details.

He moves closer to the mirror so that he

can focus, not on his body, but on his thinning hair. No one could say that he was going bald — he is grateful for that — but his
hair has lost its luxuriance and, once jet
black, is gray now, and he keeps it cropped
short to conceal the diminishment (yes, he's
admitted to himself it is a vanity, this effort
at concealment). When he saw her last, his
hair came down to his shoulders. It curled
— his aunts would say, "Those curls are
wasted on a boy. What I wouldn't give to
have them." At least he isn't so ridiculous
as to wear a ponytail at his age, as some of
his colleagues do, to the mockery of the
more hostile, or more fashion-conscious,
students. He can only imagine the contempt
Miranda would have for men who wear
ponytails. Even after all these years he is
certain of it. And, feeling himself enlarged
by the comparison that he has just invented,
he relaxes about his hair.

Turning from the mirror, he glances at his
hands. Nails round, cut short. Pianist's
hands. He has not achieved fame, success,
even, but he has not given over his calling.
She had loved his hands. She would kiss his
fingers and turn his hands over one at a
time, and kiss the palms. Her lips, moist,
their touch preceded by a warm moist
breath (he had found it quite unbearably

19

arousing). "My darling love, my genius boy. What joy you bring with these wonderful hands. You make beautiful music. You make beautiful love. I hope to see your hands the last thing before I close my eyes in death."

She was capable of speaking ridiculously like that. She was fifteen, sixteen, seventeen years old. She felt free always to overstate, to shed tears. To use terms that were too large: "genius," "love," "death." He had a perfectly ordinary pair of hands. He was, for a serious pianist, only moderately gifted. As for his skill at lovemaking: there was no skill, no art . . . no notion that there was a better way. Or a worse. They were only two young people, ordinary in their youth, their ardor.

It was easier when he thought like that. But it was not the truth, and he would not dishonor the past, the two of them as young, by such a dismissal. In their innocence, in their belief in life and in each other, in the clarity of their desire that had no residue of punishment or will to humiliate or dominate or shame, they had been a thing of beauty. Valuable. Not ever, would he betray that. His youth. Their youth. She was the love of his youth. He is no longer young. And she, too, has lost youth. But he will not betray it.

He remembers dancing with Miranda for

the first time. It was near Thanksgiving; he had not yet asked her out. Someone had a party in a basement, and although the air outside was taking on a chill, the air in the dark basement was thick with the sense of intense exertion and young lust, hanging like a curtain along with the residual smell of the family beer. He felt about to burst, burst into flame, with longing, longing quick as a flame spreading over a dry ground. A flame he could never imagine extinguishing, never going out. He remembered her writing down a word first because she liked it, second because she wanted to do well on her SATs. "Fulvous," the word was.

No one at the party dreamed of doing more than kissing. Or perhaps the more adventurous might try touching a girl's breasts. In six months, when many of them turned sixteen and the times they were a-changing, heated discussions among the girls would be the norm: how far could you let him go, after how long.

The first night when he danced with Miranda, holding her, he put his mouth against her hair and inhaled the exacting innocence of her shampoo. Clean, maddening. He did feel driven mad with desire, with shame, certain she could not be feeling anything like what he was feeling. When they were dancing, she lifted her chin so that a kiss would happen. It did not. He was too afraid.

Forty years later, he feels the clutch of gratitude. Never in Miranda was there the slightest hint, not the smallest suggestion, that he, male, was monstrous and she, female, shocked, pure. They shared ardor. It was she who suggested they become lovers. They were sixteen years old. Daring then. Now? So commonplace as to be unworthy of mention. They were sitting by the river and she said, "Adam, you need to know something. I want everything that you want, maybe more, maybe worse." Was it possible that her skin was always warm, even in winter, as if she carried with her always some hint of early June? So he could leave behind the young man's shame, like a coat he had grown out of. But not the young man's desperation. Almost impossible to recall that desperation now. The urgency of a boy's arousal. Now, at nearly sixty, he sometimes has to coax himself to be aroused by a lovely girl. And married sex? It satisfies, like a good meal, a fine painting. But desperation? Madness? Not now, never. He had asked his doctor for Viagra.

Miranda need never know that.

He turns the heavy archaic key with the gold fob shaped like a pinecone. He walks down to the Via della Reginella, a narrow street between the Piazza Mattei and the Ghetto, his hands in his pockets, weighed down by the heavy key, and lets his right hand travel over its complex indentations, the overornamented fob.

He has left the flat too early. He plans a route that in its indirectness will consume the extra time. He walks half a block in the wrong direction to the Fountain of the Tortoises, four elegant flirtatious boys, flaunting their nearly childish sex, playing with their near girlishness, arranging, seductively, the unserious angles of their limbs. As a boy he was, he knows, never elegant, and never dared to be flirtatious. If it weren't for Miranda he might never have been a boy. Only a musician. Nothing like these marble creatures offering sex as if it were a perfectly good but unimportant joke.

He turns and walks again up the street where he and his daughter live; they've lived there for two weeks and will for another three months. She is here to study at the Conservatorio Santa Cecilia, with Lorenzo

Perrotti, a master teacher of the violin. She has won a competition: coveted, worried over, prepared for with obsessive intensity and discipline. She has her chance.

The street, usually densely inhabited with work and domesticity, seems null on this Sunday afternoon. He reads the signs: the herbalist is offering consultations, free from a maharishi, assuring you that L'EQUILIBRIO E LA CHIAVE PER UN BUONA SALUTE. Next door, the furniture repairman's shop is dark, and dark, too, is the shop he never understands, Il Museo di Libro, selling pictures from people's family albums for five euros apiece. On the pavement outside the store is a sign, the words written, in a mishmash of French and English, in blue marker on a white plastic board, FIGURATION, EXPERIMENTALISM, ART PHOTOS, PHOTO JOURNALISM, CINEMA, MUSIC, FASHION, ARCHITECTURE, NUDES, GREAT PHOTOGRAPHERS, VINTAGE LATER PRINTS, LIFE LOST ARCHIVES, AMATEURS, ANONYMES, AND AUTRES IMAGES.

He passes through the Ghetto, signs in Hebrew, and thinks always of those taken away to their death. He passes the synagogue, its light extravagant façade, its palms and ground-glass roof suggesting a leisurely nineteenth-century urban civilization, a suggestion that must be quickly given up at the sight of patrolling policemen, armed with machine guns. He crosses the Lungotevere, never still, with never even the slightest possibility of Sabbath. He does this to get the benefits of the plane trees' shade: so un-American, he thinks, these trees, with their wide flat leaves, yellowing now, their high limbs seeming as if they had always found their shape in relation to these bridges, streets, and buildings. The Tiber is a slow jade snake, largely untrafficked, unlike the rivers of other great cities: the Hudson, the Thames, the Seine.

He steps onto the Ponte Garibaldi. His eye is caught by a strange knot of inexplicable color. The river rushes into a man-made waterfall. A vortex. Plastic bottles, trapped, bob up and down in the whirlpool but do not progress downstream, appearing to be tied to something although he knows that they are not. They bob and sink, they sparkle, they wink; they are a clutch of throwaway jewels, delightful but unvaluable, emerald, ruby, sapphire. Yet what are they really? Containers for sweet drinks or carbonated water. Where did they come from? Where do they go? Does someone come and collect them every night, using a special net, a long string bag at the end of a pole or stick? It cannot be a good thing, plastic bottles in the river. It must be a sign of wastefulness, of carelessness, a malign use of resources. They will collect somewhere, do harm, perhaps to innocent animals or birds. But he allows himself to be charmed by them. It is early October, but the sun falls straight and purposeful, hot on his shoulders as an August morning in Connecticut. He walks to the center of the bridge. If he turns to the right, he sees the distant specter of Saint Peter's, which he has never liked, standing as it does for everything he turns his mind against, that is, he knows quite well, the reality of Rome. Power: imperial, ecclesial. Finished now.

Turning to the left, he sees the older campanile of Santa Maria in Cosmedin, gentler, undemanding. And as if made of another substance, or an entry from another dream, the mountains, covered, even now in snow. What mountains are they? This is the kind of thing he never knows, that Miranda always knew. But what he wants to look at is not the dome of Saint Peter's or the tower of Santa Maria in Cosmedin or the snow-covered hills. He wants to be looking at the winking bottles: the color, the silly joyful purposeless activity, the vivid game of catching sun. And it seems to him possible in the improbableness of its heat, its lavishness, its wrongheaded generosity, to allow himself to give up the responsibility, the habit of northern judgment, and to enjoy the spectacle of the playful bobbing plastic bottles, the colorful unnatural blues and greens — the temporary pleasure of what, if it must be given its proper name, would be called: detritus in a vortex. But why, he asks himself, why think of what is proper? Why invoke the word "propriety"? Not in this light. Not right now.

Valerie has given Miranda instructions on how to get from her apartment on the elegant Via Margutta, just off Piazza del Popolo, to Valerie's place across the Tiber in Trastevere. The streets seem particularly empty to her, like empty aquaria, as if they were not just uninhabited, but drained. According to Valerie, the journey will be easy: you take an electric bus on the Corso, which leaves you at Largo Argentina, where you get a tram. But tickets must be purchased at a newspaper kiosk, and the one in Miranda's neighborhood was all out of tickets. It was late Saturday night when she had got around to buying them, and today, Sunday, the kiosks are all shuttered. It is one of the times she thinks perhaps it was a mistake to rent an apartment instead of staying at a hotel; in a hotel, the concierge would be of help, telling her where to get bus tickets on a Sunday, perhaps even providing them. But aside from Valerie, there is no one in Rome she knows. The woman who owns her apartment lives in London. Well, there is someone else in Rome she knows. Adam. But that is of no use to her, no use at all.

She will take a cab.

It was Valerie who had found her the apartment, Valerie with whom, somehow, she was still in touch, even though there were people she'd known in college whom she'd been much closer to, much fonder of, who interested her much more. But that was the way with people like Valerie. The energetic, organized ones who sent out Christmas letters and compiled alumnae e-mail lists. And Valerie was goodhearted, oceanically accepting of everyone, and endlessly persistent, so it would have taken a deliberate and quite cruel effort of will to cut her out of your life. And besides, what she had done was not unadmirable. She'd lived in Rome for thirty years. After traveling around, earning her living everywhere and nowhere as a waitress or a nanny or singing in the subway, she met Giancarlo, a painter. Now she made a living brokering apartments for traveling Americans; she had arranged flats for both Adam and Miranda. Valerie and Giancarlo lived with his mother in an apartment overlooking the Tiber. They had not had children.

And it was Valerie who, either not noticing that she was doing something difficult or else knowing perfectly well that it was difficult, had told her about the suicide of Adam's wife. That he had married again. And most recently, discussed with truly nauseating enthusiasm, his eighteen-year-old daughter, the reason for his being in Rome. She had most likely told Adam about Miranda's life: that she had married Yonatan, although probably she had no idea of what Yonatan really did in the California Department of Public Health: that he supervised the unit that dealt with epidemiological crises, that they lived in Berkeley, that she had two sons, twenty-five and twenty-three. That she was here without her husband because, although they'd intended to stay in Rome together after her conference, his mother had had a stroke and he was back in California with her, arranging for her care.

She has traveled farther, by cab rather than

by foot, but Miranda arrives first. The building where Valerie lives is imposing, monumental; it suggests nothing domestic. It's the kind of place where ancient lawyers, dressed archaically and charging exorbitantly for out-of-date advice, might offer you sherry when you came to prepare your will. How, Miranda wonders, could anyone think of this as home? She presses the brass button next to the name Rinaldi and hears Valerie's voice, expectant, cheerful, and her heart sinks. I have made a terrible mistake, she thinks, I can run away now and I will be free, and no one will know about it but Valerie, and if I like I need never speak to her in my life again. But then she thinks: I have to give her back the key to the flat. She will arrange for the return of my security deposit. I have no choice.

And besides, Miranda has always prided herself on her courage in facing up to things, and after all, she thinks, at my age it's important that there not be people I feel incapable of seeing. Adam had hurt her badly. Was it wrong to say he betrayed her? She is suspicious of words like that now, overlarge words she once lived by, words by which her years with Adam had been marked. She feels tender, merciful toward her young self, for decisions made in good faith that turned out badly. When you are young, she thinks, you never believe that courage isn't enough. That the imaginative, original decision isn't always the right one.

She enters the cold marble hallway. A glassed-in booth, military looking, as if a man in a police uniform should be occupying it, takes up a third of the vestibule. But it is empty.

Miranda enters the left of the two elevators. Valerie's instructions on how to get to her apartment once you were in the building were precise but complicated, and Miranda sees now that both the precision and the complications had been necessary. She enters the elevator, a small brass cage inside a box of glass, and presses the button for the third floor. And the second she arrives Valerie opens the gate, Valerie, whom she hasn't seen in fifteen years, blonde, as she is blonde, but very thin as Miranda knows she is not, in a short, wool loden skirt and brown alligator pumps, the heels so high Miranda can't imagine walking in them, a fawn-colored silk shirt, a beautifully tied scarf that seems to melt into different shades, different interpretations of red or rust. I could never tie a scarf like that, Miranda thinks. Never in my life. She doesn't know if this makes her feel superior in relation to Valerie (I don't have time for that kind of thing) or deficient (I will always look, beside you, inexpert).

"Well, if you're not a sight for sore eyes," Valerie says.

Miranda remembers that Valerie's from Omaha. "How do you say that in Italian?" she asks.

"You're not here to be educated, you're here to enjoy yourself. Come in, come in, we're thrilled to have you."

Miranda had expected formal rooms, more imposing. Larger, darker furniture, less natural light. But the apartment is as bright as outdoors when she passes through the hall. There seem to be two living rooms abutting each other, both overcrowded with many small upholstered chairs, half rose-colored brocade, half striped white and peacock blue. Every surface is covered with photographs, most in silver frames, or small objects. She sees a bronze tortoise, the size of a walnut, a ceramic cupid she could fit easily into the palm of her hand and hide in the pocket of her skirt. One table, whose top is brass, is completely devoted to toy soldiers. She thinks perhaps it is the army of Napoleon, and she believes, though she can't say why, that the soldiers have been recently played with. Each living room opens to a terrace, and beyond the balcony she sees the high hill she knows is the Janiculum, which she intends one day (not soon) to climb.

Seated in one of the rose-colored chairs is Giancarlo, Valerie's husband, who has not aged in fifteen years. His hair is still dark; his face, covered by a fashionable stubble, seems untouched by middle age. He rises, almost reluctantly, as if he'd rather be sitting, and he kisses Miranda on both cheeks. She sees that between the third and fourth fingers of his right hand he is holding one of Napoleon's soldiers.

Not rising, her bird face taken up entirely by dark glasses, is Giancarlo's mother who, directionlessly, indicating her lack of inclination or perhaps it is her failing sight, extends a clawlike but beautifully manicured hand. On the fourth finger of her hand there are three rings: a gold wedding band, a circle of diamonds, an emerald baguette. Miranda is glad the woman can't see her nails; she never gets a manicure; she clips her nails in the tub: short, round, and serviceable.

Giancarlo asks if his mother is comfortable. She says nothing. Valerie presents *prosecco.* The doorbell rings and Miranda is sick with fear. It is too late, and she knows

33

she is wrong to be here. *Let the past go,* her husband would have said, if she'd asked him if she should do it. *Let it go unless you know that it can help you.*

Why did she think that seeing Adam could do her a blessed thing but harm?

Strange to use the phrase, she thinks. A blessed thing. What's the opposite of "blessed"?

"Cursed."

No, that's too strong.

Perhaps, "difficult."

But because a thing was difficult, it did not mean it shouldn't be attempted. Fear must be got past.

She is afraid now.

It is ridiculous.

She'd gone years without thinking of him. Yonatan and her children don't know about him. If she'd mentioned his name, they'd have said, *Who?*

And yet he had been for some years the most important person in her life.

But their question would be right. *Who?* It is her question now as well. Perhaps the answer would be: *The love of my youth.* But where, she wonders, should the accent fall? On which word? "Love"? Meaning both an experience and a person. Love: she has

34

loved others, loved again. But he had been her first love. And he had gone on with his life after they were no longer in each other's lives. But if you put the accent on youth, that, certainly, was gone. Gone for good.

She has no idea whom she'll be meeting now the door opens and it has become too late.

She hears his voice as he walks down the hall with Valerie. The voices of the dead. She thinks of what happened when her friend Richard died and she called his number by mistake and heard his voice on his answering machine. She was first horrified. Then comforted. She hung up and called again and then again. As if she could, by doing this, keep him with her.

But Adam hadn't died. And yes, it is a voice she knew, a voice she remembers, and the sound of it stirs her, lights a match between her ribs, the two of them located below her breastbone, to the right of what she knows to be her heart. Something has kindled. A sharp-edged spot of heat, painful but not unbearable.

She would not have known him.

They are trying to compose their faces so that they are blanks. Giancarlo half rises from his chair; Adam comes toward him, and shakes his hand.

"So, here we all are," Valerie says.

"Valerie, that is a stupid thing to say," Giancarlo's mother hisses. "As if we were not here. Or could not be here if we are here."

Miranda knew that what Valerie said was stupid, but the old woman's saying it is hateful, and it makes her feel hateful for sharing the thought. For it isn't true, what the old lady said, at least not completely. They are here. But they could quite easily not be.

"You're blonde," he says, holding his hand out to her.

"Among other things," she says. So her first words to him are harsh. Is it that she wants to strike a blow? It's not a good beginning. But no beginning would have been good.

Adam blushes. She remembers now how easily he colored. It was meant to be genetic, she had learned. There was no helping it; it was like perfect pitch, which he had also been born with. He hated it, that because he blushed so easily his inner life was readily visible. She had suffered with him for it. She had loved him for it, too.

36

■ ■ ■ ■

He sees that she has kept her freshness. She has not diminished. She is lovely still. He wonders if she thinks him old. If she's surprised that he's no longer thin. What I said was stupid, he thinks, and he hates the loop of time that will not allow him to unsay.

Valerie hands him *prosecco.*

The old lady crosses her birdy legs.

"We are only the five of us," she says, "and only I am a stranger to you two. Please understand that I have been apprised of everything in your past. Also understand that I was educated in America. Rosemary Hall. Vassar. You read a novel called *The Group* by Mary McCarthy? I was there then. A stupid novel, still it got the flavor of the times. I mean to say that I believe, above all, in plain speech. It is a waste of time pretending this is an ordinary evening. You should learn about one another's lives, what has happened to you. I mean, of course, Adam and Miranda. Because to Valerie and Giancarlo nothing of importance has happened, or will happen. Then you will see if you have interest in knowing each other once again."

Her distressingly thin legs, her feet, fish flat in canvas shoes, her hands with their resplendent rings, her eyes, invisible behind dark glasses, further hidden by a sun shade — something Miranda had seen women wearing in America when they play tennis — render this woman if not un-, then extra-human. Oracular. Imperious. Someone to be obeyed.

"To break the ice, as you Americans say, I will tell you about my life. It has been very interesting to anyone intelligent enough to be interested in what really happened to the world in the twentieth century. You understand that I am ninety-five years old, but my mind is perfect. I prefer that my body disintegrate before my mind, and this is happening, but I am ready for that, it is all right.

"I was born just before the First World War, at the end of the Old World. You are Americans, and so history is to you an abstraction."

"Mama, that's a bit of a generalization, wouldn't you say," Giancarlo says, barely audibly. Miranda realizes it's the first word she's heard him say in fifteen years. Giancarlo is very quiet. Reticent son of a voluble mother. Perhaps that's why he married Valerie. For her chatter. For some reason she knows the Italian word for chatter. *Chiacchiere.* A good onomatopoeia. Valerie's chattering, the mother's chattering, are like a thorny maze she must walk through, abrading her skin, catching the edges of her clothing. But where must she get through to? To an understanding of what she is to do. With Adam.

He is still beautiful, she thinks. He is the first man of whom I used the word "beautiful." Still apt.

Adam looks at her, ascertaining the shape of her strong legs beneath the silk of her long skirt. I always thought she was stronger than I, he thinks, but that last day when she wept and wept without making a sound, I thought I'd broken her heart. I could do nothing else. No other path was open to me. I believed that at the time. What good can it do to question it now? I should not have come. But of the mistakes I've made, agreeing to see her again is not a great one. Nothing will come of it, nothing will lead from it. Except, perhaps, the satisfaction of a curiosity. And the reassurance: she was not destroyed. I did not destroy her. Life went on. The harm I did was not so great, was covered over by events. Time. Good fortune. Her own gifts. Her strength.

■ ■ ■ ■

"Only a small mind is afraid of generalization, my son," says Giancarlo's mother, Signora Rinaldi. Miranda realizes she doesn't know her first name. "It's like being afraid to build a house with more than one story. What would Rome be if people had been afraid of gestures that might seen too large, that took in what might at first appear too much."

No one has the courage, the will, the impulse, the energy, to contradict her. For one thing, she is just too old.

At the same moment, Adam and Miranda grasp the tone of Valerie's life. Between them stretches out a cord of simultaneous understanding. They are attached by a shared sympathy. For Valerie, the victim of a woman who never once considered that her gestures might be overlarge, who sees destruction as inevitable, unworthy of comment, certainly of surprise.

"And so, as I was saying, before I was interrupted by my son making a point beside the point, after the war, the first war, I mean, with Italy in disarray, my father, who was a physician, he treated many of Rome's first families, he was a very great ophthalmologist, my father decided I should go to America for my education. I came back home in 1932. Mussolini had come to power. I was twenty years old. Still something of a flapper. Famous for my legs."

She crosses and uncrosses her legs, thinking them, perhaps, still fetching. But Miranda can only be worried by them; to her they suggest nothing but potential fractures.

"I married Giancarlo's father the next year. He was a press attaché for Mussolini. Very idealistic. He'd been a poor boy, and he saw how Mussolini had made his life better. People like to forget how bad most people's lives were before Fascism, how badly things were run, and how much better it was for Italy to have a strong leader. You know, Mussolini came to power as a socialist."

Miranda feels a half-dollar-sized pain in the back of her skull. She knows that it is rage. She believes in the concept of evil, though not being metaphysically inclined in the least, she does not know or feel the impulse to name its source. But the old woman, with her hooded eyes, her flat feet in their canvas shoes, her blade-thin crossed ankles, seems to her, if not evil, at least to be speaking evil words.

Valerie is passing crackers with a thin layer of pâté on each, and what Adam thinks must be capers, although they are the size of large pearls, bigger than any capers he has ever seen. Their bitterness is pleasing, and cuts satisfyingly through the meaty richness of the pâté, the dryness of the crackers. He wonders if, after all these years, Miranda will have changed enough to be able to keep silence in the face of the old lady's words. If not, she will soon be saying something that will make a disaster of the evening, that will turn the room into a wreck.

Miranda is biting slowly at her cracker. She is saying nothing.

But the old woman wants something, Adam knows. She taps her cane. Valerie brings her a glass of water. Adam knows this is not what she wants; she wants something else. Discord: her thirst for it is much much stronger than her desire for the water that she demands, as if she were signaling a servant, wordlessly. Her spiteful mouth, blind seeming too because of the hooded eyes, is hungry; the dry lips are licked with relish for what she thinks she can make happen soon.

"When the Americans came, my husband was imprisoned. Twice. Once for three

42

months, right here in Regina Coeli prison. Six months here, then nearly a year in the South. It was dreadfully unfair. My husband was punished for doing what he believed to help his country. I moved heaven and earth to have him released. I wrote to the pope. Finally, because of me, or because of my father, who had made the pope's eyeglasses personally, my husband was released."

"And afterward?" Miranda asks, engaged, despite her determination not to be.

"He became a lawyer. He was through with politics."

Adam sees fear flicker in Valerie's eyes. He remembers that the apartment belongs to her mother-in-law. That Giancarlo doesn't have a job. Valerie confessed, just yesterday, that he'd been hospitalized for depression. That she is frightened, because she is in a country where family matters, and her family isn't here. Her eyes are asking him to rescue the situation. But the situation is her fault. Why did she think Miranda and Signora Rinaldi could be in a room together without a good chance of disaster? But it would never have occurred to Valerie that there were people who should not be in the same room.

He knows she is looking to him for rescue, but he can't think of a thing that he might do. What should he talk about? The weather? The new influx of Russian tourists? The weak dollar? The progress of the repairs on the Piazza Navona? His daughter's progress with the violin?

"You are shocked because I don't express shame when speaking of my husband's Fascist past. But I have no shame; I have pride. I have pride because I have understanding. My husband was punished for doing what everyone of his generation did. Now what do you think of all this, Miss Miranda? You see, I know about you and your politics and your past. That you, like so many of the naïfs of your generation, thought you would change the world, poof, like that. And then were shocked that you did not. I know from Valerie that you were political, and the young Adam was going to be a great pianist, and everyone thought you would be together forever and ever but that somehow the differences between art and politics were too great, and here you are now, forty years later, wondering what to say to each other. There is probably more to it, the kind of thing Valerie enjoys keeping from me, I would guess another woman, but we won't go into that. But you see I know about you and your political past, so I can only imagine what you think."

"I don't have an opinion," Miranda says.

"From what I know of you, this is a falsehood. Don't condescend to me because I'm old. I can take your ideas. I'm not afraid of what you have to say."

"I didn't think you were afraid for a minute," Miranda says.

"What did you think, then?"

"That you believe that I don't know enough to have an opinion that's worth anything to you."

"I can just imagine what you're really thinking, what you're afraid to say for fear of making a scene. You think that everyone who was not your idea of a hero should be punished as a criminal. This is an American arrogance spoken by a people who have never had to resort to difficult choices."

There is a sound of breakage, a sound that almost comically expresses what everyone feels. Only gradually, Miranda understands that she has broken her glass by grasping it in the effort not to say what she really means.

"What has happened?" the old lady asks.

Adam is sure she knows, but wants to hear the words. Her lips have disappeared with a spite or pleasure she feels no need to hide.

"Miranda has cut herself," Valerie says, her hands fluttering, as if she'd never seen anything like this before.

"Valerie, Valerie, *che succede,*" Giancarlo shouts, running out of the room. *"Non po sopporla."*

"Niente, caro," Valerie says, running after him to some room whose entrance is invisible.

Adam sees that no one intends to do anything about what has happened to Miranda. He takes his handkerchief and wraps Miranda's fingers. Her fingertips are bleeding, but he sees she isn't severely hurt.

"Take her to the bathroom, she mustn't stain the furniture," the old lady says.

He can hear Giancarlo weeping in the kitchen. *"Non ti preoccupare,"* he hears Valerie saying.

"Valerie, are there Band-Aids in the bathroom?" Adam asks, sticking his head into the room into which she and Giancarlo have disappeared.

She nods and points, holding her husband halfway on her lap.

Adam takes Miranda's hand and leads her into the bathroom. He opens the medicine cabinet, takes out a tube of antiseptic ointment, puts her hand under the water, spreads the ointment, and bandages each of her wounded fingers. He sees that she is crying, and he knows that she hates that she is crying and hates that he sees.

"Let's get out of here," he says.

She nods.

"I'll see Miranda home," he says to Valerie, who nods, still absorbed in her weeping, trembling husband.

"I'm taking Miranda back to her apartment," he says to the old woman, who is holding in her hand a half-eaten cracker.

"Such a shame," she says. "I was looking forward to the evening."

Miranda and Adam don't speak or look at each other in the brass cage of the elevator. Silently, they walk to the massive door leading to the street. It slams behind them like a door in a room constructed for the Inquisition. They press on the outer door. It doesn't open. They press again. Nothing.

Miranda begins to laugh.

"I remember what Valerie said now. In order to open this outer door you first have to press a button outside the inner one."

"So we're here for the rest of our lives?"

"Or until someone comes in."

"Jesus, poor Valerie," he says.

"And here I was imagining her living la dolce vita. And I was irritated by her chirpiness. Now it seems heroic. Is there such a thing as heroic chirpiness?"

"And the mother. Dear God."

"Do you think she's evil? Or just batty."

"We always disagreed about that, whether things were signs of madness or wickedness."

"Which side was I on? I can't remember now."

"I can't either. And now I have no idea which side I'm on."

"If I ring the buzzer, we'll get Valerie's apartment and she can probably buzz us out."

"No need, someone's coming," he says.

A young mother pushing a stroller puts her key into the door. She is model thin and model surly in black jeans, high heels, and a leather bustier. She looks at them impatiently and moves aside to let them out.

"I'll just get a taxi here," she says, lifting her arm.

He takes her arm and lowers it. "No," he says. "I want to talk to you. I want to know about your life."

The touch of his hand on her arm is shocking. She's disturbed by it, yet it would be absurd to show any sort of reaction.

"My life," she says. "My life is fine."

"I'd like to see you at least once more. There are things I'd like to tell you. And to ask. Perhaps we could go for a walk. Where are you staying?"

"Near Piazza del Popolo. The Via Margutta."

Ah, he thinks, so she is wealthier than I. Then he remembers: she always was. He wants to indicate that this is of no importance. So he whistles. "Ritzy," he says, purposely using a joke word to suggest that no one can take money seriously.

"A little too upmarket for my comfort," Miranda says. "You'd think Val would have been able to figure that out."

"It was always remarkable what Val seemed not to be taking in. Perhaps that's how she's got herself into this situation."

"Are we fated to always be the people we were? Always making the same mistakes?"

He assumes she knows this is a question with no answer.

"Where you live is near my daughter's school. I walk her there every morning. She has lessons from ten to three. Are you free in the morning?"

"My meetings begin in the afternoons."

"Well, then, shall we meet at the top of the Pincio at ten tomorrow morning?"

The request alarms her. She'd wanted to see what he looked like; she told herself it would be just a glimpse. But to see him

49

again: that takes things out of the realm of accident, and curiosity and chance. But to refuse: that, almost, suggests that she is frightened of something, that he is important in her present life in a way that he certainly is not.

"Just for a short walk," she says.

He is ridiculously pleased that she's agreed to it.

"A short walk in the Borghese Gardens. Just as long as you like."

"All right," she says, not knowing what it is that she's agreed to.

Monday, October 8

THE PINCIO
"Now We Are Both Orphans"

They both slept badly, and, looking at herself in the bathroom mirror, Miranda is distressed at the toll the sleepless night has taken. She can no longer be unmarked by sleepless nights; bruise-colored pouches form below her eyes; it's impossible that she enjoy the sight of her face. She showers; the hot water helps. She opens the red quilted bag that holds her cosmetics: it is larger than she would ever have predicted, particularly since she prides herself on wearing very little makeup. She wouldn't dream of wearing eye shadow before six, as some people wouldn't dream of taking a drink before sundown. But she has invested in an impressive array of moisturizers and creams to even her skin tone. One claims that it can "disappear those telltale signs." She opens a

51

two-inch-round pot of under-eye cream; it contains aloe, honey, and bee pollen. She knows she's a sucker for invisible cosmetics that claim to be found in nature.

She applies a light peach-toned foundation, a peach-colored lipstick, changes the small silver ear hoops for her pearl studs. She thinks she looks much better. It is important to her that Adam not think she's one of those women who always look worn out.

She doesn't know what she wants him to think, only that it is important that there are some things he doesn't think about her. But what, exactly, does she want from this meeting today? It was one reason for her sleeplessness: she doesn't know what she wants, and this is unlike her. Around three, when the heavy Italian furniture began to seem unreal and menacing, she understood that this is one of the important reasons to see him: only he can give her a particular kind of information that at her age seems crucial. Is she the person that she was?

And of course, there's simple curiosity, not only about him, because her connection to him didn't begin and end with him, it extended to his family. In the years that she was with him, his parents and his sister were important to her. And she knows nothing of what had happened to them in nearly forty years. Certainly, it's natural to want to know. Valerie could give her some idea of what turns Adam's life has taken, but Miranda couldn't expect her to know about Adam's sister, Jo.

It would be very good to know about these people whom, whatever had happened to her ideas of Adam, she had never ceased to be fond of. In his mother's case, to love. This is something anyone would want to do. And they're just going for a walk in the park. "It's not just a walk in the park." That was one of those phrases that people had begun using recently. But it would be just a walk in the park. She has a friend who is a rocket scientist, and he likes to say that people can never say of him, "Well, he's not a rocket scientist," because, in fact, he is.

It is, after all, a park, one of the largest in the world, the Villa Borghese, although the name suggests rather a large stone structure than the green expanse, the great varieties of trees — umbrella pine, plane, ilex, magnolia — and the running children and the strolling lovers. And how, she wonders, can the same word apply to this place and to Yosemite, dedicated to the exclusion of the very civilization this place celebrates. She climbs the stairs from the Piazza del Popolo to the Pincian Hill, the high point that marks the park's beginning.

She looks over the balustrade and sees, written in chalk on the road below, some words that even her inadequate Italian can unlock: E DOPO UN ANNO SIAMO ANCORA QUI A PARLAR D'AMORE. And after a year we are here again to speak of love. "Love," like "park," a word inadequate to all its different meanings. What will she and Adam speak about? What will it have to do with love? She wonders who wrote the words on the dangerous road, where cars come whizzing by, alarming the more timid tourists. She imagines that, whoever they were, they must have been young.

She was young the last time she was here. She hasn't been here for nearly forty years, but she remembers being happy. It made her comfortable, as other parks in great cities, Central Park, the Luxembourg, Hyde or Regent's Park, did not. It seemed somehow more accommodating, presenting more suggestions than demands. Promises. What did it promise? Something open-minded and expansive. Possibilities.

Of the possibilities connected to her seeing Adam, there did not seem to be many risks. They would simply be catching up. They would be exchanging information. They would be taking a walk in the park.

She mentioned it to her husband, but without much emphasis. There was no need, she thought, to make much of it. She would find out about Adam's family. Would she be finding out, in addition, something about herself? That would remain to be seen. She wouldn't think about that now.

Adam's sleeplessness was an intermittently pleasurable mixture of anxiety and relief. The relief made a change in the relation of his body to the world: he feels himself lighter, less weighed down, as if he'd been a hit-and-run driver who had, after years, discovered that the crumpled body he left at the side of the road had been seen to leap and dance. What does he want her to do, or say? What does he want her to say to him? What does he want? He wants to know the shape, the texture, of her life. At the same time, he is afraid of some things he can imagine she might want to say. And he wonders if he is foolish to open himself to the scalding shame that once was the medium in which he lived his days. But what can she say that would be worse than what he's said to himself? Does he want her to say that he has been forgiven, does he want to hear the words "It was so long ago. I never think of it"? That would mean she never thinks of him, and he understands that he doesn't want that.

He says to his daughter, over breakfast, "I'm going to meet a very old friend. I'm eager to find out what's happened to her. Do you realize, Lulu, that the amount of time I haven't seen her is equal to twice the number of years you've been alive?"

"Dad, you love making those kind of calculations," she says, kissing him on the top of his head. "Don't wear that shirt, it makes you look paunchy." Has she intuited something: that he was unusually concerned about how he looked all day? "Luckily, I have my fashion adviser with me," he says, disappearing into the bedroom and presenting himself to her in a light wool rust-colored shirt, looser fitting: a larger size. Then he is gripped by a new anxiety: in meeting Miranda in Rome, has he involved Lucy in a kind of deception, is she a partner in his infidelity? But he's not being unfaithful; he knows that Clare would want him to speak to Miranda; she always worries that he buries too much of the past. He'll tell her about it, of course he will, next time they talk, next Saturday. But there's no need to make a special call to speak about it now.

And he will be very careful not to say anything about his morning to his daughter.

He sees her looking over the balustrade. How young she looks, he thinks, in her black jeans and wheat-colored jacket. He imagines that people would think she is five, even ten, years younger than he.

She takes in the city's expanse. She has not, for many years, lived in a large city. And the two large cities she lived in — Boston and Rome — she lived in with him. She sees that he's uncomfortable — she recognizes, from a span of forty years, the gesture that marks his unease. His hands are in his pockets; she can't hear the accompanying sound, but she knows that he is jingling his change. Well, then, it will be up to her. She will plunge right in with wanting the news of his family. Any beginning will be awkward, uncomfortable, the thing is to make a beginning, and as a beginning, she thinks, this is as good as many, better than most.

She can't bear avoiding saying things that must be said. This is, she knows, her way, a way that those who love and admire her call directness, those who dislike her call brutality. It was always her way, but her marriage to Yonatan has made it her first instinct now.

Seconds after they have said hello she asks him about his mother.

"My mother died eight years ago."

Miranda leans on the stone balustrade, puts her weight on it, presses into it so that the stones abrade her dry palms. She looks over the Roman morning, at Saint Peter's and the other domes whose names she does not know but vows before she leaves she will be able to identify. The horseshoe of the Piazza del Popolo, with the obelisk that she has learned was built by the emperor Hadrian in honor of his lover Antoninus. But what are those terra-cotta-tiled domes? She will find out. Her father's daughter: one of her first lessons: "You must know the names of things."

"I always thought I'd see your mother again. That one day we'd meet, and it would be as it always was."

"She was sad that you never got in touch."

"We had a difficult last meeting."

She will not say what is in her mind: *I wanted her to be on my side, to vilify you, to be with me against you.* But she wouldn't. She said, "But you must understand he is my son. He has only one mother. I can never not be with him. I can never be against him. You want me to be against him,

58

and this I can never do."

Miranda is unwilling to bring up the past, a dark wave that could all too easily drown them. She does not yet know who he is, whom she is with. It is far too soon to know; she has been alone with him only for minutes, if not seconds: time in the elevator, time stuck between the two doors of Valerie's building, time when he hailed her a cab and made this plan: that they would meet for just as long as she liked to walk in the Villa Borghese.

"My mother loved you very much. She was always happy with you. You were the girl she wanted to be."

"Perhaps at first."

"My mother didn't change the way she felt about someone once she decided they were hers. And you were hers. Nothing could change that."

Miranda refuses to begin speaking this way.

"Her death, how was her death? I hope it wasn't difficult."

"A few difficult weeks. Not much pain because Jo, but you wouldn't know this, of course you wouldn't, is a hospice nurse."

"Jo, it makes me happy just to think of her. She was a perfect little girl. Her life? Has it been happy?"

"Yes, I would say she's had a happy life. She's found just the right work for herself. She always knows, she says, that she is doing good. And her husband — well, Phil seems to have trouble holding on to a job. He wanted to be an architect — but, who knows what happened? Once again, it doesn't seem to be the kind of thing we talk about. I mean my family. Her son is a sculptor, very charming, though once again we don't talk about his work. It seems to be all about rubber tires. I think she supports him, too. She was wonderful at the end with my mother."

Miranda thinks, I would love to see Jo again. Jo, whom I entirely, uncomplicatedly loved. Jo, who was fifteen last time I saw her.

An old woman is holding an ice-cream cone to the lips of an old man in a wheelchair. The breeze ruffles the man's white hair. She pats his lips with a light blue cloth handkerchief.

"My mother's mind was clear almost until the end," Adam says. "A few days of derangement, which had, even in their dreadfulness, a comic aspect. Knowing my mother, it's not surprising. When one of the doctors or nurses or helpers would come in the room she'd say, 'Oh, your son plays the piano, too.' "

Miranda doesn't think it's amusing, doesn't even pretend to laugh. She doesn't believe Adam thinks it's funny, but is used to saying it is, or that it has its comic aspects, because this is a way of breaking up the flat glass sheet of death.

"Do you still play the piano?"

"Not much. I'm much more concerned with teaching my students, directing the chorus."

So you have lost a very great deal, she wants to say, but only exhales the single syllable, "Ah."

"And what about your father?" she asks. "He was such a nice man. I don't think I heard him speak more than five sentences, ever. I don't even know his first name."

"He didn't like it, maybe that's why. It was Sal. Salvatore. He died soon after my mother. He just had a heart attack, sitting in front of the television. He died the way he lived, not making a fuss, not causing any problems. I think he had no interest in living after my mother died. It was only about six months."

She doesn't know what he wants her to say to this. Her eye falls on a dog with the body of a golden retriever and the head of a

61

cocker spaniel. She'd like to draw his attention to it, so they could take their minds off sadness, but it seems, she knows, wrong: she doesn't want him to think her unserious, unable to hold dark thoughts. And besides, she remembers: he doesn't like dogs. He'd been bitten by a dog when he was only three. There was a small scar on his right thigh. Was it still there? Were scars one of the things that escaped time? Or had age covered even that mark, that sign of history.

The dog's master whistles; he runs off on his disproportionately long legs.

"I'd heard about your parents' accident," Adam says. "From my mother, of course, who was very saddened by it. She liked your mother. I think they went on seeing each other afterward . . . but I don't know. It's the kind of thing my mother would have kept from me."

"I blamed my father for the accident. I still do. He had no business driving those icy roads."

"Well, we don't know."

"No, I suppose not. But my father and I never came to terms. Not after what happened with my brother."

"I was frightened of your father. I never got over that."

"I think he liked frightening people."

"He didn't frighten you. And I think he liked that, too."

"It's hard for me to credit him with anything. But I guess my powers of observation — which after all is what I do with my life — well, I guess he gave me that. On those walks in the woods. His teaching me the names of trees and birds."

"And Rob, how is he?"

"I'm hardly in touch with my brother now. He's still farming in Manitoba . . . he's become quite bitter, quite isolated. He thinks I'm soft and frivolous, I know it. Like many people who live entirely honorable lives he has no problems being judgmental and openly critical. It makes being with him unpleasant . . . and it's difficult to get there and, well, so many difficult things. I learned from him the pain of being the victim of that kind of righteousness. I like to think it made me less tempted by self-righteousness."

"You'll forgive me if I find the idea of you being soft and frivolous almost hilarious."

"Well, you'd be surprised. And you don't know Rob."

"Did your mother live to see your children?"

"She died when Jeremy was three and

Benjamin eight months. But seeing her with them made me kinder to her, I think. You were kind to my mother. Kinder than I, I think."

"I wouldn't say you were unkind, but you could be impatient."

"Your constant kindness to her gave me leave to be impatient."

"I knew that it annoyed you when I sat and listened to her when she offered me tea at the kitchen table."

"I was bored out of my mind. I thought you were encouraging each other to be boring."

"How you hated being bored! More than anyone I've ever known! You fled from boredom as if you were fleeing from infection."

"The plague of boredom. It does make me feel like I'm about to suffocate. Death by drowning. Death by boredom."

"I never found your mother boring."

"No one ever bored you."

"It's true. I find almost everyone interesting. Perhaps because it always strikes me as quite strange that any of us is alive."

She thinks this is a wonderful thing to have said, and it is the kind of thing people she knows now do not say. She wonders if he always said things like this, if they were always talking this way to each other.

"So now we are both orphans," she says. "I wonder how common that is, if we are statistically unlucky. Orphans: it sounds like something we're too old to be. What it means is there's no one between us and — what would you call it? — the hereafter."

"Shall we walk?" he asks.

They walk down a lane bordered by large old trees, their leaves turned nearly bronze from autumn dryness, but no less lush for that. They walk between rows of white marble heads, busts of the famous, many of whose identities they do not know. Someone has drawn, with Magic Marker, a mustache on Petrarch.

"Your mother had beautiful hands," he says. "They always seemed very soft and cool to me. They smelt of a very light perfume. I think it was her lotion: Jergens. When I smell that almond fragrance, I always think of her."

"I think about the way your mother cooked. Those wonderful thick soups. The sauces: those enormous pots of tomato sauce going on the stove all day and we'd come in and she'd dip a piece of bread in the sauce and hand it to us on a plate, and we'd eat it with a knife and fork. It was so simple, so delicious. So entirely satisfying."

"Well, she was Roman. I guess that's why I'm happy here."

"The mother country."

"Have you been in Rome since . . ." He doesn't want to say, *since the time we were here together.* He says instead, "Since 1969?"

"No, I've only been to Europe for conferences since then. And not here. Paris, Berlin, London, but not here. Not Rome. As a family we traveled in the West. Hiking and camping trips. My boys liked that. I had a horror of trooping them through churches and museums. And if we went abroad it was to visit my husband's family in Israel."

Her husband is a Jew, he thinks. Are her children? Can they be Jews if she is not: the maternal line being the important one.

"I know the city very well," he says. "I still have family here. There are things I'd like to show you. Things we didn't see when we were here. Things you wouldn't think to see when young, or living poor, as we were then, or thought we were, although of course compared to those living quite near us, it was a joke. And we were working hard here, both of us, and there were all those terribly long dinners at my cousins'." He doesn't

66

say, *And in the hours when we might have been sightseeing, we were making love,* but they both understand this.

"There's a lot of Rome you haven't seen," he adds. "Well, of course there's always a lot no one has seen, but I want to propose something to you."

The last time you proposed something, she wants to say, *we were sixteen years old and what you proposed was marriage.*

"What?"

"I suppose it's a favor to me, and of course I understand I'm the last person in the world to whom you owe a favor. But walking with you, talking with you, well, we can have conversations unlike any others. The last time I saw you I was a young man. Now, well, I'm not an old man, but today a young woman got up to give me a seat on the bus. And I took it. You're here for three weeks. If we could meet to walk, and I could show you the city, my mother's city, the city I love most, and we could talk a little every day . . . well, I think it might be wonderful."

What, she wonders, is at stake in his offer? What has she got to lose? She has three weeks in Rome, she has paid an exorbitant amount for the apartment, and it's a city where there is no one she knows, except for Valerie, whom she has no wish to see. She had thought her sightseeing would be solitary or in the company of some colleague as unlearned as herself.

And if she agrees, what will she be giving up? Her position as a victim. The pleasure, like a sharp taste in the mouth, like the taste of vinegar, ginger, arugula, the darkest chocolate: the deep satisfaction of a cherished bitterness. He would like her forgiveness. *Well,* she wants to say, *it's too late.* Because the truth is: forgiveness is irrelevant now because the pain he caused her is long gone and, painless, forgiveness is not difficult, therefore perhaps not worth much. But, then, if it is painless, why not give it? And there is that thing for which she needs forgiveness, the thing he doesn't even know.

Most probably, it is a very bad idea. She doesn't even know exactly what it is to which she is agreeing.

But she does agree. Partly because she is more off balance than she imagined she would be, more at sea. Yonatan, having lived many places, spoken many languages, never feels a stranger; she has depended on him to root her in a new place. When she'd thought of being alone here she'd considered it a luxury, one she'd been promising herself since the children were old enough not to need her.

Having felt at home in India, in Pakistan, in Bangladesh, she hadn't imagined that in Rome she would feel overwhelmed by strangeness. But in those other places, she'd had a job; she was doing something that was of use, something she knew how to do. In a strange culture without work, she'd come to realize, you are a child. She doesn't consider going to meetings at a conference real work. Talking and listening to people, foreigners themselves, in a hotel that could be any-where on earth: it isn't being part of the life of the city. You're just a different kind of tourist.

And as a tourist, there is nothing you can do for anyone, except perhaps give them your money. You must depend, like a child, on people doing things for you. And not be-ing able to be of use made her feel she didn't know herself. She had no place to stand. She didn't like feeling inexpert. She couldn't bear the idea of herself as TOUR-IST, couldn't stand the image of herself on a street holding a map, standing in front of a monument, paging through a guidebook. And even what at first had seemed exciting and charming to her in her apartment now oppressed her. The cool excessive space. The huge door with the knob as big as a cantaloupe. The marble floor where the sound of her heels seemed somehow meaningful, portentous. The window with a view onto the street, whose complicated shutter had delighted her, now seemed encumbered and unwieldy. She hadn't lived in a large city for a quarter of a century. The traffic menaced her; often she found herself getting lost. Yonatan was never afraid of getting lost; he thought it was an adventure. He had no problem looking like a tourist. "I am a tourist," he would say, "why shouldn't I look like one?"

And so, the possibility that Adam offered struck her as more desirable than it might in other circumstances. She wasn't pleased with herself, that the idea of a man to accompany her made such a difference. Of course she'd tell Yonatan about it. He knew about Adam, but it was possible he didn't remember. Yonatan's relationship to the past was radically different from hers. He had left Israel because he felt smothered by "an excessive past." Too much history, too little geography, he said. He loved America: he loved the idea of starting over. It was another thing he didn't like about Israel: everyone knew everyone, he said. So you had to be whoever everybody thought you were. He loved the idea of being a stranger in a strange land. So of course he would say, "It's a wonderful opportunity, to see Rome with someone who really knows the city. It would be ridiculous not to."

She is Yonatan's wife; she has been for more than a quarter of a century. She is Yonatan's wife; she is the girl betrayed by Adam. She is a woman, nearly sixty, who has earned the right to do something like this. But something like what? she asks herself. Of all the voices in her mind, Yonatan's is the clearest. "It would be foolish not to," she hears him say.

"Yes, all right," she says to Adam. Yes. "I'd like that."

"Some days we'll have only a little time. We can meet here, and take short walks. Then some days, we may perhaps see something, or get something to eat and drink. What I would like is to promise you that we will see one beautiful thing every day. What that thing will be I don't know. We'll play it by ear."

"Play it by ear? What can that mean to a trained musician?"

"You forget that's how I learned. By ear. I listened. Everything followed from that."

"All right," she says. "We'll meet. We'll walk and talk. We'll see what happens." She is happy with the imposition of rules, of limits. Only one thing per day. Only walking and talking.

"I think my mother would like it," he says.

She wants to cool the temperature, as if what they were doing were an ordinary thing. She doesn't want the invocation of his mother.

"Tomorrow, I have to go to Alitalia. My husband's arranged an upgrade for me for the way home. He's very good at things like that."

Tuesday, October 9

Her business with Alitalia is completed more easily than she had thought; the beautifully coiffed, beautifully made-up girls behind the counter are breathtakingly efficient. She knows she mustn't call them girls, although they are, however competent, the age of her sons. They could be her daughters, the lack of which, when she sees a certain kind of young woman, particularly a competent and lovely one, she continues to mourn.

"Let's walk up the Via Veneto," he says. "Remember when we went into the city to see *La Dolce Vita* at the Thalia?"

"Oh," she says, "we thought we were glamorous, didn't we, sitting in the Thalia

73

holding hands. Pretending we didn't just get off a suburban train. They seemed so wonderful. Those Europeans who were truly glamorous in a way that we could never be, who, however glamorous we thought we were, would always be more glamorous. It seemed a real, an important category. Glamour. The glamorous. We were as susceptible to it as secretaries buying movie magazines, but we thought we were better because our categories were European. European glamour. Now I can't even imagine that it would be important, or that it once was. Anouk Aimée driving at night in sunglasses. Why did we think that was so marvelous? It was pretty stupid, not to say insane. But she did look great."

She thinks it's all right to invoke the past this way; she can think of it as describing the behavior of a cohort rather than the behavior of Adam and Miranda as teenagers in love. The threat of intimacy has been bleached, dipped in the vat of the general.

"I watched the movie again, recently," he says. "It didn't age well. It seemed pretentious. All those people trying to be daring, trying to be wicked, like good children thinking they're bad when they can't even imagine what real badness would be like. What followed, in the way of rebellion, made their efforts look absurd. That made me sad, for myself, and for all the things that don't stand the test of time but were, for some little time, important. Like this street, the Via Veneto. This street used to be considered important, the important place to be if you wanted to meet important people. Now it's just a place for rich tourists who don't know where they're really supposed to be. But I'm still fond of it. Walking down this hill, passing these great hotels where probably only rich Japanese stay now. But I still feel the presence of the glamorous ghosts. I can imagine them happy here, in spite of everything, enjoying the lines of the buildings and the generous old trees."

"Oh God," she says, "there's that horrible church, with the crypt we went into because that weird guy told us we should."

"What was his name?"

"Dudley. Or Bentley . . . how did we know him?"

"I think he was a friend of Beverly's."

She doesn't want to say: *Well, of course.*

"It was the first thing he wanted to see in Rome," Adam says. "The Capuchin church with the crypt where the monks had taken the bones of their dead brothers and made things of them. Arches made of bones, light fixtures, working light fixtures, sockets with lightbulbs in them that were real sockets from pelvises. Bone filigrees and flowers. And then some skeletons in their monks' habits."

"I hated it. And I remember he said, 'But aren't they doing what all art does? Making something of death, something to be looked at, enjoyed. Only they're a little more literal. But isn't that just a kind of radical honesty?' "

"I remember how angry you got. And the angrier you got, the cooler, the more ironic, he became. You walked away, and left me to deal with him. I remember what you said, 'Death is not a metaphor. It is real. The dead are not material. They had their lives. They should be honored.' "

"I remember he laughed at my use of the word 'honor.' I didn't hit him, did I? I know I wanted to."

"No, you just walked away. Leaving me to deal with him and his weirdo ideas."

"I think I went just here, just where we are now, to the Triton Fountain and wet my handkerchief and cooled my face. I loved that fountain! They were my favorite thing about Rome, the fountains. Now of course I worry about the waste of water."

"Is it waste? It seems to have been going

on for a long time. I think the Romans have no shortage of water."

"Yes, it's been going on for a long time, but once it was really practical. People needed those fountains for water to drink and wash from. Now they're merely ornamental."

It occurs to him that in all the time he has been in Rome he has never once worried about the waste of water implied in his beloved fountains. And the fact that she does marks between them a very great difference. He doesn't like what she's making him feel; her concern seems willed, dishonest, and she is spoiling his pleasure for an idea he doesn't think she can really believe in.

They risk their lives crossing the Piazza Barberini to stand by the fountain. The sun is at its height; they shield their eyes, but even so they look away, down to the ground from time to time, to rest them.

"Neptune, the sea god," she says, looking up, continuing to shield her eyes from the sun. Refreshing, she thinks, refreshed, the sun is never a problem for Neptune; he's always cooled by the water. Then she notices that in fact he isn't drinking from the shell at his lips, but blowing into it: he's making music. And the music, made of water, falls back down on him to refresh him again and again. She notices, too, that his hair, drenched, falls down his back stick straight, and this is unusual; usually the gods are curly headed. If she were in Berkeley, she thinks, someone would be making a point of that, a political point. Was Bernini trying to suggest a primitivism, is it an acknowledgment of the aboriginal presence destroyed by colonialism? That is the kind of thing people in Berkeley would say. And although she loves her home, she's glad to be away from it.

Surrounding the god is a circle of dolphins. She wants to say — why is she so defensive — *On one vacation my sons and I went to a place in Hawaii where you can swim with dolphins. Real dolphins,* she wants to say, *not stone ones.* She dips her hand in the cooling water; she doesn't want to be unpleasant. Or she does and doesn't like it in herself; hopes she can keep it hidden; hopes she can keep from saying what she feels. To say what you feel, she's learned, is a luxury; you can only afford it if you've built up a balance of trust. She didn't know it when she was young, but she knows it now. It's often better not to say what you feel.

They walk uphill on the Via Barberini. He

points to a statue in an arch, flanked by two other statues. "This is meant to be Moses," he says. "It's a failure, obviously, but the artist's failure was unusually public. It's called the Acqua Felice. The 'happy water.' The pope, who was actually a peasant, commissioned it as a monument to himself, but he thought calling it the Acqua Felice rather than naming it after himself was a sign of modesty. Moses is holding the tablets, except that he shouldn't have been given them yet when he brought the water into the desert, which is what is supposed to be commemorated. The proportions as you can see are all wrong. He's stocky, like an over-age, out-of-shape wrestler."

He is doing it now, the kind of talking she dislikes in foreign cities: the tone of the tourist guide has entered, the art historian. She always dislikes commentary on the beautiful. What can you say — after you say, *Oh yes, that's wonderful* — that isn't diminishing, that isn't more about you and your wanting to be praised than it is about the beautiful thing you've seen. Language, she thinks, should at such moments be banned. Pointing can be allowed: nodding, gestures with the chin. Perhaps jumping up and down. But words, she thinks: People should be fined for speaking in the face of something beautiful.

His words have made her mind shut down, like one of those metal shutters storekeepers pull down here at closing time. She remembers that he always had that potential; sometimes when he talked to her about music, she couldn't listen. His attention to the formal details leached the pleasure for her. She calls up an old resentment: he had stolen music from her. She had loved to sing; their first encounter was about her singing. But after she took up with him, she didn't sing again. Believing anything she could do with music would be, compared with what he did, inferior and false. So now she wants to pull him down from the false heights of his aesthetic pedestal.

She moves closer to the statue of Moses. "Bert Lahr, the Cowardly Lion in *The Wizard of Oz,*" she says. "And why the horns? They make him somehow more lovable or approachable than Moses usually seems."

"I suppose if you look at it like that, it's amusing."

"But you don't want to be amused."

"No, it disturbs me. I think it's a mess. Some historians say the statue's a mess because the funds were cut at the last minute, or because the sculptor was rushed.

That it wasn't his fault. But I think it was his fault, because he allowed something to be presented that should not have been presented. People said he was trying to be Michelangelo, which he had no right even to consider, because he was nothing but a hack. The statue became a laughingstock. He killed himself from shame."

"What a terrible thing," Miranda says. "It's understandable, but that doesn't make it less terrible. You want to grab him by the shoulders and say, 'It's not worth your life.' "

"What is, then, worth a life?"

"Nothing."

"I won't accept that. Then we're only animals, living to survive."

"I can see giving up your own life to save the life of another person, certainly your own child. But for a statue, an unliving thing. No."

"I'm not sure. Isn't it possible to no longer want to live because your work is a failure? If you've lived for your work, which is not, I think, the worst thing to live for. In our fantasies about the artist's life we never include the reality that most art that is made is a failure. We believe that it's important to leave a mark, but it doesn't occur to us that it might be a bad mark, undistinguished or corrupt, a mark that would be better unleft. There's no need even for mediocre art, to say nothing of bad art. Whereas in your field to be adequate is OK; it's better to do an adequate job than to leave the job completely undone."

"You know nothing about what I do," she says, wondering when he became so rigid, so punitive. Should she take the time to educate him, or allow this to be one more thing she holds against him, one more grievance she can keep, like a stone inside her shoe.

"Mediocre work of the kind I do, of the kind people like me do, could lead to sickness and death. Real death, not just an unfortunate aesthetic moment. Nevertheless, I repeat what I said: a failure of proportion in stone is not something that should lead to death."

She knows he hasn't heard her. Or has chosen not to. Because she understands that he's not really talking about the statue of Moses, about Michelangelo and the Renaissance popes and the suicidal sculptor. He's talking about himself. He's describing his life out loud. He wants her to know something: that he has given something up. But does he want her to know it, or does he want to know it himself? She doesn't know whom his words are meant for. But she understands the sorrow behind the words, and like the sharp rattle of the lifting shutters, indicating morning on the Roman streets, some signal has been heard. Something has lifted in her, something has opened up.

"But what is it," he says, to her, to someone else, she thinks, to no one, "this impulse to make a mark?"

He wants her to talk about this with him; he wants her to say something about his life. That it is all right, the way that he has lived it. Something has lifted, but not entirely. To give him what he wants, that understanding, would require a giving over of an old grievance. And she isn't ready for that yet.

He takes her into Santa Maria della Vittoria, a church that in its overembellishment does not please her. Gold and marble: the materials of wealth and power. Everything she has devoted her life to being against. Why would he think this is something she would like? But then, why would he know what she would like? They haven't seen each other for nearly forty years.

He leads her to the front left side, to Bernini's Saint Teresa. "Is this not worth it?" he asks.

"Worth what?"

"A life."

"It's not a question I have to consider. Which is why I live as I do."

He sees that she's unmoved. He is angry with himself: he knows this isn't the kind of thing she likes. Her taste always retained something of the American Puritan: she liked bare hills, slate skies, pastures fenced with stones. He should have led her up to this; taken her first to something plainer, more austere.

Her resistance angers him. This is his favorite place on earth, and he won't allow her to spoil it for him. He wants to say: *This is greatness, this richness, this celebration of life, the gold rays, the flow of the fabric, what is done with marble that seems so light it can't be stone, her abandonment, the sharpness of the golden arrow, the sweetness of the angel's face.* But he thinks it's better to say nothing.

She wants to say, *She's having an orgasm.* But she won't. She focuses on the entirely relaxed foot, surrounded by plain air, the only plainness in the room.

"I like the pleased face of the angel," she says. "But those guys on the balcony looking on: what creeps."

"Just looking on, the donor's family leaving no mark. Bernini's life left a mark. He won't be forgotten. Do you really mean that it doesn't matter to you whether your work will be known after you die?"

"I never imagined it would. I just wanted to do something that would help people."

"I wanted to make some kind of mark. For a time I thought I would. That my work would be remembered. That I would move something forward, maybe a quarter of an inch, and people for whom music was important would know. Is it really true that you never had such thoughts?"

So I was right, she thinks to herself with a grim pride. He is talking about himself. His acknowledgment of it softens her; perhaps she can begin to be a little kind.

"Never. Your life has been harder than mine."

"Yes, I think it has."

She'd like to say, *I'm sorry,* but she doesn't think they know each other well enough for that. Not after all this time. Not yet.

"My Lucy, my daughter, is in for the same kind of difficult life. Trying for the perfection of a form, knowing perfection is impossible but trying, exhausting herself, over and over. Is that my doing?" He leans on the marble rail that keeps Saint Teresa from her onlookers.

"It's a form of narcissism to think of that.

We can't take the credit for our children. We can, I suppose, take blame."

"Your children, what do they want for their lives?"

She looks at the sculpture that she thinks her children will probably never see because they will have no impulse to. She knows that he would think her children "mediocre," uninterested in perfection. They want to be happy. They want in some way to change the world, but their ideas are vague and connected to their ideas of personal happiness. They want justice. They care deeply about the fate of the earth. But whatever they want . . . well, she knows they don't want it enough to interfere with the enjoyment of their lives. And the fate of art . . . this means, she knows, exactly nothing to them. She erases, as soon as it appears, the impulse to feel disappointment in her children. That, she has always believed, can only be destructive. It is something she will not allow.

His daughter, Lucy, is studying the violin with a master teacher. Her Benjamin is in Nepal, hoping to make a documentary film about the Tibetans. Jeremy is working for a foundation that is trying to teach environmental consciousness to inner-city children. He says he is thinking of law school, but he has made no moves in that direction. She knows that if she says these things to Adam, he will pretend to think it's fine. But he will think that Lucy has chosen the better part. So she only gives the barest outlines of their plans, suggesting that their fates are more fixed than they are.

"Their lives sound much more open than Lucy's."

Does he mean this, or is he condescending? No one speaks about the vanity of parents, that it is almost impossible to hear even the slightest criticism of your children without the impulse to take a knife to the speaker's heart. She will give him the benefit of the doubt: that he is speaking out of his worry for his daughter.

"But I know you wake up every morning grateful for your daughter's gift."

"Yes. Yes and no. I worry for her. What she's already given up. What she will have to give up. What might not come to fruition. Serious music is growing less and less central to what's considered important in the world. And yes, I think, unless people like Lucy lead a certain kind of life, give up a certain kind of life, a certain way of living, the world will be poorer. So she is, in a way, a sacrificial lamb."

"A sacrifice to an ideal of greatness."

"To a possibility."

"And if she decides it's not for her?"

"Then she decides," he says, bowing his head toward the marble woman, concentrating, though Miranda doesn't know it, on the relaxed and undemanding foot.

WEDNESDAY, OCTOBER 10

THE VILLA BORGHESE
"What Have We Given Up for an Ideal of Health?"

She has a meeting that begins, unusually, at ten o'clock; they agree to meet for a short, early morning walk.

The day before had been a disappointment to the both of them; each had found the other wanting; both telephoned their spouses, flush with the pleasure of being able to speak critically, yet truthfully: to make the point that really, there was no danger. "I had forgotten what a pedant he could be," she told her husband. "What did we do in the days before we could invoke the term 'politically correct'?" he asked his wife.

She has got to the balustrade before him. She sees him coming to the top of the staircase, that his pace is slow, and that he stops to catch his breath, holding his hand to his chest. She has noticed that she has had to alter her pace to accommodate his. Another way of saying it: she had to slow herself down. She remembers being impatient with his slowness, yet sometimes dependent on it: her safety valve, her brakes. Sometimes when she was most in love, his slowness was arousing to her, a promise of large leisure.

She pretends not to see him; she looks away. But now it is she who's been too slow. He sees that she has seen him.

Seeing him leaning heavily on the stone banister, stopping to catch his breath, she feels drenched in a wave of sorrow. How ridiculous, she thinks, keeping alive the grievances of nearly half a century, even the irritations of the day before. With a new acuteness, she feels in the bones of her back the two words "time" and "past." She thinks of a hymn her mother sang sometimes . . . did her mother miss churchgoing, was it another of her capitulations to her husband, the strength of whose assertions she never could resist? She hears her mother's voice, "Time, like an ever-rolling stream, bears all its sons away; they fly forgotten, as a dream dies at the opening day."

An incredible cliché, the river of time. But she thinks of the grievance she has cherished against Adam, and all of a sudden she wants to cast it into a river, let it be borne away . . . somewhere, into some ocean where it will be drowned, a victim of its own insignificance. He had hurt her, badly. She had not been destroyed. Her life was, by any measure, prosperous. And when he hurt her they were both young. Whatever they are now, they are no longer young.

Seeing him before her, she thinks: Soon, who knows when, soon we will no longer be in this life. And it seems to her, suddenly, of the utmost folly to cherish a grievance against this man, this fellow creature, who has, like her, lost youth, and, unlike her, health. She is full of gratitude for this opportunity: something can be done with the past, it can't be recaptured but it won't fly forgotten as a dream, and the bitterness of it need not triumph. She sees the pallor of his skin. Can she ask him, *Are you all right?*

Or: *Are you healthy?*

What is the opposite of healthy?

Unhealthy?

Unwell?

Ill?

Sick?

Afflicted?

Close to death?

She thinks of the phrase "rude health."
Odd, as if health were an offense, a carelessness, an insult.

She has always had rude health.

She has enjoyed good health.

What is the nature of this enjoyment?
How would you name this kind of joy?

He knows that she's seen something, and,
misunderstanding the nature of her work,
or assuming that because she's married to a
doctor there's a body of knowledge she has
picked up at the breakfast table, in the marriage bed, he assumes she's making a diag-
nosis. That he is being judged.

"My wind isn't what it was."

"No, none of ours is." This is a lie; she
can actually run farther now than she could
when they were together. She is never out
of breath.

He will not waste her time. "I have a stent
in my heart."

Stent, she thinks, an ugly word. It always
reminds her of a fetal pig. She won't insult
him, trivialize him, by saying something in
response. She waits for him to speak again.

"I had a heart attack eight years ago. I
thought I was dying. It did seem like an at-

tack: swift, sudden, a shocking pain. Then a kind of brightness. I became quite calm. I thought, So this is it, then. Later, thinking about it, I tried to understand what I meant by those words. 'This.' 'It.' 'Then.' "

"You weren't frightened?"

"I was sad. For so many years, I hadn't liked my life. It was too difficult for me. But I'd been given a second chance. With Clare. With Lucy. And as I thought I might be dying, I thought about how dear life was. I thought of the category: dearness. How I would miss my life. Life. Not only those I loved, but at that moment I was thinking: I will miss trees. I became quite sad thinking that, if I died, I would no longer see trees. Death seemed to me bereftness, a landscape bereft of trees."

"The trees here are remarkable," she says, knowing she shouldn't want to change the subject or steer the sentence away from the part of it that spoke of death to the part of it that spoke of trees. But she can't speak of death to him, not as they are now, knowing each other so little, strangers to each other. It seems unseemly, impolite. She has, she feels, no place to stand, as if a chair has been pulled out from under her as she was preparing to take her seat at table, as if she is standing on the quicksand from the movies that frightened her as a child. She is being cast down, sucked under, by the impossibility of a response.

"What are they, I wonder, these trees. I believe they are called ilex. And there are the cypresses. And those wonderful Roman pines. Umbrella pines, aren't they called?"

"You always knew the names of trees," he says. He doesn't say to her, *When I thought I was dying, when I thought about missing trees, I thought of you. That I would die without learning the names of trees.* He says, "I always thought someday you'd teach me."

"I thought about it," she says. "But when I tried, I saw that it made you feel overwhelmed, and I always just dropped it." She reads the sign at the corner of the road they've just turned into. "Viale Magnolia," she says. "So obviously these trees, with the glossy green leaves, are magnolias. And see those wonderful reddish ones, they're almost wine colored, the leaves, they're copper beeches."

"Well, so I've learned the names of two trees now. But I've had to come to terms with the fact that I'll never be able to identify trees. Of the humilities that I have gathered, the most difficult is accepting all the things that I will never know."

"One morning I woke up," she says, "and

94

heard my own voice saying, coming out of a dream, 'I will never know Russian.' So much followed then, 'I will never play the cello or learn to knit. I will never understand economics.' The truth is, I won't even try."

"But think of all you do know. About the natural world. And you're a scientist."

"Only a nonscientist would call someone a scientist. It's like someone saying to you, 'You're in the arts.' "

"I'll bet you understand string theory."

"Yes, I do."

"Chaos theory?"

"Yes."

"The different arguments: is energy particles or waves?"

"Um-hm."

"The uncertainty principle?"

"Enough to speak about it without sounding like a fool."

"Would you explain it to me?"

"No."

"Why?"

"You wouldn't enjoy listening. You'd try, you wouldn't understand right away, you'd work to understand, then you'd get that look, and I couldn't stand to see you looking so defeated."

He is moved by her using the phrase "that look." He would like to touch her face.

"You're right, of course," he says instead.

"Did it change the way you lived, the heart attack?"

"It changed, if not my life, my way of living. I had to change my habits. I stopped smoking. I watch what I eat."

"I can't imagine that. You ate voraciously. You ate whatever you liked, and you were the thinnest person I knew. It made me furious."

"I remember your crying once when I ate a second jelly doughnut."

"I was crying from sheer jealousy; I was trying to lose five pounds."

"You can rest now. I'll never eat another jelly doughnut. And you clearly don't need to lose five pounds."

"There's not a woman on earth who doesn't think she needs to lose five pounds," she says, then regrets her response. Because what he's said suggests that he's been looking at her body. Looking with approval. And she's glad of that. She shakes her head, a gesture of refusal she hopes he can't read. She won't allow this. Particularly her own satisfaction. It's the sort of thing that will have to be kept out of their time together.

She laughs a laugh she hopes he doesn't know is false. "Even if you knew you were going to die tomorrow? Wouldn't you say,

'I'm dying tomorrow, so I'll eat a jelly doughnut.' "

"Speaking of cuisine," he says, pointing a few yards from where they are standing. They have just passed the merry-go-round, whose tinny music seems so out of place as an accompaniment to the grand view from the Pincio, the belvedere. Mothers and children are clustered around a cart, sheltered from the sun by a yellow-and-blue umbrella. Printed on the umbrella, in white letters SABRETT'S.

"Sabrett's," she says. "What in God's name is a kosher hotdog stand doing in the Villa Borghese?"

"I think it's called capitalism," he says.

"Do you think it's an American who fell in love with Rome? Or an Italian who fell in love with New York hot dogs?"

"Maybe it was my mother sending it as a gift so we could stop, for one minute, being so damn serious."

"Shall I buy you one?"

"I don't think my cardiologist would approve."

"And I'm a vegetarian. God, sometimes I'm appalled at the amount of time I spend thinking about food."

"It was humiliating when I had to understand how important food was to me. Butter. It seemed ridiculous to say, 'I mourn the loss of butter.' But I do. And it was humbling, because I'd never exercised, and I had to hire someone called a personal trainer. Whom I grew to love. At first I thought: we have nothing in common. He has never heard of Debussy. He told me he has never read a book from beginning to end. He's from the Dominican Republic. He's twenty-three; he has a wife and two children. I have, as I said, come to love him now, to be grateful, moved by this wonderful boy because of whom I must question all the things I never thought to question. What is the value of a certain kind of music, without which I thought it was impossible to have an admirable life? And yet he does, he does have an admirable life; he's careful, he's patient, he's enormously kind, he has wonderful humor, and, well, he knows all sorts of things I don't; it's possible he saved my life, a life devoted to a kind of music he has no notion of."

"When I think of how we lived!" she says. "We smoked, we drank, we stayed up late and slept till noon, we ate French fries and drank Coke, we mocked athletes. And now I have a personal trainer, too. I will never again have a jelly doughnut either! I limit myself to three glasses of wine a week. What

98

have we given up for an ideal of health?"

"Oh, all those nights of talk, talk, talk."

"It was a way of discovering who we were."

"Who were we? Who are we now? Are we the same people that we were?"

"Impossible to imagine those young people who we were saying the sentence 'I belong to a gym.' And yet I do belong to a gym, and sometimes I think, in all the hours I spend in the gym, what might I be doing? Learning the Russian I say I have no time to learn? Involving myself in local politics."

"There's not an infinity of time. You think there is when you're young. You never imagine that there are some things that will just be given up. Lost."

"And not only negligible things. Things of great value."

"Then we lived in a way, or maybe it was a way of being alive that allowed us to feel we could use words like 'beauty,' 'justice,' 'wisdom.' Maybe you had to have stayed up all night and drank and smoked too much to feel easy about using those words. Put beside those words, how pale the word 'health' seems. It seems pathetic. Ridiculous. But it's how we live, I suppose how we must live."

"Is health life?"

"There isn't life without it, so, yes, I suppose it is."

"And pleasure?"

"Oh, pleasure, that, it seems, has become less important."

"Yes, you're right, and I think that's rather sad."

"Or is it just a kind of wisdom proper to our age?"

"But which is it — wisdom or defeat?"

"It might be hard to tell."

"No, Adam, I won't leave it at that. Pleasure now: it's something that we choose rather than something that lands on us. And I won't say that's sad. It doesn't come crashing over you, like a wave. It's a lake you see from a distance, and then enter, it's lovely, as lovely as thought, maybe lovelier. But it's not the ocean."

"So: a calm lake. No surprises. No wave turning you over and over, lifting you up, letting you down somewhere far from where you started."

"Of course there are surprises. It would be terrible if there were not."

"The biggest surprise, I suppose, will be death. Which ought to be no surprise at all."

She wonders whether his close approach to death has made him think like that. She won't indulge him in this kind of talk, this kind of thinking.

"But on the way there are some surprises that we can take real pleasure in. Just for their surprisingness. A kosher hot dog in the elegant Villa Borghese."

"Even if we can't eat it."

"Not can't: choose not to."

So, he thinks, she has not lost her faith in the power of will. He doesn't know if he likes or dislikes her for it.

She looks at her watch. If she doesn't hurry now she'll be late for her meeting. She can't afford to slow her pace for him. She walks quickly toward the stairway saying over her shoulder, "You stay here, I have to rush. Tomorrow, I'll meet you at the Campo dei Fiori. How early can you get there?"

"Nine-thirty. I leave Lucy at her school at nine."

She would have preferred an earlier time, so that the choice of fruits and vegetables wouldn't be diminished by the industrious early risers, those ancient ladies with their baskets and string bags: implacable, unerring, unconcerned for manners, justice: wanting what they want. But Adam has a duty to his daughter, and that must come first: as a mother this is something she will never be able not to know. A parent must always put responsibility to the child before pleasure. Not in this case, she thinks, impossibly far ahead.

When we knew each other before, she thinks, we weren't parents. And then she thinks: It's not only that we weren't parents, it's much more than that. We weren't who we are. We were young; we were younger than his daughter, Lucy, is now. There were things we believed; there were things we wouldn't have even begun to imagine. He thought he would be a great musician; I thought I would change the world, which I believed was open to me and everything that I would bring about. We thought that we would be each other's one true love. We believed in that idea: the one true love. Now, it is impossible that we should believe that, living as we have lived, having loved others. It is not the case that he was my one true love. Only that he was my first. *First. One.* The two words, so similar, yet calling up radically different conceptions of the world. One: the only. First: an accident of order: a series. Nothing fated. Nothing not susceptible to change. Change, therefore, loss.

She wonders: Is this the most important thing that can be said about us, that we are not who we were.

Thursday, October 11

THE CAMPO DEI FIORI
"You Might Be Surprised to Know I Cook and Garden"

It is difficult for him to find her in the riot of colors: fruit and flowers, cheap goods for sale — most undesirable to him: wool hats, plastic shoes. He considers buying a set of white ceramic cups, an aluminum pot for heating milk. Then he sees her; she is examining a hill of different-colored eggplants: blue-black; white and variegated, a marbling of dark red and cream. He sees from her posture that she is happy.

She is carrying a bright blue plastic bag.

"What's in the bag?" he asks.

She opens it; he looks inside. A jar of capers, the size of the ones they'd eaten at Valerie's (so she'd been taken by them, too); two cellophane envelopes, one of beans of various colors, one he can't identify. He asks her what the grain is called.

"Farro," she says, "a kind of barley. It's hard to find in America, but very common here."

"What will you do with it?"

"Eventually, when I take it home, I'll make a soup. With it and with these lovely beans. Look, Adam, the stripy red and white, the ruby colored, then the black and among them all the ordinary bright green peas. Aren't they wonderful?"

"You'll make a soup? You?"

"Yes. You might be surprised to know I cook and garden."

"Well, I am surprised. You who were so hostile to domestic life. My mother understood that; she said you should never learn to cook, you didn't enjoy it, it would become a tyranny. You would ask her to teach you and she would say, 'No, just talk to me, tell me something interesting, something I need to know.' She said she cooked because she loved it, so it would never be a tyranny for her, it was a friendship. But for you . . . she didn't want you to be enslaved to it, like so many women were. But then, you know, after she went back to school, particularly when she started law school, she just sort of stopped. She'd cook for special occasions, but then she'd say, 'There are just so many things I'm more interested in.' The secret of my mother was that she really didn't do things unless she wanted to do them. Of course there were a lot of things she really wanted to do, that she enjoyed doing. That was why she always made people around her feel so free."

"Your mother went to law school?"

"Yes. My mother had a life as a lawyer for a happy twenty years. She took the bar when she was fifty. She worked with a group of lawyers who did domestic law. She was terrific with women who'd been abused, who were afraid of their husbands."

"What did she know of that? If ever there was a woman who wasn't afraid of her husband . . ."

"But somehow she understood being afraid . . . even though I think for my mother the world was essentially a kind of joke, sometimes a good joke, sometimes a bad one, sometimes a cruel one, sometimes an enjoyable one. But there seemed to be a very great deal she understood."

"And when she stopped cooking, you weren't angry?"

"I wasn't living in the house. It was Jo and my father who paid the price. Only, they didn't seem to be paying anything. Somehow they both learned to cook well enough, and they did it together, and they enjoyed that. It wasn't fabulous, like when my mother did it, but it was, somehow, fine. And then on holidays my mother would produce, well, masterpieces."

What he doesn't say: that Beverly hated the holidays. She made fun of all the food, saying, " 'Th' expense of spirit in a waste of shame' is Rose in action." She'd go home and vomit in the bathroom and then say she had to stay in bed for days: she'd been poisoned.

"But you, Miranda, how did you come to it? Cooking, I mean."

"I somehow started reading cookbooks. It could only happen when I stopped being afraid of turning into my mother."

"Your mother was very kind to me. Do you remember, when I got mono and my mother was back in school, your mother would come over during the day and bring me the kind of food my mother never would have made me: Jell-O with real cherries in it, custards, very light foods that were exactly what I needed. And she was good about us, Miranda. She might not have been. The time she caught us in your bed. She might have made us feel terrible about it. But she just closed the door and never said anything."

"No, she never mentioned it. Not a word. Not even to me. Never. And you see, that was a kind of agony for me. Because I never knew what she was thinking, or when she might, out of nowhere, mention it. Or whether she'd told my father, or someday wake up and think she had to. I never knew what she thought about it. What it made her think of me. Whether it changed the way she felt about me, whether she thought I'd become a different person, whether she couldn't love me in the same way anymore. Oh, I know she loved me. But what the flavor of that love was or who it was she thought she loved — that I would never know."

"You're too exacting."

"Well, if you like. But I never knew what her love meant, what it meant to her to love me. Was she excited by her love for me, made anxious, saddened, consoled, envious, ambitious?"

"Perhaps all those things. You know from the way you are with your own children."

"She seemed afraid to touch me. Afraid of touching any of us too much. Maybe of touching anything: now that I think of it, she touched everything rather tentatively, rather fearfully, as if she were afraid of leaving a mark that would be somehow corrupting, hurtful. Perhaps diminishing. Her embraces were always abashed, they always felt provisional. My children's bodies were always so delicious to me. I kissed them and hugged them all the time. I loved having their skin against my skin. I had to think about it carefully as they got older: they were boys, after all. What should my relationship be to these new bodies? The bodies of men. The soft skin growing coarser, the round limbs thinning, lengthening, the curls becoming straight. Oh, and the first signs: hair on the legs and then the cheek you put your lips on, expecting the old swoony pillow. Suddenly whiskers. Like your father. Like every other man. And then you know they are no longer yours."

She stops, knowing it's easier for a mother to speak this way of her sons than a father of his daughter. She doesn't want to create a difficulty. But he seems not to have seen a boulder in the road.

What he sees is the statue of Giordano Bruno, at the far end of the piazza. He would like to talk to her about Giordano Bruno, who believed not only that the earth traveled around the sun but that the sun was only one of a number of stars, perhaps all equally important. Burned by the Inquisition. Adam takes in his austere unpleased countenance, his hands gripping his forbidden book, and thinks: Well, this is Italy, placing a monument to intellect in the midst of this celebration of the undiscriminating pleasures of the tongue, surrounding it by sugary pink and yellow buildings that suggest, not the life of the mind, but the succulence of fruit or the confectionary instability of some of the candies for sale in the open bins. The buildings' lightness makes them seem insubstantial: how can they stand up to weather? And yet they have, they've endured, as the statue of Bruno has endured, suggesting entirely different things about the nature of the world.

He'd like to talk about this with Miranda. But he sees that she is entirely absorbed in the luxuriant array of fruits and vegetables, and that it would annoy her if he interrupted her delights to talk about a Renaissance philosopher. He envies her ability to lose herself in the physical world, to distract herself in the pleasures of what can be tasted, touched, smelled. It is one of the things he understands about himself: he has never been able to lose himself to this sort of distraction. His distractions come from music, which, as someone famously said, has no smell.

"I often wondered where you got your

physical exuberance. Your parents were both so reserved. You were always throwing your arms around people. Sometimes, they didn't know what to do, but mostly, even if they didn't know exactly how to respond, you made them happy."

"Well, I've toned down now."

He would like to say, *That's such a shame,* but says instead, "Tell me about your garden."

"Where I live, in Berkeley, things grow easily and well, though we have to be very careful of water. But the growing season is long. I have all sorts of things in my garden, oranges, lemons, tomatoes that are like, well, like they are here, but all colors, some called heirlooms, that's funny isn't it, as if you had tomato seeds on a shelf beside the ancestral bronzes. Broccoli even. And my roses: one is called Chrysler red. Like a great big splashy convertible among the delicate pinks."

He's thinking, she can see, of something else.

"Do you remember that Rilke poem we both liked?" he says. "We both liked it so much we set ourselves the task of memorizing it. The bowl of roses, how he described all the different colors, 'the anonymous pink that picked up the bitter aftertaste of vio-

110

let . . . that one made of cambrick, like a dress / the soft breath of the warm slip still clinging to it / both flung off in the morning shadows / near an old forest pool.' "

He's embarrassed that he has said something that calls up the image of clothing cast aside. He says quickly, "A group of friends and I have agreed to memorize one poem a week. I guess that's what I do instead of gardening. I read about flowers instead of growing them. I often wish I did more things that ordinary people do."

"It was difficult for me to discover how to live an ordinary life," Miranda says. "A life in a house that didn't make me feel I was drowning. Or suffocated. There were so many things I didn't want to do my mother's way. The anxious way. I didn't want to be always saying to my children, Be careful with that . . . wash your hands. Don't sit there. And there was the other kind of domestic life, the Berkeley kind, dinner parties that were Olympic events. Decoration as a competitive sport. I didn't want any part of that either. Particularly after I'd lived in places where there was so much hardship, so little comfort. Where each decision involving food and shelter had to be carefully considered. I remember my mother sent me some cans of tuna fish when I was working in India. I would wash out the cans and throw them away, and the people in the village were shocked: they could do twenty things with an empty tuna-fish can. To them it was a sort of treasure. So I began to think of things a new way. But I didn't want that other kind of Berkeley way, that false renunciation. I think I could only live an ordinary domestic life after I had children. And after I'd known Yonatan. Being Israeli, so many things were just not issues for him. Food, clothing, shelter: they were important, and they were to be enjoyed. But not to be making any kind of point; simply for themselves."

What she doesn't say to Adam: *One of the reasons I married Yonatan was that he seemed to find so few things difficult. He liked to say, "After the '67 War, everything seems easy." One of the reasons I married him was because he was so unlike you.* But she doesn't want to be bringing her husband too much into the conversation, too much into the space where she is, with Adam, now. This hum and bustle of ordinary life. This celebration of what has been given, what can be taken. For the asking. For a price.

Instead, she says: "One of the things I had to understand about myself was how much

I wanted an ordinary life. I had thought I would spend my life working in the developing world, in India or Pakistan or Bangladesh, all of which I'd worked in. But after I came back from India the last time, and I met Yonatan, I realized that I had grown weary and discouraged. That the kind of people who were good at that kind of work had the temperament to just do what they were doing and be satisfied that they were moving the mountain just an inch or two. They didn't keep feeling crushed by the size of the mountain, as I did. So I had to live with falling out of love with myself, with falling out of love with the heroic person I had never really been, but only dreamed I was. And I wanted children, children whose safety and health I wouldn't have to worry about every day. As most of the mothers of the world do."

"You still feel bad about it."

"Yes, I fear we will all be grotesquely punished for taking much too much of the world's goods."

"But cooking, and in your garden, and with your children, certainly you must think you are moving the mountain a little bit."

"When they were younger, certainly I did. I was happiest when I had quite young children. I was tired, very tired, because I

113

was working, too, but I never wondered: What will I do today that will make sense? Everything made sense. If I made a soup I could think: Well, I did something with the day that was a good thing. I nourished my children. I bathed my children. I put them to bed. And then I went to bed, and believe me sometimes I was weeping with fatigue. And yet in those years everything made sense."

"I cook a little, but I don't enjoy it. It always seems to take so much time and then everyone eats it so quickly."

She doesn't say, *Does your wife cook? Is she a good cook?* She knows her own competitiveness and she doesn't want to create any areas of competition. She prefers thinking of, talking about, his mother.

"What I felt in your mother's house, what I wanted for my children, was a place of safety and expansiveness. I think my mother would have been better off if she'd just set the house on fire and run off with only what she could hold in her hands or in her pockets. She seemed so trapped, so frightened. I didn't want an entrapping, fearful house. I wanted a house where everyone was free and happy."

"Did you do it?"

"Who's happy? Who's free?"

"Freer and happier, then?"

"Freer and happier than I was in the house when I was growing up? Freer and happier than my mother was? I think so, yes."

She doesn't ask him about how he lives in his house. She doesn't believe it's important to him. And she knows that in at least one of the houses of his life, tragedy happened. Horror. Does he still live in the same house? She doesn't want to speak about that yet. Not here, in the Campo dei Fiori. Instead she says, "Let's buy some of these grapes." She buys what seems to him an excessively large bunch: dark purple, nearly black. She holds them to the light.

FRIDAY, OCTOBER 12

THE VILLA BORGHESE
"I Suppose You Find That Music Sentimental"

They are sitting by the puppet theater, a rough, unpainted bungalow that looks provisional and out of place among the serious official buildings that are also a part of the park, that remind you that it was once the estate of wealthy and powerful men who moved the world with their little fingers. A sign says that the show will begin in an hour and a half. Some instrument — it sounds like a player piano — is producing music that could be the accompaniment to a silent film. Miranda can't identify the melody, but she knows it's from a time when songs were required to be innocent: girls on bicycles built for two, or kissing boys in a rowboat. The music, which she has no wish to judge, pleases her, and she's about to lean back into it, like an accommodating but perhaps untasteful chair. Then she remembers whom she's with. She is with Adam.

"I suppose you find that music sentimental," she says.

Adam puts both hands in his pockets, as if he's hiding something from her. "Does it matter whether I do or not?" he says. "What would it mean to you if I said yes, I think it's sentimental."

"Now it doesn't matter. But once it would have made me very angry. And I would have been scared, and then insulted and then angry, yes, scared, insulted, angry, all at the same time that I might be accused of being sentimental. Now I think: Yes, I am, in some things, sentimental, and so what?"

"What do you mean by 'sentimental'?"

"It implies, I'd think, excess," she says.

"Excess of what?"

"Sentiment."

"By which is meant?"

"Emotion. Feeling."

"But what would 'excess' mean? Is there a fixed, a proper, amount of it that mustn't be overspent?"

"I do know there is such a thing as sentimentality," she says, "and it makes you physically sick with that sickness that tells you something's wrong. Hallmark cards.

Hummel statues."

"But my mother loved her Hummel statues and I loved my mother."

"And I loved your mother. And I loved how she loved her statue of the little girl feeding the sparrows, the one of the little boy playing the violin."

"I would never have begrudged her that pleasure."

"But me you did begrudge. You didn't know what to do when you had to support me walking out of *West Side Story* because I couldn't walk by myself, I was crying so hard."

"It was the middle of the day. I didn't know you very well. I was sixteen. I was afraid of what my friends would think . . . not that I really had any friends, but the friends I imagined I might have if they knew I had a girlfriend. I was wrong, of course, but I was young. Only sixteen years away from being born, from nonexistence. Sixteen years ago, at forty-three, I was a recognizable version of myself. A teacher, a husband, a father."

Once again, he seems to want to speak in a way she does not.

"My sons are on your side about *West Side Story,* by the way. They tease me about it. They hum, 'There's a place for us, somewhere a place for us . . .' and they hand me a box of tissues they've hidden behind their backs. My son Jeremy likes to tell his friends that his mother cried over a yogurt lid. A yogurt lid, it's true. One day I read the lid on a Dannon yogurt carton, and it told the history of Dannon, which is the story of a Jewish immigrant who brought the recipe for yogurt with him when he had to flee Fascist Italy, and he named the yogurt Dannon after his son, whose nickname was Dannone. And I cried."

He wants to say, *Did you cry because your husband and your sons are Jewish?* But he says instead, "They seem like nice boys, your sons."

"They are nice boys. You were a nice boy, Adam. A very nice boy. Only sometimes you weren't so nice to me about music."

Neither of them says what they are both thinking: that what was done to Miranda by Adam, what Miranda experienced at his hands, was far outside the category which could be appropriately described as "nice."

"You kept saying to me, 'There are certain standards, Miranda.' I sometimes thought you used music to hurt me." She doesn't say: *Because of you I have not listened again to serious music in a serious way. Because of you I have left a kind of consideration of what*

119

you called great art. I take my children to Yosemite instead of the Louvre. Neither of them has had a single music lesson. If I asked them if they knew who Shostakovich was, they might look at me in puzzlement and say, in unison, "Who?" This, Adam, is because of you.

"I never meant to hurt you," he says, and they both pretend to understand he's talking about music. "I don't think you ever knew how frightened I was all the time. That I would be discovered not to know what the standards were. That I'd be exposed as the impostor I knew myself to be. That they'd take away my place at the table. Which in the end, I gave away myself."

No, Adam, no, she wants to say. *We will not talk like this. Not yet.* "Do you remember our terrible fight about Janis Joplin?"

"No."

"I adored her. You said that she was fat and ugly, that she shrieked and howled, that she was the embodiment of everything coarse. You rarely spoke that way, so harshly. But it made me terribly angry. I said she was telling the truth about everything you and your musical friends wanted to keep hidden, that they worked to hide."

Now it is he who doesn't want to follow this line of talk. "This music, coming from

120

this puppet theater, this music you're afraid I'm going to call sentimental, well you're wrong. I'm enjoying it very much."

"Oh," she says, not knowing how to understand this.

"But I know you'll want to leave before the puppet show. I'm assuming that you still hate puppets."

"More than ever," she says.

That he knows this about her, that he remembers that she hates puppets, makes her eyes fill. And she doesn't want him to see. She pretends to tie her shoe. To stop her tears, she thinks of her sons, for whom her tendency to cry too easily is a good joke. Her sons: tall, strong, happy, or, perhaps better to say, neither for the moment unhappy. An old woman once told her, "You can only be as happy as your unhappiest child."

"You know, I liked *West Side Story,*" he says. "I thought it was Bernstein's best work."

"Why didn't you tell me?"

"I was afraid even to say it aloud. In the circles in which I moved in those days, it was impossible to say you liked *West Side Story.*"

SATURDAY, OCTOBER 13

TRASTEVERE
"Some Things in the World Have Got
Better. It's Important Not to Forget
That"

They plan to meet in the Piazza di Santa
Maria in Trastevere. She has no memory of
it. Perhaps they never came here, or perhaps
she has forgotten: it was nearly forty years
ago. But no, she couldn't have forgotten this
perfect space. The joy of a perfect space
makes her feel like a creature made of lightness; almost, she could fly. But why this
sense of joy . . . because of the color of the
buildings, all beautiful, crowded against one
another? Peach with green shutters. Dove's
wing blue-gray, ocher. Burnt sienna. Did
the names of those colors come to her mind
because she encountered them first in her
box of Crayola crayons? The box she had to
be old enough to deserve: a reward, a sign

of growth, maturity, responsibility perhaps, even expertise. In those days, just seeing the words — "ocher," "raw umber," "burnt sienna" — was exciting. Not knowing why, she knew the words naming those crayons promised a larger life. In that large box was one crayon whose name was "flesh." The assumption: all flesh is the color of pinkish chalk. She wonders if the Crayola people have become sensitive enough to have some different name for that crayon now. Maybe "chalky peach."

In the center of the piazza is a fountain around which tourists sit: disconsolate, regretful. Do they just, she wonders, want to be back home? The water sings, how can it not enliven them. But they are not enlivened. They are fagged out, spent.

She thinks at first that there are six frogs surrounding the fountain's jets of water, but then she sees that they aren't animals at all, only playful shapes, and that is what the fountain demands: an understanding of this place of playfulness. Which the glum tourists seem incapable of even beginning to understand. Beside them, young people smoke and flirt. With a hardly concealed urgency what seems like a small army of dark-skinned men are trying to sell electrified toys: mice, cats, dogs, frogs, or neon-colored circles of plastic tubing that make a whistling sound when they are swung, like a lariat, overhead. The church, with its gilded apse and mosaic saints who look down on the foolishness or beauty of the people who will soon be gone — as they are gone from life, but here now, in some way, taking part in something, stone that is, or some more permanent kind of life — these saints seem far beyond abashment. Nothing can shock them, she thinks, nothing can disappoint. Their inapproachability comes to her as potent reassurance. She does not know of what.

She sees that the square is the home for another kind of life, more habitual, more domestic. There are people who come here every day; it is their work to be here; they are homeless, and they sit or squat; they beg in a sluggish, aimless, almost off-hand way, and their dogs, flea bitten, interested only in their masters, sniff the cobblestones, forage for the leftovers of the careless tourists, close their eyes ecstatically against the noonday sun. Established in a corner of the square, sitting on a camp stool, a woman with wild hair, ripped stockings, ruined shoes, is concentrating avidly on a piece of needlepoint. Miranda looks to see if there is a cup at her feet, if she is some specialized form of beggar. But she doesn't seem to want anything from the others in the square. It is simply where she is, where she always is.

And walking in and out, chattering, seeing nothing but the place they need to be next, matrons with string bags make their way down the side streets. Some of them have settled down for a late morning coffee; two, perfectly but unfashionably coiffed, cut, with a fine precision, a *cornetto* into identical halves.

She turns up a little street, passes an ancient-looking stone building that is in fact a garage. The men inside it are wearing greasy overalls with their names stitched on the pockets. GUIDO, the names say, GIANNI, but they could as easily say BILL or RICK. The smell of oil and gasoline is a shock; she's reminded that this is a real city, and that the saints on the church are forgotten most of the time by most of its citizens. A large, hot-looking German shepherd lies in the doorway, while his master, five feet away, lies underneath a shiny, red, clearly quite costly car, whose fate is in his hands.

Adam is waiting for her at the workman's café he described. There are four tables outside; he asks if she'd like to sit at one of them.

"No," she says, "I'm too nervous about running into Valerie. This is her neighborhood."

"Oh, God," he says. "I guess I've done such a good job of blocking Valerie out of my mind I hadn't even thought of that. We must, must, get in touch with her."

"Absolutely, we must," Miranda says. And they giggle like naughty children, understanding that they won't be doing it anytime soon.

They're seated at one of a series of long tables, each covered with brown butcher paper. Only one dish is served at each meal, and your bill is calculated on the brown paper that serves as your tablecloth. When your bill is done, that part of the paper is ripped off and handed to you . . . and the rest of the paper is ripped and thrown away after you leave.

A few feet from where Adam stands, there is a salmon-colored wall covered by a bougainvillea, a blanket of sheer purple that makes the orange seem neutral, matte. How, she wonders, can these flowers grow so lush, and climb so high? It isn't, after all, the tropics. They have winter here; the hints of it are in the air when she wakes in the middle of the night.

■ ■ ■ ■

The waitresses that serve them and the others in the restaurant all seem related; their children run in and out. They are affectionate and tender to them, but to their customers, regulars and tourists alike, they are impatient, rough. A small, round-shouldered woman in English tweeds sits alone, reading a newspaper. Another — it is impossible to tell if it is a man or a woman — shares pasta with a fox terrier and takes half of it home. There is only one offering on the menu: *pasta arrabbiata,* and, for a second course, lentils and sausages. Come *contorno* they can order *insalata mista* or *puntarelle,* which Adam recommends: it's a kind of chicory with a dressing made of oil, vinegar, and anchovies. It's available only in the fall. They order wine and a bottle of mineral water but are given only one glass apiece. The roughness, the lack of *cortesia,* pleases her, as does the savory goodness of each dish she eats, the vivid flavors, spicy tomato, peppery meat and beans, bitter greens drenched in salty fish and vinegar and oil.

They walk together to the piazza. A bit over-full, her senses more fuzzy than she would like (she isn't used to wine at lunch), she makes her way to the fountain to sit for a moment in the sun.

Her eye falls on a beggar woman, hunched almost double, her foot twisted inward. She is making mumbling, supplicating noises; she is invoking the Madonna, and calling all the women beautiful, the men generous. Miranda puts a euro in her filthy paper cup.

"You see, Adam, some things in the world have got better. It's important not to forget that. This beggar woman. What do you see when you see her? Someone tragic, a victim, or someone pathetic, annoying, perhaps criminal, almost certainly manipulative? Whatever we see, she's not what we want to be looking at. We want to be seeing the color of the walls, the angle of the sun on the water in the fountain. We don't want to have to be thinking: What should be done for this woman, and who should do it? The church? The state? The family?"

"It isn't the kind of thing I think about: what should be done with her, about her. I hope someone else is thinking about it, someone like you, maybe, who has an idea of what could be done that would be of real use."

"I look at her and understand that she had polio. And that polio is gone from large parts of the world. And that it happened in our lifetime. Do you remember when we were little and every summer people were afraid there'd be another polio epidemic? Our parents were afraid of public swimming pools. They wouldn't let us go to the movies, and the movies were the only place with air-conditioning. They might be afraid of sitting near a fountain like this. And then, suddenly, it was over. That gripping fear. Poof. Over. Because of human endeavor, human intelligence.

"When I worked in India on the smallpox project, and I would see face after ruined face, and afterward, after an exhausting day knocking on the doors of strangers, urging them to be vaccinated . . . and you know how I've always hated asking for things, I would say to myself, I'm doing this so there will be no more ruined faces. Except I never said it out loud. I don't even remember what I said to the people whose doors I knocked on. We were given a script by UNICEF; we weren't supposed to deviate from it by even a syllable. I couldn't say what I was thinking, I'm doing this to work against death because the dead have become invisible. I couldn't even think of it that way after a very short while, the idea of working against death, lessening the tide of death. It was overwhelming to contemplate the millions and millions dead to smallpox. Whereas if I could make my mind focus on one face, that could be seen and known and understood; if I could say, 'I'm doing it so this one face won't be ruined,' then I wasn't overwhelmed."

"You did something that you know helped relieve suffering," he says. "When we were young together and we spoke so easily in such high terms, you said, 'I want to relieve suffering.' And I said, 'I want to create beauty.' "

"You could say we've both done something of what we wanted. And are still doing it. Not everyone can say that."

"Come," he said, "let's walk off our lunch."

They cross the Tiber, walk down the Via Giulia. She stops in front of the gigantic head, its mouth a spigot of running water that falls into its marble bowl, and she thinks how strange it is: the face is tortured, but the sound of water introduces play, the element of joy.

In the Piazza Farnese, she asks: "Why do I like those fountains. They're kind of like big bathtubs . . ." But he knows she really doesn't want an answer.

The Campo dei Fiori, denuded now of

fruits and vegetables, has become a waste-
land, a garbage dump; the Roman street
sweepers, as glamorous, Adam thinks, as
fashion models, haven't made their way here
yet; they're seeing the *campo* at its worst.
They pass through it quickly, cross the ugly,
threatening Corso Vittorio Emanuele, turning down too many streets for Miranda to
account for, and suddenly they are there:
the Piazza Navona, Bernini's lolling gods.
She imagines that if she should say to them,
*What is right? What is good? What is to be
done about the poor?,* they would answer,
*What are you talking about? There is sun and
water. Here is my galloping horse, and the
lion chasing him. How pleasant life is: how
clear and swift the flow of water, how firm and
supple human flesh.*

"You tell me, I must admit some things
are better," Adam says, sitting on the railing
by the statue of the god meant to stand for
the Danube, "but you must admit no one
could accomplish anything like this now.
We've lost the grand scale. Who would
spend what would be required on what they
would think of as useless space, space whose
only use is pleasure? For the gathering of
people and the sound of running water."

Does she trust him enough to say what
she is really thinking, to confess her anxiety:

131

her Protestant guilt for crimes committed centuries before she was born. A response she dislikes in herself, but cannot banish. Partly because it is also a source of her greatest vanity. Not physical vanity, which she gave over long ago, but ethical: *Unlike you, I do not forget.* But she wants to say it, if only because it was the kind of thing she could have said when they were young.

"To have accomplished this, grotesque inequalities were necessary. Such projects are possible only if one forgets about the labor involved, if one forgets about an ideal of justice."

"But aren't you glad they did it? Wouldn't we all be poorer without it?"

"But what about the children of the poor . . ."

"Miranda, you just can't be talking this way right now, not in this place, not on a day like today. Just save it, I promise we can talk about the poor another time. Right now, I'd like to buy you an ice cream. Fix your mind here. Choose now: three flavors."

She sees that she has made a mistake. When they were young, he might have loved her for worrying about the poor in the midst of what seemed to be a great party: the sound of the water, the delights of harmonious space, the coming and going of all these people and the great fixed stone gods. But now, she knows, she seems ridiculous to him, pretentious, even boorish. She seems that way to herself, although she knows that everything she's said is right.

"I will choose hazelnut, coffee, pistachio, and give up thinking about the impossible poor, the miserable dead." She is trying to make a joke of her seriousness, because she can see that it is laughable, really, particularly here. Yet she means everything she said. But she knows she must pretend not to mean it. She must pretend to think herself absurd, to believe that nothing is more important than the best possible choice of ice cream. Or else she will be one of those unbearable people, one of those people no one wants to be with. And she wants him to want to be with her.

"For now," he says, putting his hand on her shoulder. It's the first time he's allowed himself to touch her, and they both understand that something has changed and that they must not acknowledge that it has.

"Tomorrow," he says, "we'll only be able to take a short walk. And we'll have to meet early. Lucy and I are going to see my cousins in Orvieto."

"Yes," she says. "How nice." She's relieved. He has a life in Rome apart from her, and she is glad to take her place among the things in his life that are unimportant, provisional, able to be let go. At the same time, a small wet patch forms below her ribs, coldish, thickish: she will be more alone tomorrow than he will. He will have his daughter, his cousins. She wonders if any of his aunts and uncles are still alive. She thinks of them and the long Sunday meals she was once invited to be a part of. Tomorrow, when he's surrounded by loving, familiar people, she'll be on her own.

SUNDAY, OCTOBER 14

VILLA BORGHESE
"Certain Kinds of Weather Once Enchanted Us"

They walk up the Viale Magnolia; it pleases her that a road should be named for a tree. The park is empty, except for focused dog walkers. Serious runners.

"This is new," he says, "Italians running. A few years ago, if you saw someone running here, you knew they were American."

"How do you know they're Italian?"

"Only Italians would be that carefully dressed and coiffed even for a run."

She likes that he notices what people wear; it's something Yonatan would never do. It makes Adam seem more feminine, safer.

He looks at his watch. "I'm afraid we only have time for a short walk, before Lucy wakes up. Before I wake her. If I don't, she'll sleep and sleep. She might not wake till the sun is down."

"Don't you remember, Adam. Those adolescent sleeps. So deep. They were like heaven."

"It's hard to call back that kind of memory. For so many years now, I've woken up at dawn."

She pulls her jacket closer to her. "The weather has changed overnight. The atmosphere is different."

"The whole question of weather is different here. A different kind of question. Less frightening. Perhaps, also, less exhilarating. I do remember, about being younger, that some weathers used to make me feel exhilarated and other kinds made me feel quite frightened."

"Yes, that irrecoverable fall of darkness, like a knife blade. Just at this time of year: October. You just wanted to beg for it: a few more minutes of life outdoors, a bit more light, that precious sense of coldness, because soon you'd be called in, into warmth, into the smell of food, into safety, but at that moment it wasn't safety you wanted, it was danger, the risk of cold, to be there for that sudden drop of bluish black. Part of you longed to be locked out. As if being indoors at all were a kind of suffocation, an imprisonment. You'd never be let out again; you'd never get the air, the light."

"I used to be frightened by high winds, but of course I couldn't say it. I was a boy . . . what kind of boy would be frightened by high winds? But my house always seemed insubstantial to me. Your house always seemed safer than mine. Perhaps because your father seemed more in charge than mine."

"But your father was so much kinder."

"I can't call back the sound of his voice. But his presence, yes his presence was always kind."

"I didn't feel safe in my house."

"It was so solid, though. Wasn't it built in the eighteenth century? A stone house in a town where nearly all the houses were wooden. Oh, I guess there were some brick houses. But yours was stone. I thought that was so wonderful. And the fact that your father had built himself a greenhouse. I was in awe of that, and it seemed like a kind of holy place, I wanted to take my shoes off or cover my head. It seemed extraordinary to me, your father seemed the absolute perfection of the American man: a war hero, an engineer, so handsome and tall, and then he grew these beautiful delicate orchids."

"Ah yes, my father and his orchids," she

says with a bitterness he doesn't recognize in her. But he hears there is something else in the tone, something else besides bitterness, only he can't identify it.

She feels the effort at keeping back the pleasant memories of herself and her father in the greenhouse, the unclear light, the overheated air, and in the unclarity the brilliant flowers, so that it was an atmosphere of mistiness and certainty, a dream of peace. But she doesn't want to complicate her bitterness; she has determined she will shut her heart to her father's virtues; to allow them in would be to betray her brother, which she will not do.

"When I was in that greenhouse, I always thought there was no need to worry about certain things," he says.

"When you say 'certain things,' what you mean is money."

"Well, maybe that was part of it. I think it was more a certain kind of display that I worried might be excessive. Too much loud laughing. Too much food. Too much gratitude. Too many angry words and then too many apologies."

"My mother was both too grateful and too apologetic," Miranda says. "My father: neither. Not at all."

"And my mother was not apologetic. Nor

was my father. I think it was the grandparents. Every Sunday. Grateful and apologetic. And my father, somehow ashamed in front of them, as if he'd had too much good fortune. Not ever taking credit for how hard he'd worked for whatever he'd got. Which made me grateful and apologetic: I was always aware of how hard he had to work to pay for my lessons. And so that I wouldn't have to work so hard. I think he was always afraid that the good fortune of my mother in his life would be somehow snatched away. Which in the end it was."

"And so you think he just allowed himself to die because he didn't want to live without her. They had, I think, a great love."

"Yes, I think so, yes, a real, great love."

She doesn't want to go on talking in this way. "My mother felt she had to keep the summer light and heat out of the house. She confused light and damage. How I disliked it: the curtains drawn, the doors kept shut all summer."

"Do you remember that dread on Sunday nights? Sheer dread. I didn't even dislike school; why did I so dread the beginning of a new week?"

"Perhaps we wanted to sleep more than we were allowed. Perhaps we dreaded waking up and being tired. I do remember being tired on school mornings."

"I liked it when I lay in bed and heard the rain," he says.

"Thunderstorms, I loved. Lightning like a crack in something that needed it."

"Blue light on the snow. I loved it then. Sometimes, now, I fear the approach of winter."

"I live in a place where winter is unreal."

"Do you still love swimming? You were always so excited when you went into the water for the first time in the summer."

"I do love swimming, yes. I think I'm happier in water than anywhere else. We have a house on a small lake in Oregon. Each morning, even if it's quite cold, I dive into the water. It's a wonderful deep blue-green. There I feel exhilaration. I'm full of gratitude. I hear myself saying, in a voice I know is mine but that I can't quite recognize, 'I love everything, I love everything.' "

"Weren't the springs earlier and longer?"

"I don't know about your springs. We live, Adam, a continent apart."

"California. Land of the unreal."

"The new world. Possibilities."

"You don't have real autumns."

"No, I miss that light: that bright light on the yellow leaves."

"Here in Rome there are only varieties of

green. In autumn the greens become bronzed, like old metal. Even now, though it's October, everything is green; the yellow just becomes part of a darker green. Absorbed in it."

"America invented brilliant autumns," she says.

"Do you remember when we left home for college?"

"You got there a week before me."

"I had to audition, I had to keep auditioning . . . God, I was so afraid of failing."

"I thought, Now I must begin my life."

"We sat under a tree," Adam says. "I think you said it was a larch. The leaves were narrow, they made a canopy over our heads. I wanted to say, 'We sit beneath a canopy of brilliant gold.' But I was afraid to say something like that in front of your new friends."

"I wasn't afraid of anything then. If only I could be like that again."

"And what are you afraid of now?"

"Now I've learned to be afraid of more things than I could even have imagined thinking of as frightening," she says.

"I sometimes wonder if I am any longer capable of exhilaration. Of that sense of taking flight. Of being taken up. I am very attached to the earth."

"Maybe it's because we're more than halfway through our lives on earth and so perhaps more reluctant than we once were to take flight from it."

"Or perhaps our blood has slowed and thickened," Adam says.

She thinks: He's had a heart attack. He could have died. I'm sure he's on medicine to thin his blood. Perhaps he feels the cold.

"You look cold," she says in case he is.

"I am, a bit."

Alarmed, he turns his wrist, looks at his watch.

"I should be waking Lucy now."

She sees he is no longer with her.

"I'll stay here and walk for a while," she says. She wants to be looking at the trees in a way that she knows wouldn't interest him. Because of what they have been saying, she wants to be thinking of her father. She feels free to, as she hasn't felt for what she thinks is much too long a time.

SEPTEMBER 1964

Labor Day has come and gone; it is officially not summer, but the air is close and damp, the temperature in the high eighties. No one knows how to dress. Or rather, girls and women don't; boys and men believe they have no choice. For most activities of any kind of public nature, a jacket is required; they are prepared, men and boys who aspire to the category of "the respectable," to be too hot. But girls and women, having put aside their pastel dresses, are baffled, vexed. As long as they refuse white shoes, belts, and pocketbooks, they are perfectly within their rights to wear a skirt and long-sleeved blouse of a breathable material: cotton always the most desirable, but sometimes rejected on the basis of convenience in favor of nylon or Dacron: drip-dry. Whatever they choose, they too will be uncomfortable. Stockings are compulsory, and for all but the most brave, a girdle to hold in the

stomach, whether or not the stomach requires being held in. Also to keep the stockings up.

But even if they are not too warm, the
women and the girls will not be happy. They
have spent many days in August sweating in
try-on rooms, making important autumn
purchases: wool skirts (straight, A-line,
pleated), sweaters to match the colors of
the falling leaves. Purchases to suggest
security, dependability, a preparedness
against the coming winter.

Miranda, for example, is secretly disappointed because she spent a summer's
worth of babysitting money on a jacket
made to look like a lumberjack's red-and-
black plaid, designed by Pendleton. It would
be absurd to wear it on a day like this; she
would sweat and worry at the odor of her
own young body, still unfamiliar to her,
producing new, unacceptable substances at
a daily or alarming rate.

She does not think of it as September 7,
1964. She thinks of it as the first day of
junior year.

Four years later, September 7, 1968, she
won't consider wearing something uncomfortable. In 1968, she will wear what is easy
or amusing; no one she speaks to at that
time will be able to consider once again

wearing stockings and a girdle, which will, by that time, have become as unthinkable as a whalebone corset, a bustle, a parasol. Miranda and her friends will be proud of wearing garments others have worn before them. They will hide any designer label, anything with a recognizable name.

But of course she does not know this. It is September 7, 1964, the day she must audition for the Glee Club. It's not an ordinary audition for the Glee Club; she's already in the Glee Club, anyone can be, almost anyone who can sing in tune. But it's different today. Today she's auditioning for solos, and everyone wants a solo, and she's only a junior, and juniors never get solos, but she knows she's right to try for this because she knows she's right to say to herself, I have a good voice.

How does she know? Because her friends tell her, and so does Miss McKeever, the music teacher, whom she doesn't trust because Miss McKeever is too eager, too enthusiastic, too needy of Miranda's friendship. And Miranda is ashamed for her that she, an adult, should visibly need so much from someone like Miranda, who is still used to thinking of herself as a child.

Nevertheless, she knows her voice is good. What she doesn't know is: what is meant by "good"?

To whom should she compare herself? Most important: Joan Baez. She knows her voice is not as beautiful as Joan Baez's. She wonders if, one day, with study, with discipline, it could be, but this is something she tells no one.

Miss McKeever tells her that this year the Glee Club's solos will be taken from *Brigadoon.* So with the part of her babysitting money left over after she bought the Pendleton jacket, she buys the original Broadway cast album of the show. She chooses the original Broadway cast, with people she's never heard of — David Brook and Marion Bell — instead of the record accompanying the film, with people she has heard of and likes very much: Gene Kelly and Cyd Charisse. Because she knows that Broadway is more important than Hollywood and the original cast is always the best. How does she know this? It is one of the things she and her friends seem to know, which allows them to mark themselves as superior to others of their cohort who are considered superior — cheerleaders, athletes — but who do not know this kind of thing.

In her room, with the doors closed, when she is sure her father is at work and her mother is out shopping and her brother is practicing with one of his many teams, she sings the words to the songs.

"The heather on the hill."

"Come to me, bend to me."

She is embarrassed at her own yearning to sing these words to a living person. "Come to me, bend to me, kiss me good day! Give me your lips and don't take them away."

She has not yet been kissed.

At night in her bed she dreams of it. Her arms around a boy's strong body, his arms around her. Leaning against strength that will allow her to feel what she has never felt but imagines, through reading and the movies, is delicious: the luxury of weakness.

To be allowed to allow whatever will be bound to happen.

The music of *Brigadoon* is not the kind of music she believes in. She believes in folk music. She wishes the solo were going to be "It Ain't Me, Babe," or "The Times They Are A-Changin'." Or a song that evokes the great emotions of simple people — "Long Black Veil" or "Silver Dagger."

But when she wakes from sleep, the words on the screen between her sleeping and her wakefulness are "Give me your lips and don't take them away."

Adam takes a second shower after breakfast.

His white long-sleeved shirt is already soaking wet. He is nervous; he is mortified. This year he will be the piano accompanist for the Glee Club. He is a scholarship boy in the Thomas Arnold School; he can't refuse the job, although he despises himself for not insisting that he can't do it. He is a real musician and the music that they sing is trash.

His teacher, Mr. Levi, trained by Schnabel himself, has told Adam that this kind of music is trash, dangerous trash; he must fend off its corruption like the threat of an infection.

Mr. Levi says he thinks Adam should suggest that the Glee Club sing some madrigals.

He doesn't understand that it is impossible that Adam would suggest anything like this. For his suggesting at all would imply that he possesses an entity that he suspects is not really his. That word Mr. Levi says so casually, as if it were something permitted in the world: to speak of it, to speak the word: talent. Your real talent. Your genuine talent. And he doesn't understand that Adam would never suggest anything that would possibly hurt anyone, but especially Miss McKeever. Poor Miss McKeever — plain, unloved, even by the students on whom she lavishes so much love.

He would like to tell Miss McKeever: *If you were colder, they would love you.*

An economy of temperature he believes in but does not understand.

Miss McKeever looks on him like a young prince, a young god. She, too, uses the words that are not permitted, "your talent." Sometimes she says, "your gift."

In secret he occasionally allows himself to believe that he is gifted, talented. But it must not be said aloud. Not by Mr. Levi. And especially not by Miss McKeever, who wants nothing more than to bask in the light of his giftedness, his talent.

Which, to be safeguarded, must not be spoken of, he knows, aloud.

Every Friday when he takes the commuter train from Hastings to Manhattan he is grateful, abashed, incredulous. That he should be doing this. He, Adam, son of his parents, Salvatore and Rose, whose parents came in their turn, nearly children, traveling by ship from Italy in conditions of unspeakable filth and terror. They do not speak of it; his grandparents are nearly silent people, as if in front of their son who works in the furniture store in White Plains, and their daughter-in-law who is kind and good and cooks the food they love, but who has named her children Adam (after a man she worked for, a lawyer who went to jail because of standing up for something about colored people) and Jo (named after no one in the family, named for someone in a book she read). Their daughter-in-law who asks them to babysit (what kind of word is that, they ask each other, the grandparents) so she and their son can go to a Chinese restaurant. A Chinese restaurant? To eat what kind of food? In front of such people as their son and daughter-in-law, they believe it would be wrong to speak of where they came from, what they are. They believe they have no right.

Adam believes he has no right as he presses the buzzer at Henry Levi's apartment on Riverside Drive. No right. No rights. Those who tell him he has many rights, on account of his gift — well, he knows they must be wrong. You are my genius boy, his mother says, pretending it's a joke, kissing him over and over on the top of his head after she's heard him play anything: a Chopin nocturne, "Moonlight Sonata," perhaps not even playing them well. But she believes he has a gift, and that his gift means he doesn't have to clean the house on weekends and certainly not get a summer job. And so he tries to understand what this thing is, this music, who he is in relation to this music, and what it is to him and what are its demands; a whole world of arduous exigencies, permissions given and withheld, is his.

And the money. Money for his lessons. Somehow money is involved and is provided; he eats up family money; he sees himself at the dinner table, guzzling while they eat modestly, denying themselves the choicer morsels they might secretly crave. Or maybe it is his music that is guzzling it all. But somehow allowances are made for this as well.

They are very young, Adam and Miranda; she is sixteen; he will be sixteen in two months. They never say to themselves: we are very young, most of our lives have yet to be lived. They fear, they hope and they believe. They think: I will travel to many places/I will never go anywhere/I will have many great loves/No one will ever choose me/The world will be better for my having lived in it/Nothing I do will come to anything/I will make music of unthought-of purity/I am a fraud and will soon be exposed for the fraud I am/I will be renowned, applauded on the world's great stages/I will end up selling furniture in White Plains like my father, whom I honor/I will be the wife

151

of a great man, will be the mother of many children who surround me with incalculable love/I will marry a man, as my mother did, who forgets that he once loved me.

Of the things they do not fear, or do not think of fearing (fortunate children, spared what others alive when they are alive have not been spared, what most of the human race has not): physical illness, plague, bodily weakness. No, these are not their fears. Their fears are of the earth's annihilation by the atom bomb, the mushroom cloud, the threat of which inspires their teachers to send them under their desks for weekly air-raid drills. THEENDOFTHEWORLD THEENDOFTHEWORLD is a phrase that often spins in their minds, and they are terrified even when they forget that they are terrified. They know quite well what it will mean: the complete disintegration of their flesh and bones. The turning to ash in an instant of everything they love.

And close at hand, like an aunt or uncle living in the next town: the memories of the war. The concentration camps. The words, still whispered to themselves at night when sleep refuses: gas chamber, SS, Hitler, death to the Jews.

So these two children, or only recently no

longer children, Adam and Miranda, born in 1948, and so in 1964 sixteen or about to be sixteen. She will not allow her mother to give her a sweet sixteen party; her mother, she knows, is disappointed, but will not (she never does) press her wish.

Prosperous children, or relatively so in Adam's case. Miranda is more prosperous than she knows; her mother the beneficiary of one of those unnamed industrial enterprises common to the beginning of the twentieth century. Her father, a chemical engineer, graduate of Williams College, her mother, Smith 1941, who once worked, briefly, before her marriage, in a gallery and dreamed of cataloging English watercolors of the nineteenth century. Despite their real, or relative, prosperity, these young people have their nightmares. The flavor, the weather of their nightmares differ.

Miranda's are of explosions. Something heavy dropping from a plane. In her frightening dreams, she does not make a picture of the thing dropping from the plane; she makes a picture of the pilot: a Russian in a brown wool uniform with Mongol slits for eyes, a pig snout of a nose, enormous teeth, yellow, wolfish, that tear each night into huge hunks of meat and could tear with equal ease a girl child's flesh. The dream streets are lines of shooting flame, and people run, their skin crackling, their faces melting to monstrosity. Sirens sound, but they are useless; no one is in charge; the population hurtles toward nothing, anything, searching for anything they love, all lost, fallen into the pits the streets have become or burned to cinders. She is trying to get home to her room, her books, her mother who must be safe, her father who must know what to do, but her brother will not be home because he will be in the streets, trying to protect something, but there is no protection, no one can be safe.

Adam's nightmares unroll in a different landscape. He rarely reads the newspapers, and when his parents are watching Walter Cronkite he is practicing. But he listens, he listens to his teacher Henry Levi. Henry (Heinrich) Levi, sent alone to New York in 1936 to live with uncles and cousins. In Berlin, his family was musical; his father a violinist for the State Opera, his mother a coach for some of the most famous sopranos of the day. They lost their jobs, but they wouldn't leave, because their parents wouldn't leave and they would not abandon their parents. They gambled on their own lives, and lost, but they did not gamble on the life of their son. In New York he lived with merchants, kindhearted sellers of women's lingerie. They understood that Henry's musical training must continue. His uncle, the merchant, thought it a privilege to pay for Henry's lessons with the best teacher, and so Henry had to hide his terror and his shame. It was 1938, then 1939, then 1940, and America was still not at war. He knew that he would never see his parents, that they would be killed while he was safe, saved for his music.

For a long time, Henry Levi didn't speak to Adam of these things. Until the spring of 1963, when Adam tells him he can't come for a lesson the next week because it's Good Friday. Mr. Levi, so formal, so reserved, brings down his fist, the fist made of the valuable fingers of the valuable hand, down on the valuable wood of the piano, and the metronome jumps, the head of Beethoven jumps, and he speaks of roving gangs assaulting Jews in the name of the Crucified Christ whom the Jews are responsible for killing. You think this is only in Europe, but I tell you it is here as well. So how can he feel safe ever, he asks, on this day when he knows very well that he and others of his kind are never safe on this day, this Friday, which the people among whom he lives insist on calling good.

Mrs. Levi, whom Adam will one day (but not for many years) call Sylvia, appears from nowhere with a glass of water and a linen napkin. Be calm, Henry, she says, then something in German, and Adam is sent home.

The next week Henry Levi apologizes, says he must explain, and every week, when the lesson is over and he can be sure he is not misusing the time for which he has been paid, he tells Adam a bit more, doling out history like a rich but poisoned candy Adam must learn to digest or grow immune to.

And so, instead of reading the *New York Times*, Adam reads histories of the war. Details of concentration camps. His nightmares are not of bombed streets in flame but of piles of bodies, shoes, bones. He dreams himself a starving child in a freezing woods, barefoot; he has stolen bread which he must share with another child; he doesn't want to share it. In one book he has read, he learns of a survivor child who escaped into the woods after having stolen a chocolate coin. Each night he and his brother lick their index fingers and rub them over the slowly diminishing coin, making it last a month. In his nightmare, while his little sister sleeps, he palms the coin and swallows it all.

Who has taught him to fear his appetites, which at sixteen seem to him monstrous?

Miranda thinks of her appetites as the stuff of songs. Over and over she plays Peter, Paul and Mary (but only Mary sings), "The first time ever I saw your face." Whole hours lost, dreaming of something she doesn't even know the word for. "Boyfriend" is too trivial, too unserious, and she could not begin to form, in relation to herself, the word "lover." When she sings the words from that same song, "the first time ever I kissed your mouth" — kissed your *mouth* rather than your *lips* — she is excited and proud of her excitement. And she knows she wants to be doing something only wives are meant to be doing, but she doesn't want to be a wife, she wants to be someone's great love. She is afraid that this will not happen before the world is annihilated.

And so these children on the verge of no longer being children hear in their sleep the words "annihilation," "monstrosity."

And yet in the history of the world it is, perhaps more completely than any other, a time of safety. A time of hope. Despite the death of the young president, a time of hope.

157

■ ■ ■ ■

On September 7, 1964, Adam and Miranda
have not yet spoken a word to each other,
although they are students in the same
school, in the same year. The Thomas
Arnold School: a high-minded, old-
fashioned private school in Hastings, en-
clave of the children of the privileged, the
intellectually ambitious, the fearful, the
insecure. Adam and Miranda know each
other's names and faces. They have not
spoken a word, yet by virtue of having been
born in the same year, 1948, they share images stamped into the soft wax at the base
of their spine. For both of them, the seal is
set. Set in the spine, from which the fragile
and responsive nerves radiate out.

The smiling face of Anne Frank.

The black children of Little Rock.

John Kennedy and his wife in a formal
portrait.

Jacqueline Kennedy veiled, widowed, her
husband among the perfect dead, the little
boy saluting as his father's coffin rolls past
him in the funeral cortege.

And alongside, or perhaps pressed on top of
these, like an outline stenciled above a

painted landscape, Adam has other images which Miranda does not have.

The face of Henry (Heinrich) Levi, a young boy in Germany.

And the other Germans. Bach. Beethoven.

The face of the victorious Van Cliburn, with a mouth set like Beethoven's (not the calm mouth of Bach) and his furious, impossibly tight curled hair.

And when Miranda is reading nineteenth-century novels or learning new dances with her friends, Adam is practicing the piano four, six, sometimes seven, even eight hours a day. They have no way of knowing how the other spends his or her day: he, listening over and over to records on the phonograph his parents allow him to keep in his room so that he can better understand a certain phrasing, while she is listening over and over to Joan Baez and Peter, Paul and Mary. Adam and Miranda are from different tribes. They are both sixteen, but he is much much older. Yet in some ways, more thoroughly a child.

It is because of music that they meet and speak.

September 7, 1964. They both walk from their separate homes to the Thomas Arnold School. She is wearing a cotton shirtwaist

159

dress, blue and green flowers against a background of pinkish beige, her skirt modestly below her knees. She wears stockings held up by a garter belt, refusing her mother's semi-abashed suggestion of a girdle. Her shoes: Bass Weejun loafers with pennies in the slits made for the purpose. She is uncomfortably hot, and blames it on her stockings, which she thinks of jettisoning by the side of the road but not today, no not today. Today is too important.

Adam is too hot because the only jacket that still fits him (he is four inches taller than he was in June) is a brown herringbone wool, recently bought, looking forward to cooler weather. The sleeves of his blue-and-white plaid summer jacket now only reach a bit below his elbows, the fabric pulling shamingly and uncomfortably across his shoulder blades.

"We're going to have to put a brick on your head," his mother says, "or just stop feeding you." She says this as she ladles thick vegetable soup, pasta with meat sauce, and cuts into a cheesecake she made this morning, with a knife she ran under warm water to facilitate the removal of each slice. He sees her smile of calm fulfillment when he eats. And he is always hungry so she seems always happy. He is a boy who loves

160

his mother, loves his sister, loves, though more shyly and quite silently, his nearly silent father. He even loves his grandparents, for whom there is no silence in the expression of their love for this grandson who makes music.

He lives with the sorrow and the shame that he does not entirely belong to his family. He belongs as well to Henry Levi; he belongs to music. Music is the beam of light his eye is always focused on. He lives for music, yet he loves his family who do not live for music, not at all, could live perfectly well without it. They don't, he knows, exactly understand why he must play the same bars of a Bach invention, a Chopin polonaise, again and again. Does it drive them to distraction? They never suggest it, never say anything but the most loving words of praise about his music. He understands, he thinks he understands, that he was born for something larger, older than his family, this music that was there (but where is *there,* where was it?) long before he was born and will go on long after he is dead. And so it is not difficult for him to practice hour after hour, repeating the same phrase until the touch, the emphasis, is as right as it can be. His gaze does not stray from the beam of light whose source is somewhere higher than his sight can comprehend.

Miranda, on the other hand, has been accused of a failure of patience. But only with human beings; with objects, plants, and animals, she seems to be uncannily patient. She has been praised consistently for her enthusiasm. Her energy. A reservoir, seemingly inexhaustible, of plans and hope.

Adam has never had a real friend. For too many years his life has been too different from that of other boys his age. Oh, there are other boys whose lives are more like his, students of Henry Levi's, but they live in Manhattan and their parents seem to have more to do with Henry Levi and the music they all love than Adam's parents do, and so he feels abashed, unworthy. When Sylvia Levi suggests that the boys get together for a Coke, they do (they all revere her), but they don't know how to talk to one another, and they frequently look at their watches, eager to get back home. To practice. To be with their families, with whom they need not enter into extended conversations or talk at all.

Miranda's life is centered around her group of friends, the smart girls, who dream of not being as law abiding as they are, and who do not have boyfriends.

For weeks and weeks, Miranda and her four friends have dedicated themselves to the question: what should Miranda choose for her audition piece.

The conditions are many.

They are extensively discussed.

There is the matter of personalities: the judges of the competition.

The judges will be: Miss McKeever, who will get teary over almost everything, and, most important, Mr. Jameson, the junior music teacher, director of the Glee Club, called Jamie by the girls who swoon over him in small semiprivate groups. They love his black-rimmed glasses, his sand-colored hair, long enough to fall into his eyes and be pushed impatiently back by graceful hands that always seem to be quite tan, whatever the season. He was the first to appear in school in a madras jacket worn over a yellow shirt, something the girls had not seen in life but only in the pages of *Seventeen* magazine. It would not occur to them that Charles Jameson has a lover, with whom he lives in Greenwich Village, whose name is not Harriet but Harry. Such a category has not entered the group mind, and certainly not the group discussion.

Therefore all the girls in the Thomas Arnold Glee Club can still put themselves to sleep with dreams of their June wedding (the week after college graduation) to Charles Jameson. They speculate endlessly on the details of his current (temporary) bachelorhood. They decide he is involved with a Martha Graham dancer. Or perhaps someone who works in advertising or publishing. Or perhaps someone European. Spanish, they decide, or Portuguese.

The girls worry: Charles Jameson's tastes are unpredictable. Last spring he announced that the Glee Club would be singing selections from *Brigadoon*. Along with this, they will be singing selections from the *Messiah* and some Negro spirituals.

Then there is the painful reality that juniors are almost never given solos and the even more crushing fact of the dreaded enemy Suzanne Lazzard, who signs her notes (written to Mr. Jameson and to senior boys, never to girls) SUZZI, with two *z*'s. Her mother is rumored to buy Suzzi's clothes in Paris. Her father provides Suzzi with voice lessons from Miss Patti Richards, who was in the chorus of *Damn Yankees* and who has told everyone that she and Gwen Verdon are "very very close." Like sisters, Miss Patti Richards says. Twining her middle fingers. "Like this."

A third problem: the girls don't know whether to honor or to discourage Miranda's obsession with Joan Baez.

A trip to the city is required. To select sheet music, so that they're sure they haven't wasted their time on something that could not be presented to Charles Jameson, who can sight-read anything.

They take the same train to the city as Adam, and they greet him politely, but he blushes when he sees them and ducks his head as if their greeting were a heavy rain he must escape. He enters another car.

"Do you think he's cute?"

"Who?"

"Adam."

"He's really shy. I think he's kind of a snob. He takes these special piano lessons in the city. He's a big pianist, or something. He's going to accompany the Glee Club this year."

"Well, then, I guess we'll get to know him."

"Probably, yeah."

They don't think of him for the rest of the thirty-five-minute train ride.

They are not thinking of him, but he is thinking of them, because although he is a kind boy, a gentle boy, who loves his mother and his sister and the great music of the eighteenth and nineteenth centuries, although he is what everyone who knows him even slightly (the train conductor) or quite well (his mother, his sister) would consider a good boy, he is tormented by the wild and to him incomprehensible and unimaginable urgings of his body. He does not focus on Miranda any more than on any of her friends. He will not allow details to connect his random and generalized desire for any female at all to someone he might know, with the face of a girl or girls who exist in the same world as he, so defiling does he consider his desires. And he would never dream of buying pornography or anything approaching it. The source of his imaginings: women in bikinis seen on postcards tacked up on the wall of the garage where his father gets his car repaired. A calendar found in the same location. He thinks that he must be mad or loathsome to call up these images so often; he can't understand that the same body that dwells on these images is capable of reproducing the great pure invaluable music of Schubert and Fauré.

Miranda and her friends go to Colony Records on Broadway and Fiftieth. They find something called the *Joan Baez Songbook,* which has on its cover a picture of the singer on a beach in California called Big Sur. They plan to travel there after high school graduation. They are hoping one of their parents will lend them a car.

They pore over the book, relieved beyond all telling that it provides, not only guitar chords, but also the possibility for piano accompaniment. Now the problem is: to find a song that will not lose by being accompanied by piano rather than guitar.

They buy the book. They look over it on the train. They look over it in Miranda's bedroom. They settle on "Plaisir d'Amour," sung first in French. Miranda has studied French for eleven months, her accent is considered "excellent." But suppose Suzanne (Suzzi) chooses a French song. This is considered, then rejected. They know their enemy. They know that her imagination is set not on Paris (where her mother might be buying her clothes) but on London, where the Beatles live. She has had her hair cut in the short geometric style invented by Vidal Sassoon, and she paints her eyelids with a single thick black stroke.

They're right: Suzzi doesn't choose a French song, she chooses a song by an English singer, Dusty Springfield. "You don't have to say you love me just be close at hand." They don't know that she means it as a message to Mr. Jameson: that she has no desire, in her desire for him, to curtail his freedom.

Has Charles Jameson, though, understood this secret message? And perhaps wished to remove himself from this desire, the desire of a girl whose new haircut, new makeup, have removed her from the territory of the girlish, transporting her over the line into the territory of the womanly, a territory he finds much more dangerous, much less comfortable? What he treasures in the female, particularly as he sees it is now in the process of becoming obsolete, its form melting away like a lump of sugar in a cup of tea: innocent girlishness. Girlish ardor.

So Suzanne (Suzzi) has miscalculated. Singing her modern song with her modern haircut and short modern skirt, she represents for Charles Jameson all that he would like, in the female, kept back.

Miranda, her light brown hair unstyled, reaching below her shoulders, her flower-print shirtwaist dress, her simple song of heartfelt love and its potential sorrows, has touched, in Charles Jameson, exactly the right note. He sees that she is virtuous, and thinks of the Old English word "virtu." She is like a sturdy, unperfumed flower, a hollyhock, white, lightish pink. Her hands with their short, unvarnished, rounded nails, seem both cool and warm, as if, touching them, you might be comforted but never urged.

Miranda's eyes fall on the boy seated at the piano, on Adam, whom she looks at briefly and then looks away from. She thinks: He is beautiful. She has never in life (though she's read of it in books) seen hair like his, so black it seems shot through with blue, and she thinks "Black, black, black is the color of my true love's hair," which Joan Baez has sung night after night in the darkness of Miranda's bedroom. She wants to refuse the word "beautiful" because "beautiful" is not a word used for boys in those years. Yet it returns like a wave over a slick shoreline. Beautiful, she thinks, he is beautiful, and she thinks of this boy whose name, Adam, is the only thing she knows about him, except for the fact that he's a serious musician. Their eyes meet, and they both blush. She looks not at his face but at his beautiful hands, the traces of dark hair that make him so excitingly ungirlish.

So it begins with music, with a singing girl,

and a boy, playing the piano to accompany her song.

Plaisir d'amour
Endure qu'un moment
Chagrin d'amour endure
La vie.

The joys of love
Are but a moment long
The pain of love endures
Your whole life long.

Adam and Miranda, one just sixteen, one nearly, neither of them knowing the joys of love or its attendant, some would say, inevitable sorrow.

So it begins, the rest of the story. A love story like any other, conforming to certain patterns (rhythmic), revealing certain strains and inflections (class; gender, though the word is not yet in vogue) but most particularly shaped by its time, its moment in history: the mid-1960s to the beginning of the 1970s. Though many people would say that in 1964 the '60s have not yet begun: they will begin a year later, in 1965. But certainly we are not in the '50s. Rebellion is in the air, but it is not, for now, called revolution. Rather: "nonconformity." There are signs of change; money is not important; respectability, security, are nothing. The worst thing you can be called in those years: phony.

There is no falseness in either of them, Adam and Miranda, and what they will soon regularly call "our love."

There is one small falsity, however, a necessary one, committed by Miranda to set things in motion. Because, although she thinks of herself as a modern girl, free of the constraints that she believes have hobbled her mother and her mother's generation, she would find it unthinkable to ask a boy out on a date.

And she has never been asked on a date before, so the whole notion of "date" shimmers in the distance, desirable, unattainable, the Islands of the Blest, Mount Rushmore, Shangri-la.

So a few weeks later she pretends to just happen to be on the same New York–bound train as Adam. She knows which train he takes into the city every week because she engages in an activity that would now be known as stalking. She sees that, although formerly he took the 3:47 train on Fridays, now he takes the 11:30 on Saturdays; she assumes he is going to the city for his lesson.

For three weeks they have been in the same room three afternoons a week, rehearsing with the Glee Club. They have never been in the company of fewer than thirty others. They have yet to exchange a word.

Not only does she find him beautiful, she also finds him the embodiment of a life that is far from everything her father stands for. Her father: efficient, always certain, ready at a moment's notice to dismiss the tentative, the circumspect.

Sometimes she gets to the music room early hoping to be alone with him, but she always hears him playing the piano and when she peeks in the door his look is so intent she would be ashamed to interrupt him. And she is excited by his intensity; it creates in her a hunger as avid, and she would like to be as public in her avidity for him as he is toward his music. But that is impossible. She must pretend to be in the same place as he is by accident. She must pretend to accidentally drop books so that he will pick them up.

And when Adam sees her on the train he finds himself strangled with anxiety. Because he has found *her* beautiful, her hair like a cool stream down her back; he would like to bury his hot face in it, and her careful, sensible but supple hands, and her voice singing "the joys of love" with a clarity he yearns for when he plays, for example, the mazurkas of Chopin. But she need not strive for it; this clarity is who she is.

So when she says, "Hi, oh, we're on the same train," he can't think of anything to reply.

It is, he thinks, easy for her to find things to say.

"I'm going to the Museum of Modern Art," she says, casually. "I'm really interested in Monet. My mother has this book about him and I thought maybe I'd ask Mrs. Lucas if I could do a term paper on the French Impressionists for history. I know that's a little weird, but she's kind of, you know, easygoing."

She made that up a second before: that she will go to the Museum of Modern Art. She has never been there; she has been to the Metropolitan with her mother. But they don't visit the Impressionists there; her mother prefers the cool vaultings of the Metropolitan; she loves the Gainsborough ladies, the Goya ladies, the ladies of Ingres and David, and she once said she found the Impressionists "a bit rushed for my tastes."

Adam is in a panic because he doesn't know where the Museum of Modern Art is. He never does anything in the city but go to his lessons and then get back on the train. Unless he stops for a grilled-cheese sandwich and a Coke at the luncheonette on Broadway and Eighty-fourth Street.

"That's great," he says.

She spends the entire day in Grand Central Terminal, her eye on every Westchester train, so that she can pretend just to happen to be on the same one. He gets on a train three hours later.

"How was the museum?"

Now it is her turn to panic. She hadn't thought that she would have to tell this lie, and she thinks she's been very stupid.

"Nice," she says. "Really nice. How was your lesson?"

"Oh, good. I have a really great teacher."

"Oh," she says. "What's his name?"

And somehow, this simple question, answered simply with the name "Henry Levi," frees Adam to begin speaking. About Henry Levi, his apartment, his family in Germany that perished. And then Miranda speaks about Anne Frank, and they discuss the fact that both their fathers fought in the war in Europe and never speak of it.

"So I'll see you in school," he says as they part to walk home in separate directions from the train station.

"Yes," she says, drenched in her failure

like a hungry animal caught in a rainstorm.

But they have talked to each other, and the next weekend she gets on the train and says, "I'm going back to the museum," and he says, "Oh maybe I could meet you there after my lesson," and she says, "Oh great," and they are both frightened because neither of them knows where the museum is. But they find it, they look at Monet's water lilies and Matisse's swimming pool and Picasso's *Guernica,* and his goat. She chatters and feels a fool, he is nearly mute and feels a fool, and they go back on the train and say again, "See you in school."

And then there is the dance, his first, which he goes to only so that he can dance with her. And he smells her hair, so clean and promising, so exciting and reassuring, and two weeks later, the unthinkable: he asks her to the movies.

Zorba the Greek.

It is, for both of them, incredibly, their first date. She has never been asked out on dates because the boys in her class are afraid of her. They think she is contemptuous of them, but she isn't; it's just that she can't place them in a category she can understand. They seem to her not quite real. They aren't the little boys she'd played with easily, but they so obviously aren't men, if by men she was meant to understand someone who could be the object of desire. Her ideas about desirable men come from movies and books: Rick in *Casablanca*, Marlon Brando in *On the Waterfront*, Professor Bhaer in *Little Women*, Mr. Rochester in *Jane Eyre*. The boys she sees in school seem far too solid; there is no space in them for the depth that would call out to her. They're right that she isn't interested in them, but it isn't for the reasons they think.

She is not alone among her friends in this failure to connect. Among the four of them there is a total of two and a half dates. The popular girls, athletic or fashionable or daring, have dates every weekend, but Miranda and her friends, members of the Glee Club, the Debate Club, the school newspaper, the literary magazine . . . they don't know why . . . they feel their failure. But it hasn't happened.

Her first date with Adam is as extensively discussed as the arrival of the Beatles. They think it's wonderful that he suggested *Zorba the Greek*. It proves he's got imagination; she's lucky he's an artistic type.

She loves the movie; she's almost drunk on it, and after it (all during it, he is in a literal sweat with the desire to hold her hand

and the impossibility of doing it, not least because his palms are clammy with anxiety and she might, he fears, find that unappetizing) she takes his hand and says: That's what I want from my life, real life, strong life, life and death, and to lose yourself in that kind of dancing. I mean, his little son dies and instead of weeping he dances. God, that's what I want. I can't wait to get to Europe where people really live instead of this damn Westchester keeping up with the Joneses. Look, it's snowing, she says, and she puts her head back and opens her mouth, sticks out her tongue and starts swaying to the Zorba music she's humming. He's embarrassed, at first, on the street, but then they turn a corner, no one's on the street, no one can see them, and he lets her dance him down the street, his heart is full, she is the most wonderful person he has ever known, he would like to kiss her but he's afraid, but he does squeeze her hand, and they go on dancing. The snow falls on her hair and he would like to brush it off, but thinks he mustn't, and then does and says, "Maybe before vacation we could see another movie."

And then another movie and another, and the slow anguishing prospect of hand holding and first kisses (neither has kissed anyone before) and then meeting after school, the shock of Christmas vacation, unable to say they will miss each other, and more movies . . . it's the only place they can go that they can kiss. Hours of kissing, blissful kissing, imagining nothing more is possible for them. The pride of sore, dry lips. They kiss through the entire three and a half hours of *Dr. Zhivago* and are terrified that their parents (by which they mean her father) will ask them what the movie is about.

He is afraid of her father. Her brother makes him feel unmanly. Her mother's anxiety creates in him a terrible tenderness. It is much easier for her in his house.

And then he feels he must tell Henry Levi, and Henry is immediately practical and clinical. He speaks of "prophylactics," and Adam is abashed, and Henry sees his mistake and says, "Bring the young lady with you to a lesson sometime."

He says to his wife: It is important that he not be lost in the whirlwind of adolescent sex. It's good for him to have a girl, but it can't interfere with his music.

And so Sylvia is given the task: that Miranda must understand she, too, is involved in something greater, older, far more important than herself. But after talking to Miranda she says to her husband: It's all right, Henry, she's a serious girl.

She takes Miranda to Bergdorf and buys her a gray cashmere cardigan, which thrills Miranda because it is, she thinks, her first serious garment, the first garment that acknowledges her seriousness; it is her passport into the adult world.

They are both serious, Adam and Miranda, but in different ways, about different things. He is serious about music. She is serious about changing the world. Ever since she heard of the black girls killed in the Birmingham church she has determined she will devote herself to the eradication of the evils of the world, particularly evil caused by prejudice. They believe that it is possible that their seriousness will bear fruit.

And so for Adam and Miranda these are years of happiness. Perhaps a dream of happiness. A dream of life. Of loving and being beloved. Of desiring and being desired. Of knowing and being known. The world they see now, loving each other, is larger than they thought, but it has a place for them. Nothing terrible happens to them individually in the years 1964, '65, and '66; the sorrows of the world are public, far from them, part of the lives of others. Much of what they have been told to believe about what is called morality, they come to understand, does not, because of their love for each other, apply to them.

Later when she thinks of that time (two decades will go by during which she refuses to think of it), it seems to her that it was always early spring, the air moist, still with traces of the end of winter, but a sun insistent, white in a light sky. Breaking through.

Love, love, love. My love loves me. The love of two young bodies. Hours lying in grassy spaces, cold seeping through their clothes, the cold ignored. Half hours stolen in her bedroom when her mother is at the dentist. Kisses in the movies or on the New York subway where they believe they are invisible. And the discussions formed around an ethical problem, a question of honor, which is called respect. Where can you touch my body, at what point will it properly be called a violation? Where can I touch yours?

They don't believe there is anyone they can ask for help or advice about these things. None of Miranda's friends has a love like hers and Adam's. They might date, they might even go steady, but Adam and Miranda know they will be together all their lives, and because of his music and because she is determined to bring greater justice to an unjust world, they stand for something greater than themselves. And their families are part of the understanding, the understanding of that thing known as ADAMANDMIRANDA MIRANDAAND ADAM. So where they can touch each other's bodies becomes part of a larger question: it involves the houses they were born in and the music of three centuries.

Months and months of talking, and finally the words are hers. "We love each other. Setting these limits is false to our love."

In this decision they know they have crossed a barrier; they are on the other side of something, alone in a country of their own invention. A crossing unimpeded by regret.

In the summer of 1965 she takes the train to Harlem every day to tutor ten-year-olds, who do not love her, or who extravagantly adore her, while he increases his lessons with Henry Levi. (Three times a week in summer . . . where does the money come from? He is afraid to ask.) On the summer evenings, they meet in Central Park and lie in the grass in each other's arms and share the sandwiches that his mother has packed for both of them. Sometimes they watch Shakespeare or listen to a symphony.

It isn't true that the weather was always one way; it didn't need to be; they loved all kinds of weather. And, no, it can't be right that they were always happy. Certainly there were problems with her family. Her father, playing the jilted lover (Why don't we ever see you? Am I wrong or are they paying your bills now?). And her mother, regretful, supplicating: "I was hoping we could see a movie or perhaps one day I could meet you in New York." They are right, these parents; they have lost their daughter. Most particularly to Adam's mother. Though they do not know that the daughter and the boy are lovers. Or they do not admit, even to themselves, that they know. It is, after all, 1964, '65, '66.

What they don't understand is that they have lost their daughter, not just to a boy, and not even just to his family, but to music, which is to say to the whole idea of the past, a past beyond immediate ancestors, beyond America.

When this time is long behind them, and, no longer young, they try to understand their past, they find it hard to remember how they spent their days. What did they do in all the time they were together? They can say, *Well, there was sex* . . . but how many hours did that take up? They did, somehow, put in their days. They both look back on them as days when they believed that they were happy — and Adam, having had more unhappiness than Miranda, will do this far more often.

The way Adam's days were spent was shaped by the fact that he was trying to become a serious musician, and that happened by accident. The only boy child in a clutch of nine girl cousins, he was bored at the large family gatherings in the house of his grandparents in the Bronx and so he disappeared with his grandfather, bored also, into the back room, where Sal Sr., born in Calabria, listened to the Texaco opera hour. To the operas of Verdi, Rossini, most particularly Puccini, which were to him as accessible as the musicals of Rodgers and Hammerstein were to his children and their wives. He saw that his grandson loved music as he did, closed his eyes as he did, tapped his little feet in the Buster Brown shoes (inside them, the image of the blond boy and his dog), then walked to the piano and somehow (*Miracolo,* the child is not yet five)

183

and picked out the tune, *Là ci darem la mano.*

"He plays by ear," the grandfather said, with a pride he had never before had occasion to call up. Adam would make his way to the piano, which he loved better than his aunts, his cousins, his too expressive grandmother, but not his grandfather, with whom he shared the music. The large unaccommodating black piano was not a fine instrument; rather it was a sign, a necessary sign in a certain kind of upwardly striving house. It was opened rarely; mostly it is something to put the pictures of the children on (graduation, wedding), then the grandchildren (christening, first communion). But for five-year-old Adam the looming black complexity was the fresh green bosom of the brave new world.

"Play this, Adam, play that." They sang snatches of songs for him; he was their trick dog, their magician. "Body and Soul," "America the Beautiful." He played whatever they sang. And they didn't have to say anything to his mother, she already knew. His mother, besotted, drenched in love for her son, saw that he needed piano lessons. At seven he was taken (this is luck, but there is always a place for luck) to a woman Rose knew from church. Lorraine Capalbo, who

184

gave piano lessons. Who was, though frustrated, a real musician. She demanded a great deal from Adam, in whom she saw a gift, the fulfillment of a dream she had given up for herself. Conservatory trained, she married after the war, moved to White Plains, had three children, boys, none of whom had an ear for music, all of whom lived for sport. She taught Adam for five years; he was the jewel in the crown of the yearly recitals she presented in her living room. When he turned twelve, she passed him on (this rite of passage coinciding, though of course she didn't know it, with his first wet dream) to Henry Levi, whom she knew when she was young and serious and with whom she was still hopelessly in love.

And so at twelve, Adam entered the world of serious music, and anyone who was part of his life must be part of that world as well. His mother, shyly ignorant, but eager, tried to learn. His father came to his performances, paralyzingly ill at ease. His sister worshipped him and at night thanked God that she was the sister of a brother who did this thing she could not do and thanked God that she didn't have to do it. Music.

So Miranda, loving Adam, must be brought into this world.

It is not her world. Her world is based on dreams of justice. But there is time for both, because of all the hours Adam must be away from her, studying, practicing, and Sylvia Levi has told her it is important "to keep up her own interests but be ready when called upon to put them down." Sylvia Levi is a phlebotomist. She draws blood at the laboratory of Columbia Presbyterian Hospital. Committed to the belief that Henry's music was more important than anything she could accomplish, she found for herself a profession that would always be in demand but that would not be so demanding that she couldn't drop it at a moment's notice. Sylvia is not only skilled but charming, and so she is allowed to accompany her husband when he travels for performance dates. She suggests that Miranda keep her eye open for a similar career, but Miranda, though admiring of Sylvia, does not wish to follow her lead.

It helps that Adam's mother shares Miranda's dreams of justice. It turns out that they had a connection anterior to the one created by Adam; they both worked at the local headquarters of Bobby Kennedy's senatorial campaign. They must, they reckon afterward, have been standing quite near each other holding signs when Mr. Kennedy drove by, waving. So there is a place for Miranda in Adam's house not only as his girlfriend, but also as Rose's political comrade, long desired. Rose's friend.

Miranda's mother would like to be her daughter's comrade, companion, friend. She would like to sit at Rose's kitchen table, peeling, slicing, talking about the world. She sees the desirability of what her daughter is moving away from her to approach; she understands the lure of the smells, the laughter, above all the music Adam plays. Adam understands that Miranda's mother responds to his music in a deeper way than anyone in his family, who love him and love the music not for itself but because it was made by him.

To Miranda's mother, as to no one else, Adam can speak about his fears. He can't seem to do it in his house where people seem to come in and out at all hours as they never do in Bill and Harriet's, where no one would ever think of dropping in without calling first. Miranda's father, too well bred to say it, believes what his ancestors believed, and thinks his daughter is in the grips of a foreign influence. And so while

Miranda's parents are mourning the loss of their daughter, Miranda is celebrating the accession of the world.

She would never say aloud that she prefers Adam's house to hers, the smells of food that are insistent as opposed to the decorous anonymity of what emanates from Harriet's kitchen. The scent of strong coffee like a canopy inches below the ceiling of Adam's house. Sometimes, like a dark thread through a lighter fabric: the smell of roasting nuts. Certainly she would never say to herself that she prefers Adam's mother to her own, that she is happier with Rose than with Harriet. But somehow, especially most Sundays, she is at Adam's house more than her own.

She will admit to herself that she has more to say to Rose than to Harriet. But it's simply, she says to herself, that we have more in common. In fact, they do share two passions: their desire for a just world, and their love for Adam, whom they see as infinitely gifted, infinitely valuable, under their protection. This focus is a beam that they fix their joint gaze on, a gaze marked by its qualities of steadiness, of unswervingness. They do not ever discuss the fact that this shared focus, this shared guardianship, makes them feel safer, certainly less alone.

This watchfulness; this hopeful vigilance. Adam will be a great pianist; the world will be more peaceful and more just.

Miranda is particularly happy in Rose's kitchen, occasionally slicing a carrot or a piece of celery (Just sit, Rose says, just sit and talk to me), getting juice or milk for Adam's little sister, Josephina, called Jo after Rose's favorite literary character, Jo March. Jo is ten, and Miranda is her goddess. She believes Miranda can teach her everything in the world she needs to know. She is perfectly willing to do anything Miranda suggests or even hints at because Miranda is beautiful and intelligent and kind. She loves Jo's brother, and Adam loves her and Jo, who has since her birth found in her brother, Adam, sustenance and shelter. They have provided for each other unquestioning, unquestioned love. And Miranda basks in the drunken adoration of the younger girl. As a younger sister of a tall, plainspoken, and athletic brother, it is she who was meant to take up the stance of adoration, awe. But she never felt those things directed at her.

She is charmed that Adam's grandparents speak with accents. They pinch her cheeks, and the grandfather sings her snatches of songs whose words she doesn't understand.

The grandmother loves to braid Miranda's hair, saying it's like silk, like honey. Over-awed by her Protestantism, the grandfather calls her a princess; the grandmother calls her a treasure, but she whispers in Miranda's ear that Adam is a good boy but all boys are dirty and they only want one thing and she must keep her legs closed tight. Miranda blushes, but nods to make Nonna think that she agrees, although she certainly does not.

Miranda, daughter of Bill and Harriet, Americans for generations, now takes her place in the Old World. And in Adam's other world, also an old world, the world of Henry and Sylvia Levi, the world of tragedy and beauty, history and high, high stakes. When Adam takes his lessons in the apart-ment on Riverside Drive on Saturdays dur-ing the school year, Sylvia takes Miranda to the Frick (to which Harriet would love to go with her daughter, but is afraid to offer), for pastries at Rumplemeyer's, and to ac-company her when she buys Ombre Rose perfume at Bendel's, classic pumps at I. Miller's, creams from a lady named Florica. (Is she Russian, Mrs. Levi? Miranda asks, excited. No, Miranda, no, Romanian. In Romanian her name means "little flower.") And on her fingertips Miranda takes the powdery rose scent of the cream. She rubs it into the inside of her wrist; she doesn't spread it on her cheeks, because Sylvia says Miranda is too young to need it now, but should remember in the future.

Everyone seems to think of Miranda as Adam's wife, though they are only sixteen, seventeen. They don't know of their secret life, the real life of husband and wife, stolen treasures (half hours in Miranda's bedroom, in darkness on a beach, once, daring, on the Levis' couch when they are in Paris for two weeks and Adam and Miranda are assigned to water the plants, feed the cat). Do the Levis understand that they are providing an opportunity for illicit love between teenagers? Most likely they do.

Each time they make love, Adam and Miranda are convinced that they are doing something entirely unlike what has been done by those before them who would say they are doing the same thing. They are utterly ignorant of all but the most rudimentary sexual technique; but it doesn't matter, simply having sex is a source of ecstatic astonishment. The idea of enjoying it *more,* this is nothing they can comprehend.

It is he who pays the price of public shame, the semicriminal forays into the drugstore, purchase of that item for which there so many names, all of them unappealing: condoms, Trojans, rubbers, Baggies, bags.

Together they make their college plans; she will go to Wellesley and he to Boston University because Henry believes in a larger education than a conservatory provides: history, the sciences, the plastic arts. And his old landsman, Rudolph Stern, teaches there and yearns for a gifted pupil who will make his name. So Henry says this is just the right place for Adam; he will get special attention rather than having to fight for it as one among many. He will be introduced to a larger world, but will be protected, sheltered. It is required that the artist be protected; in his turn he must be vigilant to protect his own gift. And Miranda will be there to see it all, but not so close that her lovely body will distract him too much from the demands of his music.

They leave Hastings only three days apart; Adam needs to be in school early for auditions. Rose invites Miranda and her parents for a farewell supper, excruciating for Miranda. She has her place in Rose's house beside Rose in the kitchen, always within sight of Adam, perched in Jo's adoring regard, somewhere to the left of Sal's sight, where most of the world seems to go on for him. In her own home everything has changed. She is no longer Daddy's brilliant little girl; they can hardly speak to each other without arguing about politics: civil rights, Medicare, what her father calls creeping socialism. Her affection for her mother's light tenderness has turned to irritation.

As intelligent as anyone Miranda had ever known, Rose nevertheless cultivated large tracts of the primitive. Family was family. Everything having to do with family could be repaired by food or tears followed by loud, enveloping, even smothering embraces. The steel-cold silent daggers drawn and bristling everywhere around Miranda's house: there was no place for these in Rose's kitchen. And Miranda saw how her mother yearned to be closer to Rose, to what Rose represented, as if she were an orphan with chilblained hands afraid to approach the stove because she'd heard what happened to chilblained hands when they got too close to warmth. They bled. They scarred forever. Shyly, Harriet tiptoed into the kitchen, wanting to be of help to Rose, but it was clear that Miranda knew her way around that kitchen as her mother did not. And trying to pretend she didn't understand that made Harriet vague, confused, incompetent in a way that shamed her daughter and was untrue to her actual domestic competence, different in tone from Rose's, but well established over years. She wanted to say, *I'm a very good baker, you know. My piecrusts are first rate.* But of course she would never say anything like that.

At the dinner table, the men speak of cars, and then go silent. Sal feels unworthy to ask Bill questions about his work; Bill is a chemist; he works for a company that manufactures paints. Finally Sal asks, "Do you import any of the pigments that you use?" And Bill says, "Believe me, that's yesterday's news." And Harriet, flustered, tries to talk about the fact that some of the pigments that made possible the memorable colors of Italian Renaissance paintings are no longer available. "Yeah, it's hard to get ahold of a regular supply of donkey dung," Bill says, and everyone pretends to laugh, except for Harriet, who blushes and, too quickly, Sal says his experience of seeing the Sistine Chapel was one of the great moments of his life.

Adam and Miranda feel they mustn't touch each other, even stand near each other, or sit too close, as if the vector emanating from their bodies would provide too much information, particularly to Miranda's father.

Rose tells a story about Adam as a little boy. "I think he was five," she says. "I took him to see the movie *Pinocchio*. He was so upset when the whale swallowed Pinocchio that he jumped off my lap, ran to the front of the theater, and tried to attack the whale on the screen. 'I have to save Pinocchio,' he kept saying. I had to drag him out of the theater, screaming. He wouldn't go to the movies for two years."

Bill tells the story of Miranda's falling off her bicycle, cutting her head so that she needed five stitches, and getting right back on the bike the minute she got home from the doctor's.

Adam understands that this is Bill's way of reminding him that he isn't good enough for Bill's daughter.

It is a relief to everyone when the meal comes to an end, and Miranda's father gives a gracious toast.

"Our wandering scholars, may you go far, but never forget where you came from."

And so they leave their family houses, Adam and Miranda, never to return. No one knows that Harriet, in the large cool rooms over which she is said to preside, dim, even on the days of brightest summer, weeps because her youngest child, her treasured one, has left, and the house's spaciousness, which once seemed delightful, now seems nothing but a threat. Rose assumes that Adam will come back; she does not think of having lost him. And she is going back to school; her first classes at Westchester Community College will coincide with Adam's and Miranda's, two hundred miles to the north.

And the fathers? The fathers do not permit themselves to mourn the loss of their young to the world. The fathers pack boxes into trunks of sedans, into the backs of station wagons; they tell themselves their griefs must be unmanly. But in bed, that night, exhausted from the drive, and enervated by the highway food, Sal says to Rose, "It will never be the same," and she says, "No, it never will." Bill will not allow himself even that observation. But when they arrive at Miranda's dorm, he sends the others out to lunch while he and Miranda arrange the collapsible shelves he has built for her; she can fold them up and store them in the closet; then unfold them in case the shelves provided by the college prove inadequate. You never know, he says. You never know.

■ ■ ■ ■

Adam and Miranda leave their families to take their places in the world. Joined, they believe, hand in hand, forever, on a path that will stretch out the whole length of their lives. If you told them that the chances of this were quite small, that there were boulders and thickets and ravening animals they would encounter on their way, they would look at you blinking, puzzled, be-fuddled. Adam would go silent, but Miranda would stand straighter, look at you, her gray eyes going dark with disbelief at this display of folly, and she would say, staring you down till you agreed with her or at least pretended to, "You ask if we know where we're going? Of course we know where we're going. Why do you even ask?"

Monday, October 15

SANTA CECILIA
"What Are We Getting but Glimpses"

It is raining, and they both agree that it is odd and somehow wrong for it to be raining in Rome.

"In Paris, rain would be perfectly acceptable," she says. "In London, it would be expected. But here it seems like a cheat, a kind of mean carelessness, maybe even a dirty trick."

"I'd like to show you a place that's lovely even in the Roman rain," he says.

There's no reason not to. The rainy afternoon is open; what she might do if she were not with him is sleep. And surely that would be a waste.

They agree to meet at the Largo Argentina, which seems to her like a child's version of an archaeological dig, false, a wrongheaded offering to the tourists, a half-baked distraction to make them feel they're doing something important. She watches the people waiting to change buses; she thinks there must be fifty that stop here. She thinks of the word "hub," such an ugly word, so un-Italian, the grudging vowel barely wedged in between the *h* and *b*.

They cross the river into Trastevere, thinking guiltily of Valerie, though neither of them wants to mention her.

Miranda has no idea where she's going. Adam keeps turning up smaller and smaller streets; and they are passing Roman houses, medieval houses, Renaissance palazzi insulted by graffiti, a shop selling cakes as large and beautiful as hats, an English bookstore, a cobbler, the predictable pileup of tourist schlock: bags saying I LOVE ROME, sunglasses, soccer shirts.

They enter the courtyard of a building: rose-pink, even in the rain. The rain seems to have freshened, rather than diluted, its light stone. Through the complicated arch they see an urn: classic, restrained, unornamented, the source of the fountain's water, rising up out of an oblong of alternating black and white. Rosebushes surround the fountain, and (how can this be, Miranda wonders, this late in October) one with three salmon-colored roses, and three others, each with a single flower, buttery in the half-light.

Dim, Miranda thinks as they walk into the church. The light is dim, and the dimness is pleasurable, it has a luxurious thickness, as if it weren't really light, shouldn't properly be called light, but some other thing she can't find a name for.

"I come here because Saint Cecilia is the patron of music," he says. "Perhaps because of Handel: I love his *Ode to Saint Cecilia's Day*. Lucy's conservatory is Santa Cecilia, and so she wanted to come here for good luck. And then she was upset. She hadn't, somehow, known the story. She hadn't thought of it before: the cult of martyrs. As it turns out, when she was martyred, Cecilia was very young. I hadn't realized that she was close to Lucy's age, brutally murdered for refusing to marry the suitor her father had chosen, giving up her life because of a religious conviction. Apparently, they tried to kill her three times and it didn't work; they tried to strangle her, then behead her. Whatever they did, she wouldn't stop singing. Finally she was suffocated in a kind of steam-room prison. It was all so far from anything that had come Lucy's way. It didn't occur to me that she'd find the story

disturbing. But she ran out of the place crying and I had to chase her down the street.
I was terrified. She isn't very self-sufficient.
The way she's lived, the way we've made it
possible for her to live, she hasn't had to
cope with very much of the larger world."

"Is that a good thing for a girl, the way we
all have to live now?"

"It's the way it has to be if she wants the
kind of musical life she says she does. There
are things she has to be protected from so
that she can devote herself. It's simply the
way it is."

"Devote herself." Don't you mean sacrifice,
she wants to say. She sees by the line of his
mouth that nothing she could say would
make the slightest impression. And she
knows it's a mistake to advise him about his
daughter. Whom she has never met. Whom
she has no wish to meet.

The church is empty. They approach the
figure of Cecilia, white marble behind glass:
the simulacrum of a coffin. Her face is invisible; it is turned toward the wall of black
marble, as if this slender girl were merely
sleeping in an uncomfortable way. Her head
is covered by a veil. Barely visible: the cut
across her throat that signals her beheading.
The white marble rests itself against a

background of sheer black.

"She seems so vulnerable," Miranda says. "So girlish. Elegant. Delicate. Refined. I wonder if those concepts are of use to women now? Or if they're simply a danger."

"You want her to have spat in her executioner's face before he cut her throat? What good would it have done? What difference would it have made?"

"There's no romance for me in passive female suffering. What would your mother have said?"

"I like to think she would have found it beautiful. I like to think you do."

"I do, despite everything I know. Rome is difficult for me in just this way. It makes a mockery of everything I know is right and true. I know that it's right and true that lovely young women should not be brutally killed. And yet, being here in this unclear light, I'm touched by the poignance of her posture, of her graceful giving up. All those words, 'graceful,' 'elegant,' they required so much renunciation, and I wasn't going to stand for that. Not if I wanted to be the kind of person I wanted to be. Not if I wanted the world to be the kind of place I wanted it to be. Even this light: I feel like I can't quite see properly. But I like it, and then I think: how can you like a lack of clarity? In America, we're devoted to clarity. My house has fifty windows. Sometimes I have to shade my eyes from the sun when I walk across the living room. But I like it here and I'm not sure I should. I'm not sure I like it that I like it."

"That, I think, must be good for you."

"I'm trying to live an ethical life."

"Here, for this moment, there is nothing you can do that is right or wrong. Nothing you can do but be here with this beautiful thing."

"But if I didn't find it beautiful, if I weren't moved by it, you would use the word 'wrong.' If I came in here with a gaggle of shouting Floridians off a tour bus, eating ice-cream cones or throwing McDonald's wrappers on the floor: you would say that was 'wrong.' "

"A different kind of wrongness."

"But wrongness, nevertheless. Which is why, Adam, it's untrue to say that right and wrong are impossible here."

"And what does it mean to you if I say you're right?"

"It means I'm right."

"That's always been so important to you."

"Of course, to whom would it not be important?"

"To me. Because to me, 'It is all a

darkness.' "

"Who said that?"

"Oh, I don't know. Someone, maybe in the seventeenth century. Or maybe I made it up. I'm very drawn to the darkness. You see how the whiteness of Cecilia gets its power from the darkness. She's ready to enter the darkness at any moment. To be swallowed up. By a blankness that has nothing in it of ordinary liveliness. And yet, it's very beautiful. And that's why this thing of right and wrong, this whole business of understanding, what is it, what are we getting but glimpses in or from the darkness?"

"And the darkness, what is that?"

"Everything we don't know or can't know or understand."

"Yes, but we're not being swallowed up yet. We haven't been absorbed yet. And so now we fight the darkness. We do everything we can to understand."

"I don't want to fight the darkness. I want to understand its place in our lives. I understand that there are things I can't understand. And I think to pretend otherwise is a kind of dishonesty. Because in the end we'll be going into a darkness. And I think that's all right."

"Doesn't it scare you, Adam? Where will Lucy be, when you disappear, when you're absorbed into the darkness?"

"That's where my courage fails, so I don't think about it. Not what's outside the darkness, not what I leave behind."

"So you're not afraid?"

"Oh, often, and of many things. But of that darkness? No."

They sit again on the marble bench surrounding the urn, the bushes each with a single rose. Neighborhood children are running up and down the courtyard. They run up a set of shallow steps leading to a small wooden door. At the top of the steps: a wounded bird, flapping, taking some comic and pathetic steps, trying to fly, failing, flapping. The children are taunting the bird. Miranda wants to stop them, and then she sees from the sky, like fighter planes, six gulls swooping down, nearly grazing the children's heads. The children are frightened, delighted.

Sitting near the fountain is a slim African woman and her baby son. Miranda calculates he must be nearly two. He is about to fall asleep. The gulls continue swooping, diving, their cries, coarse and threatening, pierce the light calmness of the place. The mother speaks to her son in French but, hearing Adam and Miranda, switches to English.

"Those birds frighten me," she says.

"No, no," Miranda says. "They're nothing to be frightened of. Or we have nothing to be frightened of. They're just trying to keep the children away from the wounded one. They're just protecting one of their own."

"Still," says the woman, "I am frightened by the noise. And that they seem so close."

"Nothing to be afraid of, really. It's those children who should be afraid. But they of course are not."

A nun appears from inside the wooden door, claps her hands, shouts at the children, and they run, screaming, through the archway.

"It's quiet again," says the woman, putting her sleeping baby in his stroller. "Nice. I like the quiet."

"Yes, we're lucky to be here in the quiet."

"Yes," says the woman. "Lucky. Yes."

Miranda would like to ask her where she comes from, hoping that might help her to understand what the word "luck" might mean to her. But then she thinks: Perhaps Adam is right. This task of understanding, which she feels so often burdened by, is perhaps better let go, for now. Here in the quiet. In the dove-colored light falling on the rose-colored stone.

Tuesday, October 16

THE VILLA BORGHESE
"I Wish We Had Realized That We Were Beautiful"

A group of young men and women, ten of them, by Miranda's count, perhaps fourteen to sixteen years old, are throwing a plastic ball at one another, running to catch it. The sun is vibrant in a hot blue sky; many trees seem to have turned overnight; the leaves are lemon yellow now. And the light falls through the lemon-colored leaves onto the boys and girls who are running, laughing, catching, or failing to catch a turquoise or perhaps aquamarine ball.

"They're so beautiful," Miranda says. "I wonder if they know it."

"Do we hope they do, or hope they don't?"

"Of course we hope they do."

"But part of their beauty comes from their being unself-conscious."

"But I wish we had, at that age, realized that we were beautiful. Why was it, at that age, we never thought of it, or thought it was an impossible category for us? You were very beautiful, Adam, a beautiful young man. And when I look at pictures of myself from that time I think, My God, what a lovely girl. I wish I'd enjoyed it."

"I felt sometimes grotesque as a young man in that body. You helped me with that."

She doesn't want to acknowledge what he said. The implications would tear something open that she wants sealed up. The implications of his gratitude. And she doesn't want to allow the question: do I still find him beautiful?

"How would we have been different if we'd known how beautiful we were? Would we have been more confident? More generous? Kinder? More unkind?"

"Perhaps we would have felt free to do whatever we liked. That we, for instance, didn't have to be studious, or decent, or honest," Adam says.

"So you think beauty is a danger, then?"

"No, I don't. I walk the streets here, early in the morning, sometimes when no one is up. The street sweepers are clearing the incredible debris from the night before. They spray water on the stones, a mist comes up over them, it all seems quite unreal, the mist, and then suddenly these great stone figures, those statues — does anybody even know who they are anymore — suddenly they come alive. Everything my eye falls on is beautiful, the color of the walls, the detail on a doorway, a marble slab with ancient writing on it in the middle of a patch of weeds, and I think, How beautiful this is, and when I'm thinking of that I can't think of anything else. Or I don't allow myself to."

"But I wonder: are Romans happier than other people? I know they can't be, because if they don't have work, if they have no access to justice, if there are problems in their families, if they're ill or mad, no fountain in the world, no sun on stone, can make it seem worthwhile."

"At the hardest moments of my life, I listened to Beethoven's sonatas. And they brought me to a place that allowed me to believe that life could be otherwise than the way I was living it."

"I wish I knew what made people happy," Miranda says.

"Why do you think it's just one thing?"

"Well, what kinds of things. Then we would know how we should live, how the lives of people should be organized."

"Those kinds of ideas frighten me. I'd rather listen to the plashing of a fountain."

"Isn't it funny, the word 'plash.' A word used for only one quite limited situation. Water in a fountain. But Adam, we must think of how to make a better world or the worst people will make a worse one."

She hears a new impatience in his voice. "If I am kind to the people I encounter," he says, "if I help my daughter to add to the world's beauty, if I introduce my students to a sublime music they might otherwise not have known, haven't I made the world better? Are you saying that I don't have the right to the sound of the fountain? The joy of watching these young people?"

"But what will happen to the young people if we who aren't young aren't paying attention?"

"If we had known we were beautiful, would we have been paying attention only to ourselves?"

"I wish someone had said just once, some stranger, it would have to be a stranger, seeing the two of us, *How beautiful you are.* Because if it were a stranger I might have believed him. And if it had been said of the two of us, not just me alone."

"Do you tell your sons they're beautiful?"

"I did, when they were younger. I felt I

couldn't when they became men. Do you tell Lucy?"

"Again, like you, I can't, now that she's no longer a child."

"And do you want it for her? That she knows she's beautiful?"

"I want her, like these young ones throwing the ball and laughing, to be thinking of something else, or not thinking about anything, just enjoying throwing a ball to each other on a sunny day, just living a life. How wonderful, though, never to have felt that you were undesirable," Adam says.

He is disturbed that he's used the word "desirable": at the same time he's glad of the risk; he enjoys the heedlessness, a young man's luxury, in which, even when he was young, he rarely indulged.

"Desirable, undesirable. To whom?" Miranda asks.

"In the eye of others."

"And then what?"

"There's no 'then.' Simply to know. Always to feel worthy."

"I think that might be impossible," she says.

"Even for the beautiful? The truly, the unquestionably, beautiful? I think they're a different order from us. We'll never know."

"Isn't it odd, though, that beauty, real

211

beauty, whatever form it takes, stimulates, somehow, an impulse to praise? Where does it come from?"

It excites her to be speaking in this way, a way she no longer speaks. Did she ever speak in this way? Or is it a kind of unreal talk, dream talk . . . as their time together is unreal, a kind of dream. She is carried by the wave of their talk; she doesn't want to be let down onto the shore of ordinary speech.

"Praise, yes, a verb, intransitive, object-less. Leading somewhere. Nowhere."

He is raking his fingers through his hair; she recognizes the gesture. It's something he did when he was troubled. So whereas their talk is enlivening to her, she sees it is disturbing to him. And that his hair is much much thinner than it was in the time they were together. His hands, though, haven't changed. The fine dark hair on them has not coarsened or lost color.

She doesn't want him to be troubled. She wants him to be with her, enjoying the freedom of this talk, so different from the conversations of what she can only call their real lives.

"I prefer something graspable, like that ball flying through the air," she says, pointing.

"Until the game ends, and the darkness falls."

"Adam, it's eleven in the morning!"

WEDNESDAY, OCTOBER 17

THE VIA ARENULA
"Were We Wrong to Be So Hopeful?"

She has asked him for some help with shopping. Not the kind of shopping most people do in Rome; she is not buying shoes or handbags or jewelry, or even olive oil or pasta or wine. She is shopping for her mother-in-law, who has just had a stroke. Her mother-in-law is adamant about having only cotton, linen, wool, or silk next to her body, and she disliked the cotton nightgowns that Miranda had been able to find in Berkeley; she was too old, she said, to look like Little Bo Peep. Miranda keeps passing a store with many nightgowns and bathrobes; they appear to be pure cotton, but she depends on Adam, with his mastery of the language, to ascertain that the cotton is quite pure.

"I like my mother-in-law. I've always liked

her, even when I thought she didn't like me. Or for a long time she wouldn't even think in terms of liking or not liking me; she just didn't approve of me. I wasn't Jewish. I had a career. I sometimes think all mothers just want their sons to marry someone who will make their lives easier. Sometimes even I feel that way. When I see one of the boys with an interesting, complicated girl, I want to say, *Oh no, don't do it.*"

"But like everyone else, Miranda, I'm sure your mother-in-law came around to you."

Miranda isn't pleased that the compliment pleases her. She feels it's something she should be finished with, at her age: taking pleasure in being liked, especially by Adam. But yes, she had won Hannah over, difficult Hannah, demanding Hannah, critical Hannah, who lived half the year in Tel Aviv and half the year in Berkeley: her greatest luxury, being near her son, her grandsons. Yonatan's father had done well in the electronics business; in retirement, living two places was something they could afford. And finally, when she realized that it was only Miranda who would make the boys' bar mitzvah possible (Yonatan had no interest in it; he said all that religious stuff was only superstition) she and her mother-in-law were allies forever. Miranda stood up to

Yonatan and said, No, there are threads that must not be broken. There are threads I will not break.

And now alone, a widow, her fierceness collapsed on itself because of a blood vessel gone awry, Hannah will be a difficulty in Miranda's life. One she is glad to be away from for three weeks. Glad, and grateful, to be leaving her, for the time, to Yonatan.

"She's a wonderful grandmother. I'm glad the boys have at least one grandparent."

"Clare's parents are very good to Lucy. They live quite near us. Quite near: we all live on the campus, in faculty housing. Clare's father was, as a matter of fact, a colleague of mine. A friend. It was difficult because, well, we were friends, and he's only ten years older than I and he didn't want Clare to marry me. He thought she was trying to rescue me. 'I don't want a rescue marriage for my daughter, Adam, no thanks. Not for my only child.' But then, well, I guess everyone comes around. Lucy's their only grandchild."

She hadn't wanted to hear anything about her. Clare. But now, hearing that she's younger, rather than feeling competitive or jealous, Miranda says, Yes, that's right, that's good. She sees that Adam needed an attention and devotion you had to be young to provide. Maybe this attention had to do with sex, maybe it was estrogen level; or maybe it was based on the anxiety that you might not be chosen, that you might miss out on something essential if you weren't listening in the right way, if the man didn't feel you were. Yes, she thinks it is about being chosen. An older woman has either lived with not having been chosen or learned that having been chosen doesn't shape a life as much as she'd once thought.

She has watched younger women listening to men talk about themselves: the women rapt, entirely attending. And she's watched older women: their eyes flicking to another corner of the room: a handsome man, a woman friend, the drinks, or the hors d'oeuvres. It's a good thing, she hears herself saying to herself, surprised that the thorn in her flesh that had been Adam's wife has suddenly and simply fallen out. As if it dropped on the sidewalk and she had kicked it onto the street. Run over, stepped on by strangers. In any case, entirely gone.

They are shown cotton nightgowns. Miranda insists that Adam extract a surety from the saleswoman: that they are looking at nothing but 100 percent cotton. The saleswoman — her hair sprayed in a stiff helmet, her lips outlined in a dark, almost-black outline, her eyes shadowed in green-ish gold — looks displeased. Then Adam says something to her, shrugging, and they both laugh.

"What did you say?" Miranda asks.

"I noticed the calendar on the wall. The lettering is Hebrew; the photograph is a Jerusalem skyline. I told her you were buying these for your mother-in-law, who's Israeli. And that we all understood that Israelis are people who have the highest powers of discrimination. I told her that if you gave your mother-in-law anything but pure cotton, she'd make you get right on the plane, come back here all the way from California, to return them."

When did it happen, Miranda wonders, that Adam had acquired the skill of joking with salespeople? When they were young each purchase was an agony for him. She wonders if he is more at ease when he is speaking Italian.

She smiles at the saleswoman. But she still cannot entirely relax.

"Read the tags, Adam," she says, "make sure they're pure cotton. Read the washing instructions."

He reaches into his pocket for his glasses. He bends his head to read the tags. Leaning, reading, fingering the cloth, their faces, their hands, are closer than they've ever been. Suddenly he is overcome by a scent that is emanating, he thinks, from her face, rather than her body. It is light, unpowerful. A powdery scent of roses. It is familiar; he knows it from somewhere else, somewhere in his past. It isn't a scent that he associates with Miranda, but with someone else. It isn't his mother. Or hers. An arousing, unplaceable memory.

"One hundred percent cotton. Of the highest quality. You can bet the farm on it."

"Thanks, now I just have to get myself a farm."

Miranda is pleased with her purchases. Each of the nightgowns clearly different from the others. Hannah would be annoyed if she thought Miranda had not been attentive and imaginative in her selection. If she suspected Miranda had done it perfunctorily, as a duty, not taking into consideration who Hannah was. She very well may ask how much Miranda spent. Miranda will refuse to tell her at first, and then lie. She will tell her that the saleswoman was Jewish. This will please Hannah. Hannah will tell Yonatan, and Yonatan will be annoyed. He'll say, *If you'd crossed the street and bought from an Indian or a Chinese, you'd have got a much better deal.* Then Hannah and Yonatan would argue, and Miranda would understand (although it had taken many years) that this kind of argument, troubling to her, was something they enjoyed. They had taught her something important, very important for her life: that you could argue, you could raise your voice. Everyone in the room could see and hear and feel your anger. And the world didn't end. The world continued on its course. The world was, even, perhaps, refreshed, cleansed. In her house, the house of Harriet and Bill, really Bill's house, anger had smoldered, then burst into annihilating flame. Yonatan and his family danced around the fire of argument. And then moved on.

On the busy Via Arenula, they see three young people riding in what looks like a rickshaw with a red and yellow hammer and sickle painted on the back. Advertising their allegiance to the Communist Party, trying to gather votes for an election that will take place later in the week.

"They still believe in that old dream that turned into a nightmare. They are still capable of that kind of belief," Miranda says.

"What is it, though, that they believe in? After what history has shown them? How can they still believe in it? What do they have faith in? Right here in this place where twenty years ago Aldo Moro was killed by the Red Brigade."

"The Red Brigade: so serious once, now a kind of period piece, like transistor radios or Studebakers. Of course these young people don't see that, in the future people may think of them as an irrelevant anachronism. Perhaps for all the things they have refused to see."

"Is it possible that there can be no hope without some kind of blindness?"

"Were we wrong to be so hopeful?" Miranda asks. "We had our blindnesses, God knows. There were so many things we didn't see. Or wouldn't. How I argued with my father! I ruined so many dinners. The anguish I created for my mother, like a kind of weather she had to fear every night when the sun set. It was the age in which dinners were ruined regularly, not from private quarrels only, but for what was called principle. There were some things I was wrong about, and yet I'm certain even now that I was more right than my father. That he was deeply and centrally wrong. His vision could lead to nothing but hopelessness, suspicions, fear. The Cold War. It froze all life. It froze it dead. He said he was a person of faith, and yet he believed that human beings were inherently weak and corrupt and that it is our job in the world to stop the dark forces that are the truest thing about us."

"I think he must have been afraid."

"I know what he was most afraid of. What he feared most was disorder. The old order would be overturned: he really believed that if people just behaved themselves and worked hard, and were clean and sober and patriotic, they would prosper, as he had. But any kind of disorder made him crazy. He would come into my bedroom and see that it was untidy and that my mother was unable to compel me to tidiness and this would arouse a kind of raging despair. So I aroused despair in both my parents. In my father because of my untidiness and in my mother because of my insistence upon argument. Well, I guess my arguing made him despair, too: it was one more sign of disorder. Children were supposed to be subservient to parents. They were never to challenge them. God, if he heard some of the things my kids have said to me!"

He doesn't want to say, *Lucy is never rude.* He says instead, "The state of your room made me feel hopeless, too."

"Is Clare tidy?"

"She's even worse than you."

They laugh together.

How strange, he thinks, the first, the only, thing she's asked me about my wife had to do with her tidiness. Is it that Miranda had, in the intervening years, learned tact? Is that why she hadn't asked the first question: *What does she do?*

What does she do? Those were the words people used, and what they meant was *What is her occupation.* But after all, that was only a part of what people did all day. Nonetheless, it was the easiest way to begin an understanding of someone's identity. A better question, he supposed, than *Who is your family?* — the kind of tribal placement an Italian might be interested in. So what did it mean that before Miranda asked "What does Clare do," she asked, "Is Clare tidy?"

And he understands suddenly that he had to be asked for information about his wife; he had no impulse to speak about her. Does this mean that he feels even seeing Miranda is a kind of infidelity, something that needs to be kept separate from his married life? He knows that's part of it. But in Clare's case, it is both more and less than that. Saying what she does for a living would not shed light on who she is. It would cloak her in incomprehensibility. Clare's job does not explain her.

Clare is a dentist.

How could he explain that this was something Clare liked about her job — that, as she said, it was for people either a joke, a source of boredom, or a cause for recoil. And that it is part of what he loves about her: the slant, even ironic posture she takes toward life, a determination to be sensible and yet surprising. The way she has of blinking several times before she speaks, as if she were always standing in a light a bit too bright, whose brightness no one else seems to be acknowledging.

He has known her since she was thirteen years old. She was the daughter of the head of the history department, John Sargent, an expert on Shaw's Brigade of black soldiers who volunteered to fight in the Civil War. Clare Sargent. He couldn't remember paying attention to her; he was drowning in his own life, his life with Beverly and Raphael. He remembered a girl small for her age, with a head of curly red hair that seemed too heavy for her body, who at the school Christmas fair sold the wooden animals she had whittled; he once bought one for Raphael. A squirrel, perhaps a chipmunk. She wasn't one of the faculty teenagers who babysat; she didn't sing in the chorus. Then she was off to Yale, and then to dental school. He was one of those people who stopped listening when he heard the word "dentistry."

How did it happen, that she became his wife? It was soon after his son, Raphael, left home. Adam had broken a front tooth; he was mortified; he hadn't been to a dentist in ten years. Who recommended her? He can't remember now. She fixed his tooth. She mentioned that she was on her way to Rome. He gave her names of restaurants.

She brought him back a model of the Colosseum made of marzipan. He felt he hadn't laughed in years. She said — the awkward flirtation of someone unschooled in it — You see, I'm hoping you'll eat it and then you'll find yourself back in my chair. She told him why she became a dentist: because she had grown up among people (her father, who taught history, her mother, the school librarian) who were never sure that what they did was important. At Yale, she thought of architecture. It was clear to her she liked building things, but had no talent to design them. And no patience with the lack of concern among her classmates for how people actually lived. She thought of medicine. She disliked the premeds so intensely that when, standing on line to sign up for organic chemistry lab, she saw a burly junior push a small woman to the ground to sign up before her, she took herself off the premed list. Also, she said, she didn't like the thought of having someone's life in her hands. That you could kill someone by making the wrong decision, or not paying attention at some crucial point.

One spring break she was talking to the woman who cleaned her parents' house. She was from Guatemala. Clare noticed that whenever she smiled she covered her mouth. She dared to ask why: It's my teeth, my teeth are rotten: no one should see me smile. Clare took her to the dentist. The dentist struck her as modest and intelligent, and compassionate in a way that she found pleasingly offhand. She asked him about his work. She began exploring dentistry. It was, she found, the most neglected area of health among the poor. This interested her. She preferred the humility of the people she consulted to the triumphalist arrogance of medical doctors.

She limits her practice to four days a week. One day a week, she deals with the teeth of autistic children, who are terrified even to be touched, to say nothing of the invasive touch their troubled mouths require. The problem engages her. One of the things Adam loves about his wife is that what others call impossible she calls interesting. She also finds life somewhat hilarious. She laughs in a way that some of the faculty wives consider too loud. He loved hearing Clare and his mother laugh. And yet, the daughter of a family that was spared misfortune for three generations, she can be shocked by misfortune: she drops down to a place where no one can find her, like a stone disappearing at the bottom of a well. Was she drawn to him because, genetically spared tragedy, she saw in him her drastic other? He does not say to Miranda: *When I met her I was a dead man.* Nor does he tell her that Clare told him, "I think I've been a little in love with you since I was twelve years old. More than a little." Then she regretted it, and he, too, wished she'd never said it: it was embarrassing, a slightly indecent cliché.

"She leaves domestic life to me," he says. "She works much longer hours than I do."

He does not mention the nature of her work, and Miranda notices this. She suspects that Clare works in fashion or finance. She guesses that she earns more than Adam, and that he is abashed by this. All this makes her glad that she decided to think well of Clare even before she found she had a colleague in untidiness, which has made her feel her decision was completely right.

"And your husband?"

"Yonatan's at home in the world of things. He doesn't lose track of them. Objects obey him. They don't, as they do with me, fly out of his hands, maliciously hide themselves, disguise themselves, take themselves out of straight rows and careful piles simply out of spite."

She doesn't want to talk about her husband. He is as different from Adam as he can be (it was one of the things she prized in him: his refusal to agonize, how rare it was for him to take offense). She will certainly not tell Adam that, statistically speaking, three-quarters of their domestic arguments center on her untidiness. The other quarter arise because she finds him too indulgent with their sons.

"If you love me why won't you keep the house as it needs to be in order for me to be happy?" he says, each time with genuine surprise.

"Because," she says as if this argument were the first, "I can't."

"You aren't afraid of disorder? Of being overwhelmed by chaos?" Adam asks.

"I have been overwhelmed by it. I was, as you know, overwhelmed in Pakistan during the typhoon, and I thought that I could never do that kind of work again. But then I'd been screwing around two years, working in a coffee shop in San Francisco. Fatima's father got in touch with me. He was working for the WHO, and there was a great project to eradicate smallpox in India. He knew I was good at organization, so he invited me to join him. And I did, and it was wonderful. And yet, I didn't want a life in which I had to overcome that chaos every day. I realized I wanted a more orderly life. By 'orderly' I meant safer. So a certain kind of chaos, yes. But I'm more afraid of people who believe it's their job to keep disorder at bay. We are, as a species, disorderly."

"No, Miranda, I don't agree with that. Where would we get the idea of order from if it weren't somehow an inherent appetite? Think of this city. It gives us pleasure because of its formal beauty. And music, music isn't possible without order!"

"But Rome's also incredibly chaotic, and that's because people live here. Our pleasure in the order is connected to things, and people aren't things. People will not fall into place. That is their greatness. That's why Rome is great: it's a living place, not a museum."

He indicates the place where the bus that

she needs will stop. The bus will take her down the Via delle Botteghe Oscure. He remembers in the 1950s there was a distinguished literary journal with that name: *Botteghe Oscure.* The fifties, a time of great cultural achievement in Rome. Fellini, Rossellini, Pasolini, Moravia, Ginzburg, Montale, Morante. Now Italian literature, Italian film, are marginal to the point, he thinks, of almost total irrelevance. Botteghe Oscure. The dark shops. They are standing in front of a shop that sells cheap shoes that can only indicate a willingness for cheap sex. The shoes make him sad; he can't believe the purchase of gold plastic platform shoes, or white leather boots, red-sequined strappy shoes with thin high heels, can lead to any kind of lasting happiness.

"I think we were wrong in thinking that people who said they didn't want to change would be happy to do it if we just showed them the way," Adam says.

"How terrible, though, to be young and not to believe in the possibility of change! I felt, when I was young, as though the weather were becoming different. As if the light had changed and the shadows were thinner. My heart lifted at the possibility of the new world we would make!"

"The possibility of what?"

"The possibility of possibility. That people would be more just, I guess, was the most important possibility to me."

"I sometimes think that there are horrors now that we could not even have imagined."

"I refuse to live without hope."

"What kind of hope?"

"Is there a wrong kind? A right kind? There is patience, isn't there? Patient hope. When I came back from India, we were so hopeful. We had, you see, Adam, succeeded in eradicating one of the most lethal diseases in the world. We had got rid of smallpox. It was a fantastic success, the smallpox project. The whole world got behind it, and it was really rather simple. People going around talking to people and working with people in personal ways. We were responsible for the vaccinations of millions, and the disease was wiped out. And so we thought: Well, we have vaccines, we have antibiotics, these devastating epidemics are a thing of the past. And then AIDS appeared, and we realized that our hope had just been an illusion. That was when I changed my training from infectious diseases to environmental health. I wanted something smaller, something contained. If I could see a problem that, with patience and attention, I could do something about solving, then I could still have hope."

"Of all the people I've known, you are the most impatient. I could never understand it: you were the most impatient, and yet often the most calm. And the most able to sit still and solve a problem."

"I might no longer be that person you knew. Or thought you knew."

"Who are you, then?"

"Someone to whom, like you, a great many things have happened. So the person I am was the one I was and also another person, perhaps many other persons."

"And yet you consider yourself hopeful?"

"Because the opposite suggests a way I will not live."

"I have to go to Lucy's school now, to see if I can help her with her Bach partita. Which I hope, at her recital next month, she will play very well."

"And so if you have hope in her you are by necessity a hopeful person."

"If that is the way you want to see it, yes. But it isn't the only way."

"But, Adam, do admit: it's not the worst."

THURSDAY, OCTOBER 18

THE VILLA BORGHESE
"We're at an Age When We Must Take Care Not to Be Embarrassing"

"You see, it didn't rain, after all, like you thought it would," she says.

"And you want to see it as a sign of something."

"No, a sign of nothing. A piece of luck."

"What would a piece of luck look like? A coin? A shell? A hunk of bread and cheese?"

She enjoys this kind of play with him. It was who they were, people who played in this way. She doesn't have people now who play in this way with her.

He angles his chin toward a boy and girl in identical black pants and boots, embracing on a bench. At their feet: two helmets, one garnet colored, one emerald.

"And these two, are they lucky? Lucky in their heedlessness?"

"What do you want me to say, Adam? You want to know what I think of them? What they're doing?"

"Is this the lack of self-consciousness we were saying the other day was so wonderful in the young? I must say I don't find this wonderful. I don't understand it. How can she feel so comfortable, her legs wrapped around him, kissing him, then taking a bite of her sandwich, then looking at the trees, then going back to kissing him, all the time squeezing her legs around his waist? What can he be going through? I remember what it was like at that age. Anything could arouse you . . . an ad for panty hose. I guess it was stockings then. Somebody saying the word 'stockings.' And here she is almost fucking him in public. Yet he seems not to have lost his equanimity."

"You make it sound so ugly!"

"I'd prefer not to be seeing it."

"You're embarrassed."

"I suppose so, yes."

She thinks of Yonatan, who is never embarrassed. He might not even notice the two young people, or he might embarrass Miranda and the boys by shouting out "Go for it."

"They seem quite free of it," she says. "Embarrassment. What a strange thing it is, embarrassment, so powerful, yet no one acknowledges it as one of the important human states. And it's so physical. The accident of people's coloring makes it legible, or not. If you're fair your face turns red, and anyone around you knows you're suffering. If you're darker, well, your secret stays with you."

"I was always far more liable to embarrassment than you. I could be struck dumb by embarrassment. It never seemed to stop you. I've got better."

"Our first date, *Zorba the Greek,* when I started dancing in the street, after I went home I was terrified that I'd embarrassed you and you wouldn't want to see me again."

"No, I thought you were wonderful. Precisely because you seemed so free of embarrassment."

"If you've got better, I've got worse. I'm so aware now that we're at an age when we must take care not to be embarrassing. To dress in a way that acknowledges that some things are past. Think of hair color. You have to do it well, because if it's done badly everyone has to feel sorry for you for having to dye your hair. And you have to avoid dying it certain colors so that it appears that you're pretending not to dye it or that you're making a joke of yourself by acknowledging too loudly that it's fake. A joke no one's amused by, they're turned off by your supposition that it might be amusing. Which is why I spend what you might think is an appalling amount of money to make myself exactly the right shade of blonde. A sign that I haven't given up, but that I know there are standards, and I live up to them."

"But whose standards are they?"

"I don't know, Adam, but I know they're real, and it is about not wanting to be embarrassing. Unaware of how you're being seen. I don't want to be one of those women at weddings doing the alley cat. Or the electric slide."

"What's the electric slide?"

"The extent of your refinement sometimes takes my breath away, sir," she says, punching him lightly on the arm. "Never mind, Adam, I couldn't possibly explain the electric slide to you. Content yourself with knowing it's a kind of group dance. You can live perfectly well without knowing more."

"But can *you* live perfectly well without dancing?"

"Well, I still dance. But more formal dances," she says. She doesn't want to go on about this. It's connected to something about her marriage that she imagines would give him an opportunity for, if not contempt (Adam is not by nature contemptuous), then condescension of which he is, she knows, entirely capable. She's glad Adam hasn't asked about her and her husband, *How did you meet?*

They met, or rather they recognized each other, while taking a class in salsa dancing. Among the middle-aged hopefuls and the brilliant peacocks who by day flipped burgers or pushed clothes down the street on garment racks, they acknowledged they had seen each other at public health meetings. She was two years older; thirty-three to his thirty-one, though she wouldn't have guessed it: he was almost completely bald. Neither of them had been married.

For their tenth anniversary, Yonatan had a dancing floor built in their basement. Two nights a week they dance; they are clear with each other that, in twenty-six years, they had, as dancing partners, not improved enough to be taken seriously by the serious dancers. Which makes them very glad. She loves what Yonatan had said about it: "All day we are brilliant and accomplished. Two nights a week we are both pleased to be mediocre." She understands that this would offend Adam: he would never allow himself even a temporary sojourn into the mediocre,

237

especially if it were willed. She wouldn't want Adam to see her in her dancing outfit: purposely cheap with a low back and ruffled hem, a clinging top, high-heeled shoes with straps, and, her favorite pair: scarlet with red, blue, and purple sequins. She feels herself falling back into the idea of her husband, as if, exhausted, she is allowing herself to fall back into her own bed, their bed: a king-sized bed, with four king-sized pillows. She imagines that Adam and Clare wouldn't consider a king-sized bed.

"You seem much more aware of being looked at than you were when you were younger," Adam says.

She would like to tell him that he's both right and wrong, but to explain the ways he's wrong, she'd have to talk about Yonatan. She thinks of herself dancing, her backless dress. Her sequined high-heeled slippers. Dancing with Yonatan, she's perfectly happy to be looked at. Perhaps because Yonatan never thinks of being looked at. The unease happens when she is looked at on her own. To be looked at alone, as an older woman, she thinks, is to be unsafe, in danger. In danger from what? From ridicule, she understands. Pity, perhaps. Perhaps: contempt. With Yonatan the two categories — pity, contempt — seem entirely remote.

"It's one of those differences between men and women. As a young woman, you're looked at all the time. You can't choose the nature of the looking. It's abundant, almost a natural event like rain or thunder. A problem sometimes also, like heavy rain, dangerous thunder. Anonymous desire. Anonymous censure. Then you age, and you realize you've become invisible. You hunger for the element you once despised or took for granted. But now there's a new understanding. Being looked at, as a rare commodity, has to be considered carefully. You can no longer afford to be occasionally looked at with contempt, because the other salvaging looks — approbation, admiration — may not be coming your way any time that you can count on. Sometimes you appreciate the invisibility. You're newly free. But embarrassment, the look that says, *Don't you know who you are? You're too old for that,* I fear it like, I don't know, food poisoning maybe.

"More than anything, though, I fear being thought of as a 'game girl.' Those women traveling around in groups wearing red hats. Or maybe they're purple hats. In cafés or museums or national parks. Some game girl wrote a book, *When I Grow Old I Shall Wear Purple.* Well, the truth is, no one gives a shit what you wear when you're old unless they're embarrassed by it. So better not wear purple, just in case. Subtle, neutral shades: blacks, taupes. A bit of mourning for the end of youth is called for. A muter palette. More explorations of shades of gray. Dove. Pearl. A nice alternative to the blush of mortification. Just the right degree of blondness; a blondness that understands its relationship to gray."

"I don't want to think of you as never dancing."

She won't tell him that it's something he needn't worry about. "When was the last time *you* danced, Adam?"

"With you, I think."

With an entirely pleasant wifely pride, she thinks of Yonatan. "But if you danced me down this row of magnolias it would be embarrassing. Even these two wrapped around each other on the bench would be embarrassed. And then we would have to be embarrassed. And to be embarrassed, and embarrassing here, in Rome, in front of all these Europeans, no, that wouldn't do."

"Because to be American is always to run the risk of being embarrassing."

"I envy people from small republics whose history no one knows and therefore could never resent."

"So, let's sit here quietly, like people from a quiet country, so no one will know where we were born."

"A man and a woman, here in Rome, in this lovely place, under these old wonderful trees that have seen so much. Causing no problems. Embarrassing no one."

"Especially, thank God, ourselves."

Friday, October 19

VIA DELLE CINQUE
"Wine and Chocolates"

They meet for lunch at a small trattoria in Trastevere. Perhaps not the best choice; she is nearly vegetarian, and the specialty is grilled meats. There is another unwisdom in this choice; the restaurant isn't far from where Valerie lives, and they both glance furtively up the small streets, afraid of seeing her.

She orders *pasta peperoncini,* wanting the simplicity, the sharpness: garlic and crushed red pepper. She will not, like him, allow herself *lombata di vitello,* for which the place is famous. Veal chops: no, she knows how veal chops come to be.

He cuts into his chop, and the anticipation of the taste of residual blood makes his mouth water. He wishes Clare were here. He wishes he were with Clare instead of

Miranda. Clare loves meat. If he were with Clare, he would not have to be thinking of the suffering of animals.

"My colleagues and I were out for dinner last night," she says. "We started talking about some great health problem, tuberculosis, I think, but the food was so good we got distracted from whatever it was we were talking about. Malaria. Avian flu."

"Mussolini wanted Italians to give up eating pasta. He thought it was a distraction; he thought it made them weaker, less willing to put their shoulders to the Fascist wheel."

He sees she isn't listening to him. Her attention has shifted to a shop across the narrow street, a shop that sells wine and chocolates. A shift of attention he would never feel with Clare.

The bells of the basilica strike one. The girl closes the store; she's going for her lunch.

"Isn't she pretty, and isn't it great she's locking up that lovely store so she can go home for lunch. Her hair is just marvelous, look at those curls, so dark and rich, and that wonderful skirt: there must be a hundred pleats. I wonder if her mother irons her skirt for her."

He sees Miranda has made up a life for

her. "You haven't given that up, I'm glad to say."

"Sometimes I was worried that you didn't like it when I did that."

"I didn't like it when I thought you were getting carried away, forgetting that you'd made the whole thing up. But usually I enjoyed it. I'd enjoy it now. So: make a life for this young girl."

"All right," she says, putting down her fork. "She's going home to her father and mother for lunch. She has a pesky younger brother. For lunch her mother is serving ravioli with spinach and ricotta. Then an omelet. She's pouring water from a decanter that's made of light green glass. The girl mixes the water with her wine: she has to go back to work. The mother puts a plate on the table: the plate is white, the grapes are light green, they almost match the decanter, but they have a russet tinge. Muscat, the grapes are called. They're in season now."

"Muscata," he says.

"Yes," she says, not liking to be interrupted. Resenting, as she sometimes did, his precisions, which stopped her flow.

"She goes back to work at three. She has a pleasant afternoon full of good-natured and moderately profitable exchanges. She wraps the chocolates prettily in purple paper with that red-purple ribbon that she curls with the blade of her scissors. She puts the wine in silver bags, actually more like envelopes. She will close the store at six. Her boyfriend will meet her on his Vespa. She'll cover her perfect hair with an emerald-colored helmet; his is dark blue. He's blond, and also curly haired. Tall, perhaps a bit too thin. Maybe he takes drugs or maybe he's a runner. He stops the Vespa on a dime at a little café. They meet their friends. She takes her helmet off and her curls spring perfectly into formation. They have beer and pizza until it's time for the disco. At one they go back to his apartment where he has a tiny room; he shares the apartment with four other young men; they are all architects. The chocolate seller and her boyfriend make love for three hours. He drives her home on his Vespa. She sneaks in. Her mother hears and calls out from her bed, 'Are you all right?' She doesn't answer."

She pours herself another glass of wine and, not asking Adam, refills his glass. She leans back, very satisfied with her storytelling. It's been a long time since she's indulged in this kind of play; when they were together, it was one of their favorite pastimes.

He unbuttons the cuffs of his oxford-cloth shirt and rolls his sleeves up six inches. Did he remember, she wonders, that she found that enormously arousing. That they had agreed that he would never wear short-sleeved shirts, and that any man who did was throwing away an incalculable advantage. Like the hair on his hands, the hair on his forearms has not grayed or coarsened.

He leans forward in his chair, resting his elbows on the table.

"Suppose your story is all wrong. Suppose she goes home to a family she hates, a shrewish mother who calls her a whore, a little brother who's a meth addict. Her boyfriend's getting ready to leave her, he doesn't know she's pregnant, no one knows, she hasn't told anyone. She has to wait her turn for an abortion, which in Italy could take some time, so it might be quite a complicated operation. While she's waiting for an abortion, she's thinking, How ridiculous my life is, how ridiculous all of life is. I wouldn't bring a child into the world. How ridiculous that I spend my days selling overpriced wine and chocolate."

He is pleased about every aspect of the lunch; the meat, the wine, their conversation. Earlier, he had wished that he was here with Clare. Now he is glad that she's not here, that he's here with Miranda. It's not that Clare has no humor, but it's a humor based on irony, not story. She would never read stories to Lucy: she has very little taste for the unreal. She says she is a kind of narrative dyslexic. If Clare were here, if he were here with Clare and Lucy, and Miranda had started talking about the chocolate seller, she might have said, *But how do you know, you've never met her?* Blinking in that way that suggests that the light is too much for her eyes. And then he and Lucy would tease her, and she'd pretend to be engaged in the story to show that she is not a fool. It is one of her strengths: she never loses herself in the coil of stories. To her, life is not a story but a long interesting complicated joke. You get on with it as best you can. The joke is, most of the time you don't. You are walking down the street, dressed to the nines, perfectly coiffed, and there is the banana peel. Landing flat on her back, Clare is quite capable of staying where she is, looking around her, making note of the configuration of the sidewalk. He thinks of his young wife, blinking. He looks over at Miranda, whose eyes are on the chocolate store. Her eyes are not on him. He wonders: Were they ever?

They have taken so long over their lunch

that the chocolate seller has returned while they are still at the table. "No, you're wrong, Adam, I know you're wrong. Look at that lovely girl, and think of all the people walking out of the shop with those beautifully wrapped packages. I'm thinking of my friends and colleagues talking about avian flu. All my earnest and not-very-good-looking colleagues wanting to make the world a better place. And then there's this lovely girl, handing beautifully wrapped packages of succulent chocolates to happy people, none of them saying, *What is the meaning of life?* Only, *One hundred grams of truffles, please,* or *Today I'll try the ones with almonds.* I could only imagine the puzzled expression on the girl's face if I were handing over my ten euros for the ginger covered in dark chocolate while I asked her, *What do you think is the meaning of life?* Maybe she'd point to the chocolates, the wine, the people eating at our restaurant, and say, *All this.*"

"Well, let's go into the shop. The least we can do is let her take some of our money. After all, she's provided us with so much entertainment."

The third glass of wine she allowed herself has made her a bit unsteady, and she feels herself almost falling into him. She feels, too, that her stomach is rumbling. It began to rumble as soon as they entered the shop.

"I'm embarrassed. Can you hear the sound my stomach's making? The smell of this shop is making my mouth water. What would it be like if I got a job here?"

"You'd be fired in a week. You'd be telling people what kind of chocolate they should buy. You'd be warning them not to eat too many sweets: that it will spoil their appetites."

"I would not be fired, Adam, I'd be very good. I'd engage people in conversation and make sure they were really happy with what they bought. I'd encourage them to buy more than they originally wanted. I'd make a fortune. Then I'd open another store."

"Then who would work behind the counter at this one? You'd have to get a Vespa so you could go back and forth between the stores."

"I think I might like a Vespa."

"I know you would."

"You don't like chocolate that much, do you? Or have you developed a sweet tooth since I used to know you?"

"No, I haven't. But caviar! I have been brought to a cold sweat by the possibility that there might not be enough caviar in the bowl when it's passed to me. Or that I won't have the courage to take as much as I really want. Or that I'll take too much."

"How much is too much?"

"My mother used to say, 'Enough is enough.' "

"What's enough? How do we know when we've had enough?"

"When we have no more appetite. That's when we say, 'I'm full.' "

"Well, I am full. And sleepy. Will you get me a taxi, Adam? Is that too self-indulgent?"

"I'm shocked to the core. It will probably be in all the tabloids in the morning."

He takes her arm and leads her to a taxi rank. *"Libero?"* he asks the driver.

The driver starts his noisy diesel engine. Miranda gets into the cab; as they drive away, the engine quiets down. Miranda looks out the back window, waves at Adam, closes her eyes, and feels herself drift off to sleep.

SATURDAY, OCTOBER 20

THE VILLA BORGHESE
"Money Meant Nothing to Us"

They stop at a café known as La Casina dell'Orologio in honor of the clock that has, since its construction, never once stopped and never kept anything like the correct time.

"I like it here," Miranda says. "It's so exuberant. That enormous brass contraption for making coffee. The musical instruments on the walls. This bugle. This violin. What could they possibly be doing here? And the picture, of course, of Frank Sinatra. With one of his records. Gold: I can't see which one. Probably *My Way*."

"Sometimes I think if I hear 'My Way' one more time on the streets of Rome I'm going to throw myself into the Tiber. Or throw whoever is playing it into the Tiber. The street musicians only seem to know two

251

songs: 'My Way' and 'Bésame Mucho.' "

"Who's their target audience? Free market capitalists and lovelorn Spaniards? Do you think they all get together, all the street musicians, have regular meetings, maybe even a newsletter, and vote?"

He isn't listening to her; he can't even be temporarily amused by what she imagines he thinks of as a misuse of music. He looks around the café, displeased.

"They charge a ridiculous amount to sit here. I'll get us two coffees, and we can drink them on the bench just there. It's warm today."

"Great. Thanks."

She closes her eyes and lets the sun penetrate the bones of her skull. She allows herself the pleasure of being tired. She falls asleep for a minute and, waking, is surprised to see him. Adam. Standing in front of her, holding two plastic cups and looking terribly unhappy.

"I'm sorry for this," he says, "I made a stupid mistake." He hands her the ugly plastic cup, tan, corrugated, a quarter full of dark espresso.

"It's not important," she says, "It's lovely here. I'm happy in the sun."

"It is important. It was stupid not to take

252

a table in the garden and be served coffee in a proper cup. Here we are in this beautiful place and I bring you something ugly. I had to worry about money, worry quite a lot about it, for such a long time, and now I always worry about it, even when I don't have to."

She doesn't say what they both know: money is something she has never worried about. He doesn't realize, though, the extent of her financial comfort. That her father — resented, feared, admired grudgingly — had made excellent investments, and at her parents' death, she was left enough money so that all sorts of possibilities were open to her and her children. A house in the Berkeley Hills. Private schools. Never having to question: Shall I sit at a table or drink on a bench from a plastic cup.

"When we were young together," she says, "money meant nothing to us. We couldn't imagine that it would ever be of any importance. That it would make any difference."

Now there's something he doesn't say in return, *Yes, it wasn't important, but the way it was unimportant was different to each of us. It wasn't important to you because you were never greedy, but also because you never had to think about it. Because your mother had been left quite a lot of money.* He remembers a time when Miranda's father — perhaps he'd had too much to drink — took him aside and said, "You'll never have to worry about my girl going hungry. My wife, well, my wife's family was quite well off and I'm proud to say I've done well with what she's been left." Adam didn't want to hear it because, Miranda was right, money wasn't important to him, didn't interest him, but also because he had a feeling it suggested what her father really thought about him. That Adam couldn't, on his own, provide for his daughter. That he was a better man than Adam: more a real man.

Adam's family had very much less money than Miranda's but always made him feel that he need do nothing to make money, nothing that would interfere with his music. He could never be entirely without guilt for that, a guilt that changed its tone as he aged, as he began to understand his father's thoughtful kindness at keeping from him the details of what he had to do to make the money. And sitting on the bench beside her, he doesn't say, *But you see your having more money means you can live in the Via Margutta while I live in the Via della Reginella,* because he knows she would actually prefer living where he lives. And he knows she has more money than her husband because Valerie has told him. But what he doesn't know is if she understands that her money comes not from her father, but from her mother, that gentle woman who would not have known how to say the first word about it. So he decides to speak of money in a different way.

"Even the young now believe money is important. They think about it in a way we never did."

"I know that it's important to them, but I don't know in what way. And perhaps I don't think about it as much as I should. I know that we have enough money. A house we like very much. A small cabin on a lake. Our sons have gone through college. If they want more education, it can be made to happen. And yet, for the first time: I would like more money. But I don't know what for. More clothes than I can wear, more houses than I can live in, more food than I can eat?"

"More time, perhaps. Fewer hours working."

"Time is money, right. I don't like saying that, but it's the truth. Then I ask myself: Time for what?"

"To be still. To go where you want when you want. Not to have to be fatigued."

"Are you tired of your work, Adam?"

"Yes, I suppose, and yet I think it's quite important, and I think I'm good at it. It frightens me that, in a generation, the music that I love, that I have lived so much of my life for, will almost disappear. It was considered a necessary acquisition: people, ordinary people, had pianos in their living rooms. Everyone took music lessons, even if they were doing it only to be perceived as doing it, to be thought of as cultured, worthy to be taken into the middle class. Now almost no one thinks it matters one way or the other whether you take lessons. Most of the young. Most of the world. It's important to me that I can influence some of them so that they will be moved, consoled, set on fire. Of course, it's nothing like the importance of what you do. You save people's lives."

"Only at several removes, and I don't know what the long-term effects will be. I told you, I gave up that kind of ambition because I wanted an ordinary life. A life for my children with the things money can buy. Health and safety."

"Is that what money buys? Health and safety?"

"And quiet. And privacy."

"And beauty. Tomorrow I'll take you to a beautiful café."

"No, Adam, tomorrow I will take you to a place I've wanted to go. It is, I think, quite beautiful. The kind of place we would never have dreamed of entering when we were young. It's expensive. But I can afford it. It's the kind of thing you can almost never say: I have enough money. People will talk about almost anything else, the most intimate, the most mortifying things, before they'll mention money. We don't want to be poor, but we don't want to admit we're not."

"And if we had lived poor, as we said we would when we were young, going to this kind of restaurant is the sort of thing we would never have hope of doing. Would we be more or less happy? More or less unhappy? I know people, my God the money some of my students come from, people who think about money all the time. They have too much money, and they aren't happy. I know that's the wrong thing."

"And the right thing?"

"Ah, that I can never seem to settle on." His face seems to her to have darkened; but perhaps it's only that he's moved into the shadow of the overhanging leaves.

Sunday, October 21

THE RESTAURANT,
THE MUSEUM OF MODERN ART

The restaurant is actually part of the Museum of Modern Art. They walk up the elaborate marble staircase, through the doors flanked by Corinthian columns, not even stopping to buy a ticket. He's told her the collection is undistinguished, not worth the steep admission price. "You don't come to Rome for museums," he tells her. "There are only one or two that are really world class."

They're more dressed up than they've been since their first night at Valerie's. She's wearing a black silk pantsuit; underneath the jacket, a silky jade-colored shirt. He wonders if the shirt is sleeveless. He thinks of his memories of her arms: freckled, lightly muscled.

In all the time they've been together, all

these days in Rome, he hasn't seen her legs. She wears long skirts or pants. Her legs were always a vexation to her; he had found them beautiful, arousing. Worried that he knows she's thinking in this way, he doesn't compliment her on her outfit, as he'd thought of doing, before his imagination took off in a direction that causes him unease.

She's reserved a table outdoors, on the veranda. They look out over the park, the park that she's come to know well because of their daily walks.

"The sky is white today," she says. "The flat pines are beautiful against it. The pines of Rome."

"I like the pines, and I always wanted to like the music, the Respighi, but I can't."

"Umbrella pines. I love the shape they make against this white sky. I think what I love most in Rome are things seen against the sky. And things that are what they are because of water. Bridges. Fountains. The sound of fountains. The reflections of the bridges, of the arches of the bridges, repeating themselves in the river. Particularly at dusk. At twilight. What's the difference between twilight and dusk?"

"That's the kind of thing you know, that you wonder about, that I never would. And

I meant to ask you, what's the name of those trees with the small leaves. In all my years in Rome, I've never known. And it seemed like the sort of thing I should have known, so I was always embarrassed to ask anyone. It always seemed too late to be asking."

"Ilex," she says. "I'm glad you're not embarrassed to ask me."

"Because you know it's the sort of thing I've never known."

"It is, Adam, the sort of thing you could learn."

"But you learned very young, from your father."

"Yes, those were times I know that we were happy, walking in the woods."

Her father, she knows, wouldn't approve of spending so much money on a meal.

"Every time I've passed this place, I wanted to have lunch here," Miranda says. "The view is wonderful, but there are some places you don't want to eat alone. Or with someone who'd fuss about the price. It might be different for a man. Although things have changed. When I was younger, it was rare to see a woman in a good restaurant eating on her own. Traveling in India, it's almost impossible. If you're eating on your own reading a book, a young woman of the restaurant family will come and take your hand and tell you it's terrible for a woman to be eating alone with a book, and you're just swept up, into a family life that I am simultaneously delighted by and appalled by — I mean, I'm appalled by the theft of my privacy."

"There's no Italian word for privacy."

"How can that be?"

"There's a word for solitude, but that's different, almost religious. The right to privacy: that's very northern."

"You only have to travel a bit south or east to be shocked at how northern you really are. How important things like people arriving on time become. When you have to understand that when you say two o'clock you mean two o'clock, and the people you are with mean 'sometime between two and seven.'"

"You're no longer habitually late."

"No: Yonatan cured me of that." She doesn't want to be talking about her husband now. "Let's order something luxurious. The sort of thing that would shock my father. Have the most expensive thing on the menu."

"But suppose the most expensive thing on the menu isn't the thing I want?"

"Yes, that would be a problem. Then let's

say: have whatever you want and don't think, for a moment, about money."

This is impossible for him. And he is not entirely at ease with a woman saying those words to him, implying that the check will be paid by her. Still not entirely at ease that his wife earns more than he. But he knows that is a foolishness, one he can just let go. And this is Miranda, and he is Adam, and it is much too late for that; he knows it is beneath him.

"Lobster risotto," he says, "to start."

"Yes, and then?"

Cinghiale, he says. "Boar."

"Oh, yes, I've been told it's the season. How frightening boars are: those tusks. Digging for truffles. What a strange animal. Threatening, but discriminating. Bloodthirsty, yet a friend of the table."

"Look around: most of the men are gray haired, like me. It's because it costs a lot to eat here."

"But the women are not gray haired. Not one. Even I'm not; though without chemical help, I would be."

"I think you're more worried about getting older than I am."

"It's harder for a woman. A finality occurs. One day you're fecund and the next day barren. Bang. No more children for

262

you. Do you know how lucky you are? I won't have the chance again. You must have been in your forties when Lucy was born. And there wasn't the slightest worry attached to that. You could have another twenty-five children if you wanted."

"But I don't, of course, want."

"I may have had too much to drink, or they're taking too long bringing the food, but I want to tell you something. It happened last night. Someone who gave a paper at the conference was staying at a very fancy hotel. Not the Hassler, but something up there like that. He invited us all for drinks. It was one of those very modern places where the bathrooms make you think you wandered into a conceptual art installation by mistake. You think maybe some German did the sinks, some postmodernist you're not hip enough to know the name of, and you can never find the water faucets. There were only two toilets. I went into one, and before I sat down I saw there were spots of blood all over the seat. So I went into the other toilet.

"After I washed my hands I noticed the Asian woman who was handing out the towels. At first I was horrified that she'd think the blood was mine, and think of me as unclean. But then I hoped she thought it was mine, so she would think of me as still young. Young enough to menstruate. Still vital. I gave her an enormous tip, because I wanted her to think both things at once: that the blood was mine, and wasn't mine, that I was not unclean but not infertile. I suppose I am not ready to be seen as no longer young."

The waiter brings the food; it's not very good. Neither of them wants to remark on this.

"We're more than halfway through," Miranda says.

"Through what?"

"Our life."

"Nel mezzo del cammin di nostra vita," Adam says, making a face so she won't think him pretentious.

"Past the median."

"Postmeridian."

"Postmeridian. It just means after noon."

"Dolce?" the waiter asks. He hands the menu to Miranda, and translates for her, "Sweet?"

SEPTEMBER 1967

She knows he doesn't want to go, and that it's difficult for him to tell her.

The march on the Pentagon. The biggest antiwar demonstration ever planned. The government will have to understand that they are wrong to be in Vietnam. The war will have to end.

Miranda and her friends have been planning for it, negotiating with bus companies, attending training sessions: what to do if you're teargassed, if the cops approach you intending to beat you up. Miranda's father doesn't believe that any policeman would dream of harming his daughter. He would not, however, have dreamed that his daughter, in blue jeans and a work shirt, a bandanna around her neck, would be carrying in a knapsack bottles of water and tubes of Vaseline (smear the Vaseline on your face, then douse the bandanna and cover your face in case of teargas). Small bottles of iodine to treat potential wounds. He would never have dreamed that his daughter would be a "demonstrator," that she could imagine she had anything to fear from the police, that she would be shouting (so unladylike! he had raised her to be a lady like his mother, like her mother) phrases that were ridiculous to him, "Hey, hey, LBJ, how many kids did you kill today?"

There is not, she believes, anything more important than stopping the war. When she arrived at Wellesley, in September 1966, a little more than a year before, she did not know she would be thinking this. She thought the most important thing was choosing the right classes for her first semester. Would she study Russian or continue with French? Should she do her science requirement in her freshman year? What would her roommate think of her new blanket, a Hudson Bay (cream, trisected by three bands: turquoise, orange, gold), which she and her mother had shopped for and which she loved, the first domestic item owned only by her, not by her mother, her father, though paid for, of course, by them.

Two days before he will leave for Boston, she spreads the new blanket out on the floor of her bedroom. Her mother is shopping in the city; she has read about a special kind of cloth bag that will prevent clothes from being wrinkled when they're folded in a suitcase. She is determined that Miranda will have several.

Adam and Miranda lie on the blanket; he is running his palms against the soft wool. She tells Adam she's signed up for a course in music theory. He is rarely angry, but he looks angry now; a beautiful russet creeps up toward his brows and he says, "I don't want you to do that," and that, too, is odd; he never asks her for anything, but she can ask him why because they love each other, nothing can hurt their love or weaken this bond, which she knows will go on unto death. So without fear she asks, "Why?" and he says, "I want you, when you listen, to listen to *me* playing. To listen to me, not the music. I need to know you love me as a man, not as a musician."

She is thrilled to hear him speak this way. To refer to himself as a man. He is, after all, only eighteen and perhaps has never before used the word to describe himself. And because his using it in her hearing frightens them both at first (as if they were inhabiting a room they'd been told they had no right to enter), and then seems entirely right — they have moved not only into another room but to another country: they are citizens of the grown-up world.

"I need to let my eye fall on you sometimes when I'm playing and not be worrying that you're judging every nuance, every
pressure of the pedal, every tempo of every
phrase. I live with being judged, all the time,
I'm judged and judged and judged. I need
you to be in a place away from it all."

She is ennobled by his words; he's asking
something of her, something womanly,
saintly, asking her to give something up (a
kind of knowledge), to be willing to empty
herself of something she doesn't even yet
possess: to enhance her own emptiness.
(She thinks of the word "womb," which she
prefers to "uterus"; her womb is empty, but
only temporarily, waiting for his child.) Her
emptiness will help him give birth to his
own greatness. He wants her to be *not music.*
He wants the blankness, a blank slate, no, a
blank shoreline, dry firm sand where he can
set his foot and feel safe.

She takes her model from Sylvia Levi, who
enjoyed her work as phlebotomist, enjoyed,
as she said, colleagues who didn't know
Bach from boogie-woogie, and yes she
missed her job when they agreed that Henry
was earning enough money and didn't need
her salary, what he needed was her attention, that she should be able to listen to

him. Like that dog, she said, cocking her head in imitation of the RCA Victor dog in front of the gramophone. What he wants is for me to listen and respond, without musical training, without criticism, just listen, and make a place where he can eat and sleep and entertain his friends in comfort and of course after all these years of listening I have learned enough so that I know something about what he does but not so much so that he has to be afraid. They are so afraid these men who have given themselves to music. What they do is so demanding, in a way so dangerous, that it is our place, as their women, to make a safe harbor. To make the harbor safe. Miranda believes it is an honorable role and the one to which she has especially been called: the woman behind, beside, the great man. Enabling, rather than possessing, greatness.

Miranda never asked Sylvia *Is this why you never had children?* because she would then have to say, *I will give up a great deal, but that I will not give up.* She and Adam talk about their children; he will teach them music; she will teach them to swim, and to know the names of trees and the varieties of birds. Which she was taught by her father. Who taught her brother as well. Her brother to whom her father now vows he will never again speak. The three of them sharing binoculars. Her father whispering: Listen. Or pointing: Just there.

It is in some ways a mistake, his keeping her away from the world of his music. Because it takes up most of his time, and all the people he knows use their time in the same way, but she is using her time differently, meeting people very different from anyone he knows or has known. Almost immediately, she is taken up by people she likes on campus who tell her that to resist the war is the most important thing, and she knows they're right, because it's life and death they are talking about, real lives, real death. What is at stake is more important than anything that has come into her sights before.

And then there is Rob, her brother, who has left home, who has mortified his father, terrified his mother. He is now in Canada, in some town they have never heard of, somewhere in Manitoba. And he cannot come home.

Her brother resisting, evading, or, in her father's words, dodging the draft.

Her brother, running for his life.

Her father shouting. Her father, insulting, accusing. "We risked our lives to make the world safe for little punks like you who think your lives are too good to risk for the idea of freedom."

And her mother wringing her hands. "Oh stop Bill oh don't."

And her brother, his hair golden in the sun that pours through the windows that June day, despite her mother's trying to keep the damaging light out. Not answering, his jaw clenched, saying, "I know you'll never understand."

But Miranda understands; she fights her father; she tells her father her brother is a hero; it is more courageous to say no to evil than to go along with it. What about Nuremberg? We are more like the Nazis than we are like the English and Americans in your war. She calls it "your war," as if he'd started it. And he says, "Little girl, you don't know a goddamn thing."

Her brother, five years older, looked at adoringly, although they do not inhabit the same world. Her brother who rode her on the handlebars of his bicycle and gave her piggyback rides and took her camping, just the two of them, cooking their meals on the Primus stove. Her brother, quiet, practical, his father's son, the two of them in the garage, sawing, painting, hammering, her brother, engineering student at Cornell, her brother with the lovely girls and their stiff hair and their swishing skirts and their high sharp scents driving away in the convertible he saved and saved for . . . now her brother has left home, can't return, and her father says, "And don't think of coming back to this house, you've burned your bridges." Her mother says nothing, but her lips thin into an invisible line of paralyzed grief. And Miranda cannot give her mother sympathy because she won't stand up to her husband on her son's behalf. But Miranda will stand up to her father, so every dinner is a fight, every night's peace is destroyed, and Rob is somewhere in Manitoba, homesteading, he says, and she will visit him in the summer if she can save the money, and of course she will. She will go with Adam; she will be sure she does.

By 1967 the weather has changed; it is no longer early spring; it is high noon; the sun falls like a blade on everything, shedding its overclear light. Everything is as clear as it can be. Or it is entirely invisible, entirely incomprehensible to sight and understanding. So if it is not high noon it is black midnight; it is the land of death and darkness or it is the land of unprecedented hope and transformation. But it is not the land of their birth.

Now Miranda's brother has left home, as it turns out never to return from a place they all had only thought of as *prairie,* featureless on a map whose details they had always believed were of no importance to them. So with all this happening to her family, to the world, how can she think anything is as important as the war, the source of unnameable horrors and one grief she can all too familiarly name. How can she believe it matters if she studies French or Russian. She would like to take a course on seventeenth-century poetry, but she will not allow herself. She will study economics, history, biology. She will be premed; she will become a doctor and serve the poor: in rural Appalachia, in Harlem, or in Africa or India, she's not yet sure.

But what is important to Adam in September of 1967? He understands that Miranda is right; nothing is more important than stopping the machine of death. On the other hand, or at the same time, his allegiance is to the great music of the past, and he must honor that allegiance by attending to the demands of the music, which requires many many hours a day of practice. Playing and replaying the same notes, the same phrases, trying to master the *Hammerklavier,* agonizing over fingering as Miranda is agonizing over napalmed children and the destruction of the land and culture of Vietnam. He believes Henry Levi (shouldn't he know best, given his history?). When Adam talked to him about his guilt for not being more involved in Miranda's antiwar activities, he had said:

"Wars have always happened and human beings have always done hideous things to one another, more hideous than you can imagine. And above all, or underneath it all, this music goes on, must go on. The question must be not only why do we live but what do we live for? And one of the most important answers, Adam, you must believe me about this, is for beauty. For beauty whose greatness goes on and on.

"Don't think, Adam, that I don't question all this. That I don't sometimes think I'm misusing or wasting my life. But when I begin to feel this way, I think of the curators in the Hermitage during the Siege of Leningrad. They were starving, hiding themselves in the museum while unimaginable horrors were going on outside. People selling human flesh in the black markets — you can't even imagine. But the curators stayed on in the museum. The great paintings had been taken away, hidden. But they took each other on imaginary tours, pointing to the empty spaces on the walls where their beloved paintings had been. They described them in detail to one another, knowing that some of them might not survive, that the paintings might not survive, and that at least the memory of them should be preserved, somehow. To me, these people were heroes. The kind of heroes that help me live my life."

And walking down Riverside Drive, waiting to meet Miranda for their last time in the park before they go back to school that September of 1967, Adam feels at peace. He will serve the world through his music; Miranda will serve it through protesting the horrible unjust war.

Then in September Miranda asks him to come with her to the demonstration at the Pentagon. It will be a great event, she says; it is necessary that everyone participate; it is their moment in history. Not to go would be like not standing up to Hitler. Adam thinks of Henry Levi, who left Germany because of Hitler. Henry Levi left and his parents did not. Henry Levi lived and his parents did not. But Henry Levi tells him he must not participate in demonstrations because if he were beaten, if something happened to his hands, if they were injured, there would be no hope for a career. He suggests that Adam try to organize other music students to present concerts in protest against the war. But he must not go to demonstrations himself. He must not put himself in danger.

Adam sews (he will not ask Miranda to sew for him) a black armband onto the sleeves of all his jackets so that wherever he goes and particularly if he is performing in public he can be seen to be opposing the war.

He knows this isn't enough for Miranda; she praises him, but he can hear the reservation in her praise. And she can hear that her political friends disturb him; he doesn't trust them, he thinks they love violence because they are confusing it with something else, some other romantic category: courage or sex. The boys with their uncombed hair and dirty jeans talk about stockpiling guns in basements, about blowing up banks or laboratories. And Miranda's friends look up at them adoringly, and then invite the boys with their uncombed hair into their beds.

He doesn't tell Henry Levi that refusing to accompany Miranda on the march will put him in another kind of danger. The danger of losing her. Whom he is not afraid to think of, to speak of, even, as the love of his life.

They are slipping away from each other as if they were standing on a muddy bank holding on to each other, trying to be completely still although they feel their footing giving way.

Only a year earlier when they were both leaving home for college, it seemed everything would be quite easy.

From the day that she moves into the dorm, Miranda knows that she is lucky in her roommate, Valerie, from a small town outside Omaha, bouncy and pleasant and pleased with everything. She wants to major in art history. Miranda's arriving at college with a boyfriend, a musician, gives her, for Valerie, a great cachet. There are what are called parietal hours, two hours on Sunday when boys are allowed in dormitory rooms. Quite early on, Miranda confided her sexual status to Valerie, who was honored to leave the room on Sundays. And so for the first time Adam and Miranda are free from the fear of intrusion and surveillance. For the first time, they are safe in her bed.

Miranda makes a new friend every week.

Her closest friends live on the same dormitory floor: Lydia, from Needles, California, who likes geology, and tall Renee from Philadelphia who urges Miranda to take Russian, and Marian from Chicago who is one of the first to major in African studies. They think Adam is wonderful; his distance from contemporary culture makes him seem precious, a museum piece, a fragile porcelain. They tease him about his ignorance of rock and roll. When he says, "Some of it's very good, the Beatles, for example, some of their harmonies are quite complex. They're very interesting," "Oh, for God's sake, Adam," Renee says, and laughs that laugh that makes everyone want to be standing next to her. "Saying the Beatles are interesting is like saying ice cream is interesting. Maybe it is, yeah, and you could analyze it: there's cream, there's sugar, there's the ice and the machines that make it. But in the end it's just fucking fabulous and you're really glad it's in the world."

Everyone suddenly seems to be saying "fuck," using the adjective "fucking" in the easy, habitual way they used to say "groovy." Renee denies it, but Valerie and Lydia admit to being jealous of Miranda's wifely status. They all feel free to say how good-looking he is: his beautiful hair, his beautiful eyes, how easily he blushes. Lonely and inadequate in their single beds, they dream of what she has. Adam's shyness, his seriousness, touch the maternal in them. If Miranda isn't in when he calls, they speak to him as if her absence were a deprivation he must be protected from. As if not hearing her voice, he will feel starved and they must feed him.

They are very young, Adam and Miranda. Their bodies are continually miraculous to each other. They have never seen other bodies, and so for them both, the body of the other is all bodies, or the first body: they are Eve and Adam in the Garden, and the apple has not yet been thought of, tasted, known. Their skins are fresh, unblemished; not having touched other skins, they do not fully understand this; their joy in each other is absolute; there is nothing to which it can be compared. Each touch is arousing; they can hardly wait to be in each other's arms. Having come together first as almost children, they had not had time for the malice that corrupts desire, that mixes it with punishment and blame. Making love soon became quite customary; it was as if it were something they had never not done. Customary, and yet still miraculous. Often they say to each other, lying in each other's arms, "I am happy. I am very happy."

How did it darken? Was it that the world was getting darker in those days, a daily darkening, a cloudy thickening? Miranda volunteers for draft counseling; the sister of Rob, how can she not, and Rose at home is counseling neighbor boys to resist the draft: assuring them that they're behaving justly; helping them relocate to Canada, directing them to psychiatrists who will swear that they are psychologically unfit for battle, that they would bring danger to their fellow soldiers; that this risk should, in the interest of the war effort, be avoided at all costs.

For a time, Miranda moves in a well-meaning pastel-colored clutch of colleagues and companions: Quakers, Unitarians, left-wing Catholics and Jews, people whose parents had voted for Adlai Stevenson. She sings in the dormitory lounge the songs of Peter, Paul and Mary. The edgiest lyrics that come out of her mouth are "Accept it that soon you'll be drenched to the bone . . . For the times they are a-changin'."

Was it because the music changed? That Dylan became ironic, angry, that the Beatles moved from vaudeville to LSD? And then there are no more parietal hours; the young

280

women of Wellesley will no longer accept that they should be told when men are or are not allowed into their rooms. And so now they are allowed in more and more, and suddenly there are male voices in the hall, male presences in the dining room.

Tall Renee experiments with drugs because of her new boyfriend, Arnold, who is from Florida and insists that only through pharmaceuticals can enlightenment be found. Two weekends into the second semester of sophomore year, Marian decides that she no longer wants to be friends with Miranda and Lydia and Renee and Valerie; she doesn't even want to live on the same hall with them, although they'd gone to great trouble the year before to assure that they'd all be together. She is put off because they are so uncomfortable with her boyfriend, Roger, who has hair unlike any hair they have ever known (it's called an Afro, Marian tells them), who is silent and sullen and makes no attempt to engage the girls in conversation, who disappears for long periods and then is suddenly there, who is not a student; they don't know exactly what he does. They fear that their anxiety is racially motivated, and they try to conceal it; but even with Renee, who is the most relaxed, the tension is clearly there. Some of

281

the groups with which Miranda is involved have given up an unequivocal commitment to nonviolence.

Adam does, in the end, go with Miranda to the march on the Pentagon. He sits with her on the bus, but what he does at the march isn't enough for her and they both know it. He's uncomfortable; she knows he's worried about his hands. He is too shy to shout out slogans and can't bring himself to walk in silence with his two middle fingers formed into a V. He knows that she's grateful to him for going. He knows, too, that for the first time she considers the possibility that she might wish he were other than he is.

During spring break 1968, Adam and Miranda visit Rob on the farm in Manitoba. The bus trip takes them two days; they are filthy and tired when they arrive in Winnipeg, picked up by Rob in a battered truck, and filthy as they are. He lives on a commune; they are shocked at how ramshackle everything is, how hard everyone works, how humorless the people are. No sign of spring has come; the snow melts halfheartedly in puddles that half reflect the empty trees. The people with whom Rob lives, many of them draft evaders, are too exhausted to care about music or poetry; they seem too worn out even for ideas. Rob is affectionate, but he speaks to Adam and Miranda as if he were speaking to slow, though good-hearted, children. She sees that he thinks, like her father, that he knows more than she will ever know. She feels around the edges of his love a flickering of contempt, which he tries to stifle, but she senses that what has always been between them is now like a page saved from the fire, but nonetheless singed.

On the bus ride home, she weeps in Adam's arms, and he consoles her, saying, Rob is tired, he's overworked, he's still in shock, he'll come around, he loves you. Thinking of his feelings for his sister, Jo. Unconditional love. The older for the younger. The stronger for the weaker. My sister. My brother. Nothing, he believes, can change that. Inherited from Rose the primitive conviction: blood is thicker than water.

This belief makes him different, he knows, from his fellow serious musicians. His place in the family headed by Rose and Sal. His love for his family. His easy breathing of the family air. Who don't know exactly what he does all day, but believe his grandfather when he says, "It's in the blood." What blood? Adam wonders. Can what I feel for this music have to do with blood? And yet, of course, he knows it does; his blood makes his fingers move, makes his head swoon and his heart sing. Yes, of course, it is a thing of blood. As is his love for Miranda, which he cannot talk of to his friends, who seem never to have breathed ordinary human air, only some other element, not oxygen enriched, or perhaps superenriched: the air of music. They don't understand the ordinary world, the give-and-take of ties that are called familial affection. Nor do they understand what he has for Miranda, this love, necessary, automatic as breathing, natural as swimming in the sea.

They don't have girlfriends, or they have too many girlfriends because girls like throwing themselves at musicians, thinking they are making themselves a place in the world of high culture. Or they have difficult girlfriends, or they discover that it is men they love, and the musicians who are girls weep and are exhausted because the boys don't understand them and they are exhausted from their incomprehension, and then the boys become more fractious, trying to handle their own exhaustion, and the exhaustion of the girls, and the mutual incomprehension. So Adam goes to Miranda often in the evenings and every Sunday (you are my Sabbath, he says to her) for refreshment, renewal, rest. The release and replenishment of his desire, which is, he says, like Moses's burning bush (Boy, they got you with that religious imagery, Miranda says, temperamentally uninterested in religion). Well, perhaps; nevertheless my love for you burns and burns and is never consumed.

On the Greyhound bus on the way home from Manitoba their skin turns livid in the bad false light. Adam is ashamed when his eyes fall on his pale hands, remembering the look of them beside Rob's: callused, bandaged, chapped. Capable hands. The capable, he knows, are always contemptuous of those whom they consider the merely accomplished. Rob didn't used to be contemptuous of him. But Adam knows that he is now.

"My brother's changed," Miranda says. "He's become a bitter person."

Adam knows that Miranda is right. Her brother is bitter about his country and his family. Bitterness is eating him away. There is a core that is there, steely, undiminished. It has not been reduced; rather it has hardened. He is himself, but harder. Adam

285

allows Miranda to weep in his arms. His heart is broken for her; she has suffered a loss that has something to do with blood. He had always admired Rob and somehow feeling that Rob liked him, approved of him for his sister, made him feel more valuable; it was good to be valued in the world of men like Rob.

Normal men.

He is glad to be comforting Miranda. It's so rare nowadays that she needs anything from him. His need of her is so obvious, so constant, everyone acknowledges it: that he needs Miranda and he always will need her because people with musical gifts like his need other people in the world to get them through. Because what they do is so difficult, so impossible. Requires so many hours of practice: hours behind closed doors, the hands, the back, put in unnatural positions, positions which must be held, repeated, held. Such heroic concentration. All of it taking its toll on physical and mental health: these breakdowns must be warded off, kept back by a vigilance that cannot come from the musician himself: he hasn't the time for it, the mental space. But without it: the music will be lost to the world, or its quality diminished beyond recognition, even beyond worth.

The war escalates; the numbers of the dead pile up and up, the cities burn up, and Miranda has to work harder, pull her mind away from what she is really thinking about to concentrate on his question: should I prepare the Schumann sonata or the Beethoven bagatelles? He says he doesn't want her opinion as a trained musician; he just wants her as a sounding board. For the first time, she feels, by this task, rendered inanimate; for the first time, she isn't sure she likes it. Being a sounding board. It occurs to her that a sounding board is not a person but a thing. Unliving. Unalive.

Just as Adam has chosen the Schumann over the Beethoven, Martin Luther King Jr. is shot. Dr. King, whom Miranda continued to revere although some of her friends grew contemptuous of him and his insistence on nonviolence. As Rob has become contemptuous. Contempt is in the air. It is a space at the front of the shelf now, easily reached for, easily available. And then Robert Kennedy is shot, shot in a hotel kitchen by someone with a name and an origin that seem bizarre. How can it be: another violent death, another Kennedy cut down by violence? How ridiculous they now seem: the

287

endless heated arguments: *Do you support McCarthy or Kennedy?* When anyone can be so easily, so absurdly, cut down. She runs to Rose, and they weep in the kitchen because they saw him, they saw him up close, and they did not see Dr. King, and Bobby is the second brother to be killed, but they worry: is that saying something wrong, something bad about them? Rose still believes one must vote for Hubert Humphrey, she is working for him at Democratic campaign headquarters; Miranda says, No, I won't support him until he disavows the war. The war is the most important thing. And Rose says, I don't believe anything is *the most important thing.* There are many important things which Nixon will prevent. And Humphrey is a good man. Nixon is not.

Rose and Miranda don't like to argue with each other. Does Rose understand that Miranda is moving away from her son? It is possible that even Miranda doesn't understand it.

All spring, Adam prepares Brahms's *Seven Fantasies;* in May, he will enter a competition. His principal teacher, Madame Rostavska, and Henry Levi, in consultation, decide that this is a good choice for him. It avoids the expected competition choice: it is not a virtuotistic piece, but it will show off Adam's talents, his ability to range among moods and tones, his gift for subtle, deep interpretation. If he is selected, he will study in Rome with Stuarto Roncalli. He is putting in more hours in the practice room than he has ever done. He listens to Henry Levi, to Madame Rostavska: he listens to everyone, everyone is telling him different things. Henry Levi says: You must concentrate on the transition between note and note. Every transition must be clean, crisp. You must honor the emptiness, the silences. He concentrates on no. 3: the Sturm und Drang Capriccio in G minor. He urges Adam to emphasize the stately processional aspect of the central section. Madame Rostavska is most concerned with no. 4: an intermezzo in E major. She reminds Adam that Brahms originally called this a nocturne; she urges him to imagine moonlit descending figures, the calm transformation that results in a serene end. He dreams the notes; he hears in his nightmares his teachers' conflicting advice. Miranda brings him sandwiches and tea with lemon and honey; these are their suppers every night for the month of May.

When he plays for the judges, he feels he is outside his body. Miranda greets him backstage, and she sees that he is drenched with sweat. He tells her he thinks he's never played worse: how could he have imagined he had a chance? How could he have imagined he had the right to play this piece by Brahms, so full of great themes, great feelings, when he is nothing but mediocre, no, less than mediocre. A total failure. An utter fraud.

But then it is announced: Adam is the winner. And Miranda insists that all her friends take time off from demonstrations and teach-ins and strategic arguments, and they take over a pizza parlor on the North Side and toast Adam with endless glasses of Peroni beer.

Through a Wellesley alumna, Miranda secures a job in Rome that will pay her almost nothing, with the Food and Agricultural Organization, which everyone calls FAO, pronounced "FOW." She hopes to work on projects connected with the distribution of food in what is then being called the Third World. She lies to her parents, tells them she is living in a woman's hostel. She suspects that her mother knows she'll be living with Adam, and she encourages Miranda's elaborate lies at the dinner table. In the hostel for girls only, she tells them, she will be watched over by nuns.

■ ■ ■ ■

On the plane (it is her first time in Europe, but Adam has been with his mother twice; no one is left in Rome, but she still has family in Orvieto; all of Sal's family is in America now), they are once more only Adam and Miranda, only Adam and Miranda to each other. "This is good, I think we needed this to get away," they both say, and she is delighted by everything her eyes fall on. They play a game with the color of the walls: find your favorite wall today and pretend we work for my father's paint company and we have to make names for paints. First-dawn blue, they say, sun-drenched sand. The trees seem older to her; she sets herself the task of learning their names.

Life is easy for them in the apartment owned by friends of the Levis, where she is for the first time a housewife. Although they never eat at home, except for breakfast; two doors from where they live in the Nomentana is a trattoria. The owner, who finds them charming, serves them meals for a dollar apiece. Why would she cook? She doesn't know how. Adam wouldn't dream of asking her.

The arrangement for the apartment is part of Henry and Sylvia Levi's plan, the plan to ensure that Adam is taken care of by Miranda. Later she will resent this, feel they were implicated in her entrapment, but for now she revels in the high ornamented ceilings, the dark wood of the furniture, the maid, very young with the single long braid, who comes three times a week and calls her signora and leaves behind her the smell of beeswax and lavender.

In Rome that summer, there is none of the dark buzz, the dangerous downed wires that seemed everywhere on every road Adam and Miranda walked on in the America of 1968. She needn't argue with Renee and Marian (she is speaking to them again) about the Black Panthers. She needn't worry that Lydia seems to be taking too many and more frightening drugs. She needn't keep it from Adam that she is smoking pot with her friends; she wouldn't dream of smoking marijuana here; she wouldn't know how to go about finding it even if she wanted to, which she does not. She needn't argue with Toby Winthrop, the Harvard junior, her fellow draft counselor, about the fascist implications of monogamy; she needn't listen to him taunting her as "the suburban radical, the Westchester liberal." She is tired of arguing with so many people and of trying to understand so many things. Here, it is impossible to think clearly about politics. Italian politics are so complicated that she thinks that in the course of a summer she could never come to understand them; they inhabit terrains ranging, from what she can gather, from Byzantine historical complexities, old grudges and old loyalties, to a dangerous love of violence. It isn't her responsibility, and she feels she can "lay her burden down." Just for a few weeks; she'll take it up again when she goes home.

But here they are happy. Happy having their coffee and *cornetto* in the morning, served by an elderly man, who tells them they must not call him signore but Giuseppe, who adores Miranda, tries to explain to her who Padre Pio is, tries to explain the stigmata, and Adam is embarrassed because his grandmother also has a picture of Padre Pio, in her bedroom. Adam tries to explain to Protestant Miranda that this picture of the smiling, bearded monk, below which they drink their *cappuccini* and eat their *cornetti,* is the image of a man who was meant to bleed from wounds, like Jesus, in the place of Jesus, every Friday and most days of Lent. And that both Giuseppe and his grandmother believe this man could fly.

She listens to his explanations as if he were speaking of initiation rites in Papua, New Guinea: she finds the story charming, not entirely understanding that these are the stories Giuseppe and Adam's grandmother live by.

They are happy shopping, buying their peaches, their cheese, their tomatoes, their bread. Though she won't cook, she loves buying picnic food and planning the location of their outings. Calm and pleased, she walks the aisles of the ancient covered market in Nomentana: rows on rows of fruits and cheeses and salamis, fish she doesn't know the name of and wouldn't know what to do with but enjoys looking at. She allows herself to be distracted. She follows Adam's lead: this is his other home, these are his people. Certainly, it must be in his blood, this way he has of picking up a peach and turning it over, smelling it, putting it to her nose, telling her to bite it, taste the juice, no wait, he'll take the first bite so she won't have the trouble of the fuzzy skin, and he brushes the hair from her cheek with the edge of his palm. And surely he must have been born to it, to talk this way about food, to speak without embarrassment about the richness of the tomatoes, the sharpness of the basil, the smooth texture of the cheese. He praises the olive oil; he says its taste is the taste of comfort and hope.

He is passionate about Roman water. He shows her how to cover the hole in the spigot with her middle finger so she can drink more easily, so the delicious water can go directly into her mouth. He fills bottles with water from the different fountains and insists that she discriminate and choose her favorite. He talks about the way the color of the stone changes as the day progresses and the shadows lengthen. She allows herself to believe that it's all right to enjoy the world, to pay attention to the kinds of things he is paying attention to. It's a kind of slowness, a kind of attentiveness that would mortify and perhaps even frighten the people she was raised among. She can just imagine what her father would say if he heard Adam going on and on about a peach. He would call it, she knows, unmanly. But it is the opposite to her; never has she desired Adam more; never has he seemed more the man with whom she delights in sharing her bed. Their bed.

Except when they are in bed, to sleep or to make love, they are hardly ever indoors. All summer she reads almost nothing. They walk the streets from 9:00 a.m. to 9:00 p.m.

on Saturdays and Sundays. She asks him: Do you ever want to go to church. And he says no and blushes. So they do not enter a single church. Except to hear music: Palestrina, Monteverdi, sung in the places they were meant to be sung, part of something they were meant to be part of, not cut off, no longer museum pieces, but connected to something still alive. But he will not kneel and stand when the others kneel and stand, and he refuses to take communion.

Adam says he knows that his not going to communion would make his father sad. He tells her that it is Sal who has the religious life, Sal who is saddened that Adam seems uninterested. Rose knows why: Adam will not take communion because he knows that he is understood to be in a state of mortal sin on account of being Miranda's lover. Since the papal encyclical *Humanae Vitae,* which reaffirmed the Catholic church's stance against birth control, Rose herself has not entered a Catholic church. Sal is an usher at Mass on Sundays and often a communicant at Mass during the week. Each year he makes a retreat for five days with the Redemptorist Fathers, someplace upstate; no one ever questions him, and he says nothing to anyone about his religious life. Which Adam knows is serious, extensive, because of the books that line his shelves. John of the Cross. Meister Eckehart. Julian of Norwich. It seems not to come between his parents, Rose's rage at the church, Sal's devotion to it. Adam doesn't understand why it doesn't come between them, but the fact that it does not raises in him an enormous pride, as if his parents were great players in a long, demanding, but intensely private game.

Miranda knows that she and Adam are only playing house, but why not, she thinks, why not enjoy it? When they meet for dinner, tired after work, tired for the first time as adults are tired, she allows herself to be distracted as well by this new kind of adult exhaustion. And distracted by her job, a job involving the analysis of data, a task that, to her surprise, in its cool comfort, she enjoys. At her job she meets people from all over the world; she is the youngest, they indulge her, they are amused by her, but, at the same time, admiring her facility, they take her seriously. A competence with numbers, with what is called data, is something she didn't know she had. She believes she is learning about the world. She likes her job; she likes the color of the stones and the sounds of the fountains; she likes their endless walks, though she never remembers for long what it is they saw. Only the color of the stones, the sounds of the fountains.

Adam feels himself being stretched, and yet relaxed, closer to becoming the kind of musician it is his life's work to be. He does not spend the time in the practice rooms that he did in America. But none of his Italian friends do. They do not seem distorted, misshapen, his new Italian musical friends. They may be mad, he tells Miranda, but they're not neurotic. I think it's because serious music isn't an oddity here, something people only pretend to think is important. It's more ordinary, and it makes them much more normal.

They have families they live with, these new friends, and they invite Adam and Miranda for Sunday dinners that go on for hours and that have a cast of characters it is impossible to remember, sometimes, even, to count. And they are invited to Rose's family in Orvieto, who do not ask the details of Adam's and Miranda's living arrangements; they are shopkeepers, the family; they sell cheese and bread and olive oil. Afterward Adam and Miranda get on the train back to Rome dizzy from the funicular and stuffed from a day of endless, interlocking meals, carrying bags and bags of food as if they were returning to the Arctic rather than the great city of Rome.

And so they spent that summer walking the streets, avoiding the American students on the Spanish Steps (We're not like them, Adam, tell me we're not like them), a month of streets marked by fountains and public sculpture and concerts which seem to be everywhere, every night, and free, and the scent of flowering trees and frying food and laundry flapping in the heartlessly blue sky, the sound of whirring sewing machines and snatches of songs flung out onto the Via Nomentana way past midnight.

She had meant, originally, to go to Pakistan that summer to work in Lahore with her friend Fatima in the clinic of her father who is a doctor there. She has told Adam she must do it the next summer, and he says, yes, of course, but this is a once in a lifetime chance, and afterward she knows that he was right; she wouldn't have missed it for anything. Even for the responsibility of saving the afflicted poor.

The things that vexed and separated them seem far away. Miranda reads the *International Herald Tribune* occasionally, but there is no television in the apartment so he doesn't have to hear her every night railing as Walter Cronkite describes napalmed bodies as he would back home. She leaves the railing to the Italian radicals, whose slogans she can't begin to understand. She takes the bus each day, a forty-minute ride beside ordinary Italians who seem absorbed in ordinary lives, and that seems right; it's all right for her to be absorbed in what seems ordinary Roman life: colors and smells and textures. After all, she is working hard on something important, reports on sorghum and terracing and irrigation. Adam and Miranda can hardly remember what seemed so troubling between them; whatever it was has disappeared, dissolved like the miles that turned to nothing as the plane rose up over New York and crossed the fretful cold gray-green Atlantic. It seems that they have all the time in the world. Each day they tell themselves that they are lucky.

Then they go home; the days shorten; the October sky turns blue-black at five o'clock; there are no longer enough hours in the day. Is this the same sky, they ask each other, as the Roman sky? Is the sun the same sun? Why is the light so different? It is only with Adam that Miranda can have this kind of conversation: tender, speculative, playful. This habit of mind has no place in the diction of her serious friends, who know it's their job to change the world.

She is spending more time in the biology lab; her real love is botany, but after her summer at FAO she has decided on a double major in biology and economics, which pleases the premed adviser: she thinks Miranda's prospects are excellent. Miranda is still counseling draft resisters. She is back to smoking pot.

And Adam is doing as he has always done: practicing, practicing. He is absorbed in the relationships among the last Schubert sonatas: when he tries to speak about this to Miranda she says, "Um-hm, interesting," but he knows she isn't interested. Madame Rostavska, a Russian, continues to believe that the technical training he received from Henry Levi is all wrong. Henry Levi insisted on his doing stretching exercises that were painful; he believed that without a certain amount of pain the proper stretching could not be accomplished. Madame Rostavska says that that's "typical German sadism," and gives him a new set of exercises, which do not hurt but are more time-consuming than Henry Levi's.

He eats most of his meals with people who make jokes about musical figures. "What's half a bottle of Four Roses? A diminished fifth." Some of them ask and then forget and ask again, "Why are you wearing that black armband on your jacket? Did someone die?" And he thinks this continued questioning must be aggressive; if it weren't, they would be afraid to ask him in case someone in his family had really died. He knows this subtle aggression reflects an appetite for perversity in his semifriend Ronald, who is in love with Shostakovich.

On January 10 of 1969, Beverly Marshall, a piano student a year behind him, makes a suicide attempt in the practice room beside his. Adam barely knows her; he has noticed that she waits for him often outside his practice room, seems to want his attention in a way that makes him uncomfortable. He's surprised that although they barely know each other she always wants to speak to him of her abiding sadness. When he hears what sounds like a fall, he knocks on her door, turns the handle, finds it locked, becomes alarmed, and persuades the janitor to open the door with one of the hundred keys that hang from a ring he carries on a chain attached to his thick webbed-leather belt.

It is the first thing he has been reluctant to talk about to Miranda.

As she is reluctant to tell him, or to remind him, that this summer she will go with her friend Fatima to Pakistan to work in her father's clinic.

When she shows him her airline ticket, she can see that he is struggling: of course she must go, of course they had agreed on it more than a year ago, but she sees a flare of panic in his eyes, as if someone had lit a match inside his skull. He is afraid to be without her.

She is afraid of his being without her, but she knows it would be wrong to say that she is afraid of being without him.

But when she gets to Pakistan she is afraid, often afraid, at the sight of blood and hunger and too early death. She isn't good at dealing with the sick, the dying; and Fatima's father, a kind man, suggests that perhaps she'd prefer going into villages, teaching women about nutrition, which she does succeed at moderately. Back at the clinic, she listens to the staff's complaints about disorganization, and there she succeeds, not just moderately, but brilliantly, at organizing the records, the rotas, at creating systems for ordering medicines and apportioning tasks. But she can't love herself for this; she would love herself more if she were better at dealing with the sick and the dying. She determines that she will work on her nature; she will make herself better; this is the important work in the world and she must make herself take part in it.

She returns to Wellesley knowing that she is happier in the lab than at the bedsides of the dying, but she will not allow herself to make decisions based on accidents of happiness. All that fall, and into the winter, Adam can't shake a cold, and finally, after they come back from Christmas vacation, he goes to the health service and is diagnosed with mono. He is sent to the infirmary, and then sent home.

At first, all during March and the beginning of April, she goes back to Hastings on the weekends, to help with nursing him, to keep him company. And then the world is different: Nixon invades Cambodia. She phones and speaks to Adam, who is so sleepy, he says, just so sleepy, but she also talks to Rose, who says she must stay in Boston, she must be involved in the demonstrations: Adam will be fine; he has plenty of people here to look after him. She is having to learn words like Pol Pot and Khmer Rouge and who Sihanouk is and who is the hero and who is the villain and who is to blame and what is the role of the North Vietnamese and the Chinese and the Russians. And how to absorb, how to understand the shock of Kent State: the National Guard is shooting students, students like herself; the world has gone mad, and in order not to go mad she must be with people like herself, devoted to acknowledging the madness. But Adam is, literally, sleeping through it, sleeping eighteen hours a day, sleeping under the blankets of his boyhood with the blinds half drawn. Rose has gone back to school; she is taking courses at the community college and is busy, and somehow it is Miranda's mother, Harriet, who seems willing to check in on Adam several times a day, to bring him soup and custard, grapefruit and orange juice. And to play cards with Adam and Jo when she comes home from school.

Adam tells Miranda that the three of them are very happy playing cards in the time when he can keep awake, but it makes her impatient to hear about it; her days are spent at meetings, mimeographing leaflets, making demands on the university, mourning the dead. And listening to a new conversation: the women who say they're not going to mimeograph, not going to make coffee; they have their own issues, they want a voice. They do not want to be the servants of men. And so when she is called to come home, it feels like she's being called to be a servant, and she understands now she has no wish to be a servant. She can hardly bring herself to go home for even one weekend. Rose senses her impatience, sees how Miranda tends her son and says, "You might want to rethink being a doctor. I'm not sure you like being around sick people very much."

In his bed at home, Adam, exhausted, frightened, missing her, is terrified because he is playing the piano less than he has since he was seven years old. He can, for minutes at a time, study the scores of the Schubert sonatas, perform Madame Rostavska's stretching exercises, but to sit at the piano for any time at all: he simply doesn't have the strength. And the piano, he knows, is a jealous lover. He may very well be punished by the loss of a technique he will never be able to recoup. Because although he is a boy who enjoys life, and he is kind and infinitely sympathetic, he is also the terrified lover of a dominating beloved, who can give or withhold, whom he has no choice but to serve. And when Miranda comes to lie beside him in the half-dark room, the smell of his insufficiently washed body, the indolence that lodges in his beard, make her feel clammy and suffocated, and for the first time his body is not a delight to her;

for the first time, being next to it is not where she wants to be. She wants to get away, outside, into the cold, into the icy spring wind, back to school, back to the fire of this moment.

And one night, high with fatigue and the sense of purpose, she somehow allows Toby Winthrop to convince her that not to have sex with him is to give in to an oppressive hierarchy of monogamy. She thinks of Adam lying heavy and sweaty underneath his childhood blankets, and Toby's body — wire lean and bristling with rage and contempt — seems to her newly desirable.

Afterward, trying to sleep beside Toby, she is struck cold with the wrongness of what she's done; she gets up in the middle of the night, runs back to her dorm, and weeps in Valerie's arms: "What have I done. I'm awful. I'm despicable. I don't deserve him." And Valerie says, "Look, it's crazy times, everyone's a little crazy . . . just don't ever tell Adam. For God's sake, it won't hurt him if he never knows. The cruel thing would be to tell him. What you did was stupid. But don't be cruel."

And Miranda allows herself to believe this is the best course. She doesn't speak to Toby Winthrop again; she does not work again with his organization, but joins another group, less militant, with more women in charge. When she sees him somewhere — at a demonstration, or on the street — he always smiles and makes a gun shape of his hand and pretends to shoot her, and the contemptuous look in his eye is simultaneously humiliating and arousing to her.

Her last weeks of college are sluiced by her shame. Her graduation is overshadowed by Cambodia and Kent State; her last classes were anticlimactic, and she has missed so many she does not graduate summa, magna, or cum laude as she had always expected, as everyone had thought she would.

Adam must make up the course work he has missed, so he takes some summer courses. He wants to do more theory; he will also study voice and conducting; Henry Levi criticizes contemporary pianists because they don't sing their music, they concentrate only on their fingers and don't allow their bodies to follow the line. Miranda likes this plan; she doesn't want to go home to Westchester and fight with her father about his support of the war machine and, newly versed in the language of women's liberation, to be complicit in her mother's oppression. She gets a job in the office of Planned Parenthood in Somerville;

she and Adam move into the top floor of a white clapboard house. At work, she begins a program of sex education for teenagers who, healthy, though defiant, even deluded, she likes better than she likes the sick.

He wants to talk to her about chromatic scales and contrapuntal structures; his theory classes and composition classes are teaching him a language to which she has no access and in which she has no interest. She is a worker now; she must get to a desk at nine and not leave it till five; she leaves their apartment in Somerville at eight and gets home at six, if there's not a meeting, and Adam, proud of her and her work in the world, is also excited by the music coming to him in new ways through his learning about singing and conducting, and Miranda says, Yes, it's wonderful honey, wonderful sweetie, but he can tell she isn't listening as she used to, and he is frightened by her distance, by her new energy as a woman of the world.

Most of the time, except on the weekends, they are apart. She's at work; he is in the practice room, the one next to Beverly, who has returned to school after her time off ("Both of us, Adam, lying in half-dark rooms; you in your mother's house, me in the bin, much fancier, much more costly"), and she does listen to his excitement about voice and conducting, and the relationship among the last Schubert sonatas. And she signs up for those classes with him. Madame Rostavska, a Russian, and a sentimentalist, calls him into her office one day and asks him to do "a mitzvah, Adam, do you know what a mitzvah is? In Jewish tradition: a kind act, a good work. Beverly would like you to work with her on the Messiaen 'Amen.' She's a fragile girl, very gifted, she's suffered a great deal. I think, as musicians you could learn from each other. She's a passionate pianist, but lacks your discipline. You could benefit from a touch of her wildness."

Adam blushes; he says he'd like to think about it. He does not speak about it to Miranda. He doesn't speak of it to anyone, but he is drawn to the challenge of expanding his range as a musician. Messiaen is not someone he had ever thought of much, but the technical demands of his keyboard music, he knows, are enormous. Certainly it will be good for him to stretch himself like this. The question: will the stretch be painful, like Henry Levi's stretches, or mysterious in their effects, like Madame Rostavska's? He tells Madame Rostavska he will

310

be glad to do the two-piano piece. Beverly throws her arms around him. When she lifts her arms, he smells the rank uncleanness of her sweat mixed with the harsh sweetness of a perfume he will later know is called Ma Griffe. He is disturbed that it excites him. He will learn that *ma griffe* is French for "my claw," and he will wonder if it was for the suggestion of animal aggression that Beverly chose it.

And in November, Fatima, back in Pakistan, gets in touch with Miranda after the Bhola cyclone: the worst natural disaster in the subcontinent in the century. A telegram: old-fashioned in its brief imperative. "Come now. All is chaos. We need you here."

MONDAY, OCTOBER 22

THE CLOISTER OF
THE QUATTRO CORONATI
"Some People I Have Just Let Go"

"I want to take you to one of my favorite places, a restful place in this city that seems to have no interest in rest."

Looking out the bus window, she sees the Piramide, and then the headquarters of FAO, the Food and Agricultural Organization, where she worked during the summer of 1969. She can hardly remember the details of her work, that work that was so crucial to her at the time. She can hardly remember her office or rather her cubicle. She seems to recall that all the American women she worked with were named Lois. She can remember, as if trying to discern them in a dream, or in a fog, some details of some faces, sometimes a dress — navy blue with white polka dots — or a pair of shoes, red high heels, open toed.

They pass the Colosseum, which, without saying anything, they both understand they will only glance at. They leave the bus and pass the church of San Clemente.

"San Clemente is famous for embodying the layering of Rome. At the bottom is a Mithraic temple, where bulls were slaughtered, above that an early Christian basilica, and on top a seventeenth-century church that includes Byzantine mosaics and Renaissance frescoes. But let's not go there. You have to give me credit, Miranda: I've kept my word. Only one beautiful thing a day."

She laughs. "I appreciate your restraint," she says.

They climb up a hill to a much older brick structure, walk through a courtyard whose simple grand proportions, its emptiness, its openness, seem a desirable sign of something large and fine. They enter the dark church. Adam walks toward a far wall and presses a bell that for a time Miranda cannot see. As her eyes grow used to the dimness, a nun opens a door, and Adam says, so low Miranda can only just hear him, *"Grazie, suora."* She wonders how he knows what to call nuns in Rome.

■ ■ ■ ■

The nun, tall, pale, and smiling, closes the door behind them. They are directed to a cloister, a place that seems entirely apart from Rome, from everything she has known or ever thought of as Rome. The quiet falls, at first quite heavily, on her shoulders, then she feels it on her eyes, like a poultice, as if, without knowing it, she had been running a low-grade fever. Sitting on a stone bench, she gives to the stone all the accumulated tiredness of the unfrivolous traveler. She closes her eyes. Four sounds come to her: the sound of what she understands as seagulls, raucous, querulous, reminding her that Rome is near the sea, something she has not had the slightest sense of. Then there are the cheepings of better-tempered birds. Are there sparrows in Rome? she wonders. They somehow seem so Anglo-Saxon, not a bit Italian. Then a siren, then the sound of children's heels on stone, and then their challenges, given, thrown back, and against it all the mother's voice: *Sta'zitta.* Quiet down.

On the inside of the arches that surround the cloister is a pattern, bright red against ocher, of what appear to be teardrops. In the center of the cloister, the grass surrounding the well seems wild. Uncared for. And yet the wildness seems deliberate, an allowance rather than a neglect, and once more she is amazed that late in October there are roses, white, blooming only on one bush, the farthest from the door. She remembers that of the qualities she liked most about Adam, among the most important was his ability to be with her in silence. A silence that seemed like a very special kind of accompaniment. She allows herself to bask in silence now; she lowers herself as into a warm pool, or no, she thinks, a lake with just enough coolness in it to make you feel movement is possible, any movement you might like.

It is difficult to leave, to go back to the outside world. He feels this strongly and, as if to take the difficulty in his teeth, he brings up a difficult subject.

"What shall we do about Valerie?"

"Oh, Lord, Adam, you would think of that. You were always so responsible about that sort of thing."

"Well, yes, OK, I've thought of it, but I haven't the slightest idea of what to do about it. You were always better at that than I. Figuring out what to do. Then doing it."

"That's because then I believed there was a right thing to do, and if I just put my mind to it I'd discover it. That's another one of the things I've given up."

"We could send her a note. Thanking her."

"For what? For a disastrous encounter? For the dinner we never got to eat?"

"For the drinks. For arranging for us to meet."

She refuses to take up this last statement. "And what would the note say, 'Thanks for the drinks. And by the way, Adam and I are meeting daily, and we haven't invited you once, and we have no intention to do so.' "

"Couldn't we just say, 'Thank you for having us for drinks, your apartment is lovely and thank you for making our holiday more enjoyable.' "

She feels annoyance rising, an oblong at the back of her neck, heating the cool place that was left there by the cloister's silence. "First of all, Adam, we can't say 'we.' And this isn't a holiday for me; I've been working."

Ah, he thinks, she hasn't lost her anxiety that she isn't working hard enough. That she hasn't done enough. What were her words? That she's "let herself off the hook." As if any kind of pleasure were an unearned release. From what? He never knew what it meant to her to be "on the hook." It seemed somehow desirable to her, in a way he never understood.

"It would be good to write some kind of note, though," Adam says.

"Of course you're right. And you probably will write a note and I probably won't. I'll get paralyzed. I'll go silent because of the impossibility of finding the right thing to say. Something that's truthful and not wounding. But in my own defense, it's not just this situation: I'm terrible at writing thank-you notes. My husband writes the thank-you notes, if any get written.

"So you see we're different now," Miranda goes on. "It's you who thinks of the right thing and does it, and I who somehow can't. I who don't know what to say or how to say it. It's because of just this sort of thing that there are some people I have just let go."

"I was always astonished at the number of people in your life. Wherever we went, it always took much longer to get there than I thought it would because of all the people who wanted to greet you. And whom, therefore, I had to greet."

"Well, yes, I came to see it was too much. I came to the point where I didn't want to have any new friends. I wanted to have a card printed up that said, 'I'm sorry I can't get to know you because there are already too many people in my life.' "

"But of course you would never do that, because you really hate hurting people's feelings. Although you like being witty, being thought amusing and sharp. I never knew you to hurt anyone out of malice. You hurt people when you weren't paying attention. When you were distracted."

"That kind of carelessness, I've come to see, *is* a kind of malice."

"No, Miranda, no, it's not. I've known people who take pleasure in hurting. Who enjoy humiliation. That was never you."

"Nevertheless, I have hurt people. And then, in my guilt about that, my inability to face the harm I've done, I turn away from them. We can forgive those who trespass against us. We can't forgive the ones we've trespassed against."

"I have very few friends." He sighs. She can't bear to see the sadness that is shadowing his face. It's not right; he should have more friends. She doesn't want him to suffer an additional burden: the conviction that it's because of something wrong in him.

"But you, for example, kept in regular touch with Valerie all these years. I never answered her cards. I think I sent her birth announcements and changes of address and, well, when she came to the Bay Area I think I saw her, maybe once or twice in twenty years. But you, I know, kept writing. I only phoned her because I read in the Wellesley alumnae magazine that she had the business renting out apartments in Rome."

"My friends are of long standing. But sometimes, we don't see each other for many months, sometimes years. And I suppose, like you, I'm not that interested in making new ones. The people we see, well, we see them because of Clare."

"I don't think I want new friends and then I meet someone and I fall in love with them. I long to know them. I feel my life will be impoverished unless I get to know them. Like this German woman I met at the conference. She's trying to set up mental health facilities in the former East Germany, which is much poorer than West. Her kids are just my kids' age, though they're girls, so of course we've planned marriages between our children and she was just so interesting. I wanted to order everything she ordered for dinner, and I admired her scarf, so she gave it to me. It turns out we wear the same scent. I know we'll be friends now."

"But you have too many friends, you said."

"I do, but this woman, well, she's wonderful, I'll learn so much from her."

"So it will be an educational experience."

"Yes, like my trip to Rome."

"No holidays for you!"

"Of course not, Adam. Don't you remember: I'm a very serious person."

"So I can't buy you a gelato here."

"Yes, maybe you can . . . that will be an intellectual exercise. To train my powers of discrimination. And increase my vocabulary. *Martillo:* what's that, blackberry? You see, I'm learning something. And choosing something completely new."

"A brave woman you are, Miranda."

"Yes, a woman of discernment. And what will you order?"

"Strawberry," he says. *"Fragola."*

"Strawberry. That's all you ever ordered. Here where you could get all these flavors you couldn't get at home, why ever would you stick to strawberry?"

"Because I like it," he says.

She punches him lightly on the upper arm. She feels herself leaning into him, and she hears the false note in her voice, in both their voices. She recognizes it: they're flirting. But she and Adam? Flirting? No. This is wrong. Flirtation. Adam. No, the two words inhabit different universes. He was the love of her youth. There was no flirtation. They loved each other. Simply and directly they acknowledged their love. Simply and directly, they pledged themselves. And then unpledged. Flirtation, no. She tries to breathe more slowly. She tries to stop the vision she has of them walking somewhere. She cannot stop herself from seeing them walking together in a high, dim place she's never been, a place that could be taken from a dream. Her own or someone else's.

TUESDAY, OCTOBER 23

THE VILLA BORGHESE
"Vitae Laudae"

Down a path called the Via del Orangerie, they come upon three stone figures: Satyr father, mother, child.

"What a strange statue that is. Or is it a fountain?" Miranda asks.

"A fountain, I think, though not in working condition. That's a little sad. This is where I feel the failure of my education. I have no idea who these figures are. Those great travelers, those eighteenth- and nineteenth-century Englishmen buried in the Protestant cemetery, they'd know who these people are in a minute."

"Let's try to read the inscription. I'll try to make it out using my pitiful Latin, which you didn't have to take because you were given a course release to practice."

"Well, I'm paying for it now."

"Not at all. I've forgotten ninety-eight percent of any Latin I ever knew. I'll try to pick out these few words. Of course, I don't know the cases. It's something about life and praise. Maybe that's it: 'Praise life.' "

"What kind of life are they praising?" Adam asks, in what she recognizes as his jokey tone. "The father's a satyr, that tail can't mean anything good for family stability. And those hairy arms holding all those grapes. The mother has very well-developed calf muscles. She probably supports the family treading grapes."

"But look at the child. He's sitting, happy as he can be, clutching grapes, too. Is he a baby drunk? But look at how comfortable he is. They've joined hands and made a bench, or a platform for him, of their arms. Perhaps they're dancing. Just look at this child. He's perfectly secure. Perfectly stable. A well-adjusted little boy."

"What if they turn too fast or let go of each other's hands or drop him?"

"It's what we think, isn't it, that pleasure-loving parents will produce monsters. Babies dead in their cradles or splattered on the sidewalk in front of some seedy bar," Miranda says.

"*Vitae laudae.* Who could praise life when it's so full of horror?"

"They obviously don't think so. We're the ones who are afraid. I remember on holidays when my cousins got together and my cousin John and I, whom I always loved, whose company has always been a sheer pleasure to me . . ."

"I liked your cousin John so much. What happened to him?"

"He did very well. Made a fortune in the dot-com bubble, whatever that is. Lives with an ex-priest in the Napa Valley. They have a vineyard."

"Why were you talking about John?"

"Well, on family holidays John and I would sit together and laugh and laugh and my mother would start to get nervous, and John's mother, who was really as mean as a snake, would separate us. She would say of our laughter, 'This will end in tears, mark my words.' Just this year, John said to me: 'It was the first time I thought: Maybe grown-ups don't always know what they're talking about. Why do they think laughter will end in tears? Maybe it will end in laughter?' "

"What if the satyr parents dance with their baby and then go home for a nice meal and put him to bed and then get into bed themselves and make love and fall happily into a healthy sleep?"

"And the kid gets two eight hundreds on his SATs and gets a scholarship to Harvard."

"There's something in us that doesn't want it to turn out that way," Adam says.

"What I most fear as a parent and a human being is that disaster will occur and I'll be called upon to do something heroic and I will fail."

"Once I was with my son in New York and we were surrounded by a group of boys and they demanded my wallet. I just gave it to them. They took it and ran off and my son ran after them. He was only twelve. I stood there, frozen. He couldn't catch up with them, thank God, but he came back, defeated and despising me. And I despised myself. He said, 'I had to do something. You didn't even try.'"

She feels a little thrill of alarm. A son. That's right: he had a son. His child by Beverly. It's the first time he has mentioned him. She guesses that his history has not been happy. Of all fates, she has always believed the worst is to feel that you have failed your child. Even though she has no evidence to support her, she feels she must reassure him, because you must always reassure parents that whatever they did, it was the best, at that moment, they could have done.

"You were right to do as you did," she says.

"It was the beginning of my son's conviction that he couldn't depend on me. He was, in a way, right. I can't defend myself or anyone. I have never been in a fight. Never. When I was young I had to be careful of my hands. Suppose people I loved died because I couldn't use my hands to save them. My precious hands. Musicians' precious hands."

She thinks of Yonatan, who fought in the '67 War. The thought makes her want to protect Adam.

"But, you see, that hasn't happened."

"Vitae laudae."

"Something like that."

"Will you tell your cousin John I asked for him? And tell him that I hope he's right."

"Right?"

"That it won't end in tears."

Wednesday, October 24

THE PANTHEON
"The Smell of Drains"

She is, she tells him, feeling guilty about avoiding the great classical sites. The Colosseum. The Forum.

"I never know what I'm supposed to be looking at and looking for," she says. "I always feel I'm pretending to be seeing something I don't see, something that I'm sure isn't there and other people seem to believe is there. To know is there. I go into a kind of trance. I pretend I'm seeing things I don't see. And I end up saying things like 'Oh, yes, the scale is massive.' And then I want to leave. Also I keep expecting Victor Mature to be appearing from behind a column. There's a part of me that doesn't believe it's real, that it was just made up for some heroic scene in a movie I wouldn't dream of going to anymore."

"Well, what we'll do is look at the Pantheon. But only from the outside, the inside's been destroyed, turned into a Christian church. And we'll go at night, when the massiveness isn't somehow quite so threatening."

"They insisted on the massive, didn't they? They had no ambivalence about the desirability of power."

"None, absolutely none. Not being an imperial Roman, I wonder if I might just suggest that I take you to dinner. There's a restaurant by the Pantheon that has wonderful *pasta con vongole.* That is, if you eat clams."

"I do, actually, eat clams. Maybe that's not the most consistent thing in the world, but clams are something that I eat."

It's the first time they've met after dark and the first time he has treated her. She feels a little ripple of unease. Is this breaking the rules, or bending them? She makes sure that she calls Yonatan before she leaves; she has told him about Adam; she mentions that they'll be having spaghetti with clams.

"I envy you," he says. "I sometimes wonder if my passion for shellfish is a kind of compensation for their rejection by generations of my ancestors."

■ ■ ■ ■

They meet at eight by the church of Santa Maria sopra Minerva: Bernini's saddled elephant.

"It's such a funny presence here, this elephant, as if someone had set up a petting zoo down the road from the Pentagon," she muses.

"At one time it was known as Porcino, 'little piggy,' then it was called Pulcino, which means 'little chick,' people don't know whether it was called that because it was short or because the church belonged to the Dominicans and one of their major charities was to help young women needing dowries; apparently they made a procession here in the courtyard every year. By the way, right here to your left, this building was the headquarters of the Inquisition, where Galileo was tried."

"So how do I understand this place: the little pig, the little chick, and the murderous Inquisition."

"I have no idea. I never try. I just try to take it in, as if I were some kind of creature without a mind, one of those flies whose eyes are disproportionately large in relation to its body. A creature who doesn't have a brain at all. Just an eye, a skin. A sense of smell."

The restaurant is between Piazza Minerva and the Pantheon. The evening is unseasonably warm; she's wearing a sleeveless silk shirt, lemon-colored, which she covers with a pumpkin-colored scarf she'd bought just that day. The conference is over; her friends have gone home. She knows that it's something she won't do with Adam, shopping, so she spent her day buying gifts for Yonatan and the boys. For him: a white straw Borsalino; for the boys, who seem to have no interest in clothes, cotton sweaters: two apiece, in shades of blue whose subtle difference one from the other they would never take into account. Having thought of her husband and her sons, she felt free to indulge herself; agonizing over the scarves — pumpkin or turquoise — she knew she should not choose both. In the end, the pumpkin won, though all day long she mourned the turquoise, lost for good.

It is warm enough for them to eat outside, although she sees that the regulars make their way into their customary inner tables, and although she enjoys the last of October's warmth, she'd prefer that they were inside, away from the tourists, who order in English, all the wrong things. But the waiter seems to know Adam, seems to approve of his selections, and she relaxes in the pleasure of feeling that she is perceived, not as a tourist, but as someone who belongs.

He orders an expensive bottle of wine, and she worries that it is something that he really can't afford.

"It's from Orvieto," he says when it's presented to them. "Rose's home. I thought we'd drink to her."

She begins to tear, and pretends to have dropped her napkin. *Forgive me, Rose,* she says to the beloved ghost. *Somehow I always thought there'd be more time.*

"OK," she says. "Tomorrow I'm going to call Valerie. Let's meet her for lunch, maybe Friday."

"Yes, all right," he says.

Their pasta arrives and, although she's said clams are something that she eats, she eats them rarely, and she feels a bit transgressive: they taste, after all, more like meat than anything she's had in quite a while. But she thinks of Rose, and needs to believe that Rose forgives all her transgressions, among which the eating of clams is not, by a long shot, she knows, the worst.

The food and wine have made them quiet, and they walk the hundred yards in silence.

Above the Pantheon, the sky is inky, blue-black with hints of silver. Miranda leans back to look above the overwhelming roundness of the dome. Tracing the insistent curve, then contradicting it, breaking the contact between stone and sky, two birds dive and wheel. Miranda wonders if they are the same gulls whose presence always comes to her as a surprise here. The lights meant to illumine the dark stone turn the birds' wings metallic. The first birds, the irritable gulls, are followed by smaller birds . . . swifts, swallows (she had an English friend who insisted she know the difference) who quickly disappear in the night sky. What birds are these, so long after the sun has set? She can't think of another place where birds seem so much a part of the look of the great monuments, a formal element rather than an intrusion. Not like the pigeons on Nelson's Column in Trafalgar Square. It's one of the things that pleases her most about this city: the easy in and out of natural and man-made.

She is struck, suddenly, by a smell she hasn't taken in for a long time. The smell of drains.

"Do you smell that, Adam? Just here. Now."

"That bad smell? The drains."

"So if we're creatures with a sense of smell, we have to come to terms with bad smells, too. Like this one. It was everywhere when we were here before. To me, it was the smell of Europe. Suggesting a whole life more physical than I was comfortable with, really, though I would have died rather than admit it. It worried me at first because, of course, I knew it was the smell of shit. But it seemed to me that it was corrupt in the way I wanted Europe to be, in the way I wanted Europe to corrupt me. It reminded me that I had really got away from home. It was in the air; it was the air. And now, it's gone. I wouldn't have thought I'd regret the absence of what could only be described as a bad smell. Now I feel the loss of it is something I want to mourn."

"I guess it's one of the American victories: the triumph of excellent plumbing. Kind of like the Romans and their aqueducts."

"When you smelled it you immediately thought, This is foreign. Now nothing's really foreign."

"When I read those old travel books I love, especially English ones, which I seem to have a particular fondness for, I come upon sentences beginning 'The Italians.' Just beginning a sentence with those words showed how much of a gap they felt between

333

themselves and the people they were writing about. But now, those kinds of generalizations aren't true, and to use them is only an affectation. MTV, the Internet, Italian kids listening to rap music: we're not strange to one another. Not strangers. And yet we don't really know each other. I still worry about presuming too much, carelessly giving offense."

"It's hard to know in what ways we've become the same and in what ways we're different when we all look the same."

"When we were young, Italians looked different from Germans, you could tell the Spanish from the French. Now everyone's wearing baseball caps backward. Except the girls: they're wearing baseball caps the right way round."

"When we were here in '69, there were nuns and priests everywhere; you were always nervous bumping into them, young men in long skirts walking unlike any young men I'd ever known, kind of like they were on roller skates, and the nuns, women almost entirely invisible, always in black, always in pairs. All of them, you felt, making sure you weren't going into one of the churches in a sleeveless minidress."

"The churches are empty now. The cafés are smoke free. Italians jog and have salad as a first course. It's no longer chic to be a Communist; it's only now for ill-dressed fringe types."

"I very much dislike nostalgia," Miranda says. "I fear it. But the smell of drains . . . why do I want to weep because of it? I wonder what, some years from now, we'll mourn the loss of. Something that we now think of as an irritation. Even a curse."

"I think before we have the chance for that we'll be taking our place among the dead."

The mention of the dead is shocking: they look at each other, a bit frightened.

"I want to be like one of those marble effigies on the church floors here. Arms folded over my breast. Dog curled under my feet. Stepped on by people on the way to something they're eager to see," she says.

"You want to be unregarded? Underfoot?"

"I think of it as supporting the passage of the living."

"The living in their backward caps, not knowing what they're walking on."

THURSDAY, OCTOBER 25

THE CHAPEL OF SAN CARLINO
"I Don't Want a Face"

"I'm feeling a little guilty that I haven't given Bernini's archenemy a chance."

"I didn't know he had one."

"Borromini," he says. "He kept losing commissions to Bernini . . . Bernini was charismatic and he was dour, a Northerner, a Swiss, and his aesthetic was demanding and austere, I thought perhaps the plainness might appeal to you."

"Yes, sometimes all the ornamentation is overwhelming."

They walk up a steep hill to the Street of the Four Fountains. She's worried that the steepness might be a strain on his heart. She thinks she's walking slowly, at a pace that won't cause him strain, but she keeps stealing glances to make sure his color is all right.

At the top of the hill, she's surprised that there actually are four fountains, one on each corner, each representing a lounging neoclassical goddess, filthy, moss covered, good-naturedly presiding at the top of the frenetic traffic-clotted street.

The entrance to the church is unremarkable: she hardly takes it in. But once inside, she is flooded with whiteness. Above her head, a dome that is a honeycomb of pure white circles, interrupted by crosses, not a hint of ornament. The arches are like waves of snow: they alternate, concave, convex.

She closes her eyes, opens them, allows herself to be carried by the alternating waves.

"I thought you'd like this," he said.

"I like it very much."

They make their way to the cloister. She's struck by its emptiness. Not a possibility here of bush or flower: white stone, gray paving, black plain ironwork providing a canopy for the well which one could only imagine had always been and would always be empty. Her heels strike sharp on the gray stone; the sound flies, unencumbered, through the deliberate, neutral air. Her eyes travel upward to the windows — perfect ovals: plain, transparent glass recessed into the wall whose whiteness seems, though she's been told this is impossible, pure white, without a trace of color.

"I'd like to look at the dome again," she says, "and the wavy arches."

The chapel is entirely empty. Pleased at the emptiness they take a seat at what they have determined, without speaking, is the exact center.

She opens her eyes. Closes them. Opens them and looks at what he understands is nothing he can see.

"Do you pray?" he asks, embarrassed, as if he has asked her to confess indecency.

"I have," she says, "converted to Judaism. Still, I can't say I've become a Jew. Or I'm a Jew. Or I am Jewish. It's a strange thing. I don't quite believe you can claim to be a Jew if you weren't born one."

"Did you do it for your sons?"

"You know me well. Of course I couldn't stand to be at the margin of one of their important moments. So before they were bar mitzvahed, I began to study. But it wasn't just that. I wanted a larger life. I wanted to be saying words people had said for thousands of years. I chose Judaism, yes, because of my sons, but because a Jew doesn't have to believe in anything particular. We just have to behave in a way that . . . oh, I don't know . . . that does the world good. I guess I like the sense of endless responsibility without the promise of reward."

"You haven't answered me. Do you pray?"

"In a very special sense. I don't pray to anyone. I don't want a face. I like the Jewish interdiction against making an image for God. I want to be able to say certain words: words that conform to certain categories. 'Praise.' 'Lament.' And you, Adam? Does Rome make you feel more a Catholic?"

"No, less. I don't have it, the ear for faith, the way some people have no ear for music. I feel it doesn't fit me; I've seen people whom it does fit. My father, when he died I found he had a lot of books on mysticism, and in the end, when he retired, he went to Mass every day. You remember my mother stopped going to church when the pope declared birth control illegal. Of course she was Italian enough to go on Christmas and Easter. And Ash Wednesday and Palm Sunday. But when we came to Rome she'd go into the churches and look in the back for anticontraception propaganda and pick it up and take it outside and throw it away. My father was mortified, but, I think, also secretly pleased. She would rail about the gold and the marble in the church, and carry on about the starving poor. Oh, where have I heard that," he says, patting her on the head.

She sticks her tongue out at him. But she's delighted that her scruples were shared by Rose, her beloved ghost.

"My father and I would visit the churches and let her walk the streets, talking to people, drinking her endless *espressi.* I would watch my father pray and think: My father is a good man. My father has the ear for goodness. And I knew that I did not."

What he doesn't tell her: how Beverly, in her last madness, became obsessed with a vision of the Holy Ghost and the saints, obsessed with Messiaen, convincing herself she was his unacknowledged daughter, making Adam's father take her to Lourdes (he never told Adam a thing about it, only that he thought, Beverly had a hard time). She kept hoping Adam's father would join her in her mad vision; she wanted him to go with her to Latin Masses at an ultratraditionalist church, but he wouldn't. Adam found it all sickening and frightening. And the thought of prayer, after that, sickened and frightened him.

"If there is a God," he says, "it is the God of music. If there's a life after death, it will be, I think, some kind of music."

"I think it will be nothing or I will be with

everyone I love."

The door bangs open and a tall muscular man, cameras dripping from his neck like heavy vines, walks up and down, around and around, snapping pictures.

"Aren't you not supposed to do that?" Miranda says. "This is where I'd like a police state."

The man is flipping open several guidebooks, handing them to his companion, a slender, languid, unfresh-looking bottle brunette, whose long thin feet look tired in their platform espadrilles. He keeps telling her to look at things, pointing to pages in the books, pointing to the dome, the arches, the stones on the floor. She sits down and puts on her sunglasses. He leaves her, and they can hear his boots clomping on the stones of the cloister next door; they hear the swish swish of his camera lens.

His companion sits with her eyes closed. She has taken off her sunglasses.

He comes back into the chapel, nearly pulling her into the cloister, insisting that they make their way downstairs to the crypt.

"Tell me their story," Adam says.

"Oh, that's easy," says Miranda. "He's a professor of entomology at Tübingen. He met her on an expedition studying beetles in Latvia. He got drunk one night and let his colleagues take him to a brothel. She had the bad luck to draw him. He woke up beside her, in love, and said he would marry her and bring her to Germany. Of course she took him up on it, as she'd been sold into sexual slavery in the brothel as a twelve-year-old. But now, she's thinking of going back to the brothel; she thinks it might be preferable to his endless enthusiasm, his endless attempts to educate her. It will break his heart, but in the end, he'll find a graduate student to console him."

They hear the man shouting in German words that Miranda thinks mean "marvelous" or "a marvel." The woman says nothing.

"I hate to leave this place to them," Miranda says. "I'd like to protect it from them."

"I'm sure it's been through worse. Though poor Borromini did kill himself here. Not right in this place, but here in Rome."

"Maybe it was types like this guy who drove him to it."

Immediately she is horrified at herself. What has she just said? It's not a good idea to make jokes about suicide to the husband of a suicide.

She doesn't know if he's pretending that he hadn't heard, but he says nothing, leans his head back, opens and closes his eyes.

"A dream of whiteness," he says.

"Yes," she says, swallowing her embarrassment. "Yes, a lovely dream."

FRIDAY, OCTOBER 26

THE ENGLISH CEMETERY
"Writ in Water"

"I'd like to take you to the Protestant cemetery," he says. "I have such sympathy for those nineteenth-century northerners. Down on their luck. Out of their element. Living here on nothing, going to the Anglican church on Sundays, with their headaches and their grand palazzi full of moth-eaten furniture, freezing all the time, knowing they should feel grateful, in love with the place but pining all the time for home."

They cross a terrifying street surrounding the Piramide and walk along the Aurelian Walls. Ornately decorated brass wreaths celebrate the partisans who died fighting the German invaders.

"This is how the Italians live with their past," Adam says. "It wasn't them. It was never them. They never elected Mussolini. Everything bad that happened was someone else's fault. The Germans. One of the rare human things is to tell the truth about the past."

"Or even to know it," she says. She is thinking of her infidelity with Toby Winthrop. It happened more than forty years ago. Adam never found out, because she kept it from him. She kept it in the dark. She allowed him to think the only infidelity was his. She would like to say, *I too am guilty of lying, by omission.* But she lacks the courage.

They pay to enter the Protestant cemetery. "I feel like the temperature's dropped ten degrees here," she says. "It's so un-Italian." They make their way, like everybody else, to John Keats's grave. They bend to read the words carved into the stone:

This Grave contains all that was Mortal, of a Young English Poet, Who on his Death Bed, in the Bitterness of his Heart, at the Malicious Power of his Enemies, Desired these Words to be engraven on his Tomb Stone: Here lies One Whose Name was writ in Water.

"Well, he really got it wrong," Miranda

says. "It's a good thing to remember. None of us, really, has any idea of what we'll leave behind. But look, Adam, it also says he wanted this written because of his enemies. So he died bitter because of bad reviews. That seems a kind of waste. And maybe it's not so bad, something writ on water. At least the words were written somewhere. Which means they were thought. Does it matter so much that things should last? And for how long? And for whom?"

"It matters to me. I don't want the music of Bach and Beethoven to be just washed away. And sometimes I think I'm just building sandcastles, or tending them, hoping they won't be obliterated by the inevitable wave."

When Adam talks this way, Miranda yearns for Yonatan, who does not fear the future. Who very rarely allows himself to mourn the past. Except at those times when the wave of what has been lost knocks him over. He thinks about his brother, killed in the '67 War. He retreats into the bedroom, closes the blinds, turns out the lights. She does not go near him. She has learned that, after a certain number of hours, he'll come out of the dark room. Finished with something, ready to go on. She'd like to shake Adam by the shoulders and say, *If Yonatan,*

*seeing what he has seen, living through what
he has lived through, can be hopeful, why
can't you?* She won't do this, but she won't
continue what she considers a useless, a
debilitating conversation.

"Look at this," she says, pointing to a
poem carved into the wall near Keats's
grave.

K-eats! if thy cherished name be "writ in
    water"
E-ach drop has fallen from some
    mourner's cheek;
A-sacred tribute; such as heroes seek,
T-hough oft in vain — for dazzling deeds
    of slaughter
S-leep on! Not honoured less for Epitaph
    so meek!

"I never noticed that before," he says.
"I wonder who wrote it?" she says.
"Let's ask the man selling the books and
postcards."

A young man is sitting beside a computer,
making stacks of postcards and bookmarks.
Adam asks him who wrote the acrostic
poem. *"Non so,"* he says, and turns to his
computer. The computer does not yield the
information. He asks his older colleague.
Miranda thinks he must be nearly seventy

347

in an impeccably cut gray suit, his silvery hair just the right combination, Miranda thinks, of straightness and wave.

"Hemingway," the man says.

Miranda hears the name Hemingway and is outraged. "You must tell him that is impossible. Hemingway could not possibly have written that poem."

"I will tell him, Miranda, but it won't do any good. Italians feel that if they don't know something and tell you so you will be disappointed. And he doesn't want to disappoint you. He knows Hemingway was an English writer, so he tells you Hemingway wrote the poem."

"But he must stop giving out that kind of misinformation," Miranda says, really irate now.

"He probably won't," Adam says. He tells the man that he is sure Hemingway didn't write that poem. The man looks at him regretfully, shakes his head, opens his hands in a gesture meant, Miranda guesses, to indicate helplessness.

As they leave, they pick up a single Xeroxed page headed "Guardians of the Departed." It is a request for funds from an organization that cares for the cats who make their home in the cemetery. Miranda reads aloud: " 'Shielded from the outside commotion, the cats are safe from harm here. The green tangle of vegetation creates a secure haven for these little friends of the departed. As territorial animals, each cat has his adopted turf, overseen with pride. These feline guardians provide loyal companionship to the deceased, giving at the same time life and vitality to their resting place.' "

"I can't bear thinking of these English spinsters devoting their lives to the cats. I much prefer the plates of spaghetti left randomly for the cats around the Forum, with no notion that they are 'little friends of the departed,' " Miranda says.

"Perhaps it gives the English ladies a sense of meaning and purpose."

"Well, Adam, that's truly grim. Let's get away from all this gentility and take a walk on the rough Roman streets. Maybe we will be lucky and someone with a switchblade will demand our wallets."

"Let me show you this," he says. "This hill is made of the shards of old amphorae. The port was here and after people had used the oil from their amphorae, they didn't know what to do with them, so they just broke them up and made a hill of shards."

"I wonder if Keats knew about this," she

says. "I wonder if it depressed him that this is what lasted. All those broken things no one wanted."

They stop for a coffee. On a wall that must, she thinks, be ancient, a young man and a young woman are affixing political posters. For a few minutes, the young man makes desultory efforts with a brush and a pot of paste. Then he puts down his pot and brush and waves his arms around, giving animated directions to the young woman, who works faster now, attaching to the stone the bright-colored posters: a middle-aged man with a lot of teeth, representing a party Miranda has never heard of.

Adam sees she's entirely absorbed in the comedy across the road. She isn't thinking of Keats or Bach or Beethoven or the English spinsters. She puts her head in her hands. He doesn't understand why she is weeping. Then he sees, she isn't weeping, she's laughing. She takes her hands away from her face, throws her head back; her whole body is taken over with her laughter.

"Hemingway," she says, hardly able to catch her breath. "Hemingway."

"Down, girl," he says, reaching across the table, pretending to take her pulse. "You're going to have a heart attack." He is a little alarmed at her hilarity; he remembers now that he was always a little frightened when she laughed like this. Perhaps because this kind of laughter took her somewhere else, somewhere far away from him.

"Well, so maybe I'll die laughing. That wouldn't be so bad."

"Not on my watch, please," he says. And he is struck, as he is more and more lately, with the simple fact. At some point we will not be here. On this earth. At some point, Miranda and he will be . . . where. Not here. He takes her hand and kisses it, and they are both embarrassed, so he drops it quickly, and calls the waiter for the check.

What will I remember of this day? she wonders. Will it be Keats's grave, or the Hemingway misinformation, or the cat ladies, or the couple and their posters across the street. Or his taking my hand and kissing it. Or my embarrassment. When I recall this day and start the sentence "That was the day when . . ." I wonder how the sentence will end. And how will it end for him?

SATURDAY, OCTOBER 27

SANTA SABINA
"Why Is It There Are Some Things
We Aren't Meant to See?"

"How about a picnic?" Adam says. "It's a wonderful day, and I'd like to take you to a place I love, orange trees and Rome in front of you, all laid out. We can buy food in a market where the locals shop . . . you don't hear a word of English or German or French, just people shouting insults and giving in or not giving in."

They met at the church of Santa Maria in Cosmedin. He runs up to her, takes her hands and spins her around three times.

"I called Valerie last night, to see if she wanted to join us for the picnic. She seemed really overwhelmed, incredibly apologetic that she hadn't been in touch. She was just on her way out the door. Apparently her mother-in-law is going to some spa in

Switzerland, and they need to be there with her for three weeks. She said she'll be in touch with you about the details of your leaving. She's sending her cleaning woman to pick up the key, you're not to worry about anything, but she'll phone from Switzerland."

"I have to change my entire understanding of the universe. I now believe there is a loving God who cares about my personal well-being!"

"Maybe that's not it at all," he says. "Maybe she didn't want to see us either."

"Why wouldn't she want to see us?" Miranda asks, genuinely puzzled.

It occurs to Adam that Miranda finds it difficult to understand that anyone wouldn't want to be in her company. He remembers a conversation; they were still in high school. She was talking to one of her friends about another girl, whom she intensely disliked. "She's so conceited, she's really dumb, she's a total brownnose," Miranda had said.

"She doesn't like you either," Miranda had been told.

And she had seemed genuinely surprised. He thinks she might have even asked, "Why?"

He understands that he will actually have

to explain, a task that makes Miranda seem endearingly young to him.

"Maybe she was so mortified by what happened when we were at her apartment, or maybe she's horrified that we know what her life's really like."

Miranda shrugs, unconvinced, still puzzled. They both agree that they won't take their place in the line of tourists putting their hands in the open mouth of the appalled or outraged god. The Bocca della Verità. The mouth of truth.

"You remember that moment in *Roman Holiday*? Where Gregory Peck pretends to have his hand cut off in the god's mouth? Because the lion is supposed to snap off the hands of liars. It's a moment of complete charm, when Audrey Hepburn screams: she knows she's a liar, too, pretending she's not a princess."

A wire thrums in the space separating the two sections of Miranda's rib cage. Does not saying something that should have been said still constitute a lie?

She wants to bring the conversation away from anything like this.

"I wonder," she says, "how many people have their first, maybe their deepest, impressions of Rome from the movies. How many people thought of Rome first as the place

354

where Anita Ekberg jumped into that fountain. They might only learn later that it's called the Trevi."

They make their way to the large covered Testaccio Market. "There used to be many more of these," he says. She is happy, he sees, going from stall to stall, looking, tasting. Being elbowed by ordinary housewives who insult one vendor's tomatoes, praise the plums of another. She points to the different cheeses in the showcases: he names them to the salesman, and she is given taste after taste. She takes a bite, then passes it to him. She hopes he hasn't grown nervous about germs; but she sees that he's content to share the morsels with her. She wipes his lips with one of the rough napkins that the salesman offers. As she does it, she thinks perhaps it's something she shouldn't be doing: it's infantilizing; he's not a child. But she enjoys the fondness of the gesture, the plain tenderness. If you start worrying about this kind of thing, she tells herself, you'll never be spontaneous; you'll always be looking over your shoulder. For whom? Afraid of what?

They reach the top of a hill, a long climb; he is breathing with effort. She is worried for him: his weak heart. On each side of the street are prosperous, heavy-looking villas, some of them, she guesses — seeing a sign on the door of one, 1932 — built by Fascist grandees.

At the highest point, they pass the church of Santa Sabina (for after lunch, he tells her) and walk through a square arch. The park, she sees, is dedicated to the memory of a minor comic film star. The scent of oranges surrounds them. A sign forbids playing with balls, but all around them children, teenagers, even old men, are throwing and catching a great variety of balls.

This seems to be the place where brides are photographed. She wonders: Are they all getting married in the church? All today? There is one spot — before the splendid view of Rome — that all the couples covet. They are literally lined up in the few feet before the balustrade. She finds the assembly-line aspect of it all mildly saddening: she is disappointed for the brides. If she were one of them she would resent the erasure of her singularity on this day when a young woman wants to believe herself particularly singular.

She remembers the time that she imagined she would wear a long white dress and walk down the aisle to marry Adam. Is he thinking of that now, too?

She hadn't been married in a long white dress; she'd worn a sleeveless purple silk sheath, a scarlet shawl, high strappy black sandals.

She and Yonatan were married in the house of one of their friends; twenty people were invited; there was champagne, canapés, then everyone went home. She and Yonatan had lived together for two years; they were both too busy for a honeymoon.

The day was nearly spoiled for Miranda because of her father's grim face; he hated that his daughter was being married under a chuppah, by a rabbi. Her mother had asked if she wouldn't consider having a minister as well; she had stubbornly refused. Now she regrets that she didn't do something that would have made the day, if not happier, then easier for her mother. That would have softened her father's wrath. But she didn't think he deserved to be humored; she found his responses insupportable. "I'm not an anti-Semite," he'd said. "I'd just like my traditions honored, too." When Yonatan's father raised his glass and said, *"L'chaim,"* her father had said, "Doesn't anyone speak English here?" mortifying Miranda and her mother. She was almost as angry at her mother for standing silent, wringing her hands. Her brother had declined the invitation, as she knew he would.

She imagines what the day would have been like if it had been her and Adam's wedding. Probably they would have married in his parish church. It would have been a day of easy happiness; everyone's believing their marriage a sign of something hopeful in the world, a new beginning, a fine fresh start. Forty years later, she feels cheated of a day that never happened: that she had been denied the moment of being seen as the perfect embodiment of an old idea.

Adam is remembering his and Clare's wedding in the Hartford City Hall. They very well understood that to some people, not the least Clare's parents, their marriage was an embarrassment.

Miranda notices that, among the couples, one pose seems to be popular: the bride stands, wraps the long train of her gown around the groom, down on one knee like Al Jolson singing "Mammy." She wonders what this means: *I've got you now, for good? We are entwined forever?* Wrapped in the train, the couples hold hands, leaning back, looking up at the sky. Miranda doesn't understand why this pose might be appealing. She notices the dresses: none seems well made or expensive. One bride, pushing a baby in a stroller, is wearing a dress that is entirely see-through. Another, very young, her dark hair piled on her head with an elaboration Miranda feels ill equipped even to consider, stands simply beside her new husband, who is four inches shorter than she. The family, speaking Spanish, take what seems to Miranda to be the same photograph twenty times. Some feet away, at the balustrade that marks the frame of panoramic Rome, the tallest of the brides has the most trouble managing her train. She has just married someone who is clearly a captain of industry: older than she by at least twenty years. They are photographed by a professional who moves them around with no enthusiasm, as if they were stiff, expensive dolls.

Adam and Miranda eat their cheese, their tomatoes, their rolls: thin crust, then air. Furtively, he chews on his salami, which Miranda would never eat. The brides, the grooms, their families, make them feel intruders, so they don't linger, but walk quickly toward the church.

"These wooden doors are very old," Adam says. He takes her hand and tells her to tilt her head way back. It is still unnatural for them to touch, and the same wire that she felt thrumming when she considered the implications of her past untruth starts up between her ribs again.

"There," he says, "at the very top, there on the left, that panel is meant to be the oldest depiction of the unclothed Christ."

She takes steps frontward and backward. She bends her neck back, then straightens it. She squints. She makes a frame of her hands. Then a tunnel. She closes her eyes. Shakes her head. Opens her eyes again.

"I can't see anything," she says, not concealing her annoyance. "What's the point of all that work, just for the sadistic pleasure of letting people know there's something they can't see? What's the point of something that's there for us to see that can't be seen?"

"Perhaps we've lost a certain way of seeing," he says.

Her neck hurts. She's afraid she's twisted something in her back and will suffer in a minor way that will intrude on her last days. This, she knows, is a function of age. This, too, annoys her.

"I think it's ridiculous," she says. "Perverse."

She walks ahead of him, clicking her heels aggressively on the stone pavement of the courtyard.

They make their way down the hill. In a

garden, alongside a small brick church (Why do they need another church so close to the basilica? she wonders), three homeless men sit at the edge of a fountain. They are smoking cigars and washing their clothes in the fountain. They have constructed a clothesline by hanging a rope between two orange trees; under the leaves socks, underwear, T-shirts, flap recklessly in the light breeze. The men wave at Adam and Miranda, comment on the beauty of the day, and cheerfully ask for money.

Miranda gives them five euros each. Adam would like to stop her, but he sees that, in giving them money, her good temper has been restored.

SUNDAY, OCTOBER 28

THE GALLERIA BORGHESE
"My Head Aches and I'm Tired"

It is a brilliant day; the sun has no inflection, no modulation, and it falls like a fist on the white obelisk of the Piazza del Popolo, the bemused lions, the lounging gods. The bright light is only a trial to Miranda; the night before she went to a dinner party given for her new German friend, given by Germans. She ate and drank too much, woke in the night with an overwhelming thirst, and when the alarm rang in the morning, she was headachy and nauseated. If she'd known how to telephone Adam, she would have called to cancel. All she wants to do is spend the day in bed. She misses Yonatan: he would bring her oranges and herbal tea and provide aspirin and cool cloths for her head. She wishes she were home with him. She's tired of it all, the crowded noisy city where she does not understand and is not understood, the endless talk with Adam, full as it is of unanswerable questions. Am I the person who I was? What has become of me?

A creature, man or woman, it is impossible to tell, has silvered him- or herself and is standing stock-still in the middle of the piazza, representing the Statue of Liberty, at whose base is a paper cup with some paper euros and some coins.

"What a ridiculous thing to do," Miranda says. "Why would anyone think that was interesting or amusing? Worth paying money for?"

"I have great news," Adam says, as if he hasn't heard what Miranda has just said, or the tone in which she said it. "I've got us tickets for the Galleria Borghese."

"Without asking if that's what I wanted to do?"

She is pleased and not pleased by his dashed look. A taste, a delicious remembrance, of her old power. The quick slice, the quick blow, she always had a feel for it. But in the end it was he who delivered the blow that was, if not mortal, then nearly. It had not been quick and it had not been over quickly, as her blows were. But unlike her, he hadn't meant to hurt. After all these years, she is still sure of that.

"I'm sorry . . . I just thought . . ."

"No, Adam, that's just it. You didn't think. You just went ahead. As it happens, I'm not feeling well today. My head aches and I'm tired. I ate and drank too much last night and I slept badly. The last thing I want to do is go to a museum and push my way through a crowd of retired Americans and Germans looking like oxen struck by a mallet, longing to be back home so they can use their own toilets."

"I'll make a deal with you." She hears the old, patient, conciliating voice. She is determined to resist the pull of its comfort. "We'll just look at three things. Three Bernini sculptures. We can leave as soon as you like after that."

She would like very much to childishly refuse. But she knows there's a chance that she'll regret it later. So they cross the piazza, navigate the death-defying street beside the church, and climb the stairs into the park. She hears herself making the sighing noise her boys make when she asks them to help her to carry groceries.

They are at the opposite end of the park, and she walks beside him sullenly. When they get to the Galleria, she sees that the line for collecting their tickets is endless.

Then there is another for required checking of all bags, and a third to present their tickets to enter the museum.

"This is absurd," she says. "Can it really be true about the Italians having no talent for organization? Maybe Mussolini was right; maybe they should give up their pasta."

"On the other hand," he says, pointing to the view from the balcony, the long avenue of trees, the statues flanking.

"There is no other hand," she says. "Let's try to get to the front of the line so we don't have to wait another half hour to be let in."

The guard opens the doors and they are shown to the first room, each surface covered, embellished. What she might have thought of another day as richness strikes her now as assault.

"My head aches so," she says. "This is not a good room for me right now."

"Just do what you can," he says, taking her elbow, steering her past the monumental heads, the allegorical walls and floors. They stop before Bernini's *David.*

This David is not young, not boyish, not in the slightest delicate. He is tall, well muscled, anything but innocent, adamantly unpoetic. Miranda's eyes go to his mouth, the lips rendered invisible by resolve; this is a mouth not used for love or speech or the taking in of food; it is a mouth that finds its purpose in one thing only. Resolve. Resolve to beat the odds. No one can stop the damage he will do, gripping the slingshot, his body torqued by the determination to do harm.

From her past, a memory swims up. Of a clenched mouth. That tightness. The resolve against all impulse. She remembers: it was her own mouth. And she remembers that her mouth went like that because someone had put a hand against it, had put a hand before her mouth to silence her. And she had acceded to the silencing. But the will, her will, had not succumbed.

She knows very well whose hand it was. Rose's hand. The hand of Adam's mother.

Out of her mind, beside herself. The phrases overused had become real. She felt herself watching herself from another place, a place of wildness where any words or actions were allowed. With Adam, she had been silent. Her vanity had enabled her restraint. Now, with Rose, who loved her, whom she loved, Rose, the mother of the man who she had said was her whole life, she turned into the animal she felt she had the right to be. She allowed sobs to be

366

ripped out of her body. She made no effort to be quiet. She shouted words without a thought of their propriety. "Traitor. Liar. Coward. Thief." It couldn't have been long, that she shouted those words, that she pulled at her hair and lost the center of her breathing. It couldn't have been long before Rose put her hand over Miranda's mouth, a hand that was not cool, as Miranda's mother's hands were always cool, and was not smooth or cared for, as Miranda's mother's hands were smooth and cared for. Her vanity about her hands was the one vanity Miranda's mother felt she was allowed. Miranda felt the rough, overwarm pressure of the palm of Rose's hand, making her words impossible, stifling her wild, furious sobs. And then Rose's own words, "But you must understand. He is my son."

And she understood what this woman required of her: silence. Having no choice, as David had no choice, murdering something (her love for Rose, her belief that the ideal of justice was more powerful than the accident of blood) as David murdered the gross giant. Just feet from Bernini's willful murderer is Caravaggio's version: a luscious boy, desirable, remorseless, holds by the hair the pathetic head of Goliath — his eyes shocked, his mouth appalled — far more sympathetic than the brash boy killer.

And on that day when Rose put her hand against Miranda's mouth, Miranda put her lips together in this way and silently composed herself and left the house, the house where she believed she learned how possible it was to be exuberantly and yet securely happy. She never saw Rose again. And never again was she the child of any house.

How long ago it seems, she thinks, those scalding tears, those sobs raised from what she had believed would be an endless well of sorrow.

Adam takes her elbow and leads her back the way they came, through the ornate room of the monumental heads which, minutes ago, she found threatening, and now finds consoling. Huge. These gods, she thinks, are unsusceptible. Beyond us. And the possibility of unapproachableness sluices her hot brain.

He brings her to another room, the walls, the floors, devoted to the stories of the violent gods; a sculpture, white against a blur of color, commands everything. A man, bearded, not young, his biceps perhaps not as impressive, not as threatening, as they once were, is grabbing a much younger woman by the waist. His face is the face of nothing but appetite. His fingers press into the flesh of her thighs, denting them, dimpling them. He can't see her; he sees nothing but his future pleasure or, perhaps, simply, future release. She is miserable. The face of plain abandonment. Despair. On her face, sculpted tears. The position of her feet, the distortion of her toes, signal that she has given up the fight.

"Pluto and Proserpina," she says, reading the brass plaque. "How can I not know who they are?"

"But you do know. I know you know. I remember a paper you wrote about the story in college. Pluto and Proserpina are Hades and Persephone. Hades, the lord of the underworld, who abducts Persephone, the daughter of Demeter, the goddess of the earth. She says that if he doesn't send her daughter back she'll arrange for eternal winter. Demeter and Hades come to a compromise. The girl will live half the year with her mother and half in the underworld with him."

"My God, Adam, you remember that?"

"What you wrote was beautiful. It taught me something. About a woman's desire for the dangerous male at the same time that she's just longing for her mother."

"Was I really that smart then? I've lost

that way of thinking. I read much less now. No poetry at all."

"Your life is full."

"Overfull, you mean."

"No, Miranda, I said what I meant."

"Of course, now I understand much more about Demeter and her destructive rage. The bereft mother threatening eternal winter. The death of everything. Give me my child back or there will be no grain."

"I can imagine you might like that kind of power."

"Well, who wouldn't, Adam?"

"You might understand that not everyone would."

"Bullshit. They would if they thought they could get away with it."

"Can you bear to see one more?"

"Of course, Adam, I'm not that pathetic."

"I was just worried that your head was bad."

"I'll decide how I'm feeling, Adam, and believe me, I'll let you know. Now that we're here, I'm very glad to be seeing this. He understands it all, Bernini, how vulnerable women are to that male force. And he understands her anguish: those wonderful tears on her cheeks . . . The pressure of his fingers into the flesh of her thighs: he's denting her flesh, and he doesn't even know

370

it. He doesn't know anything, he doesn't see anything except his own desire. He really understood it, Bernini: that male blindness."

"And yet he was capable of the most terrible brutality to a woman. When he found out that his model, with whom he was passionately in love, or at least he was sexually obsessed with her, well, when he found out she was also sleeping with his younger brother, he tried to kill his brother and then paid his servant with two flasks of wine to cut up his mistress's face. The servant did as he was told. He cut her face up for two flasks of wine."

"What happened to her? Did she die of it?"

"No, she lived on to old age, or a relatively old age. But she was sent to prison for adultery. Bernini went unpunished. The pope said: 'Rome is not Rome without Bernini.' He was told to marry, which he did, and fathered eleven children and then got religion."

Her head pounds now and she says, "I wish you hadn't told me that. Now I will always have to think of that when I think of anything of Bernini's. It makes me feel there is no hope for people. If someone can have the understanding that he did, and for it to have no effect on the way he acts!"

"I'm sorry, perhaps I shouldn't have told you."

"Why, Adam? I'm not a child. It's always better to know things." She is contradicting herself, but she doesn't care. She means both parts of the contradiction equally, and she's too tired to articulate this for his sake.

"I should have waited to tell you until we'd seen this," he says, taking her into a nearly empty room. Just left of the center of the room is a statue: two figures, a man, or boy perhaps, a woman, or perhaps a girl.

"Daphne and Apollo," he says, "do you know the story?"

"No, I never wrote a paper about them."

"It's in Ovid. In the *Metamorphoses*. Apollo is taunting Cupid, calling him a foolish boy, saying he had no right to use arrows, which were the weapons of a man. To punish him, Cupid shoots two arrows, the golden one, the one that excites desire, into Apollo's breast, and the leaden one, the one that repels love, into Daphne's. Daphne was a girl, a nymph, who never wanted to marry. She loved the woods, she loved her father. She told her father, who by the way was a river god, that she wanted to remain unmarried, like Diana, and to stay with him. Her father said: 'Your face will not allow it.' She doesn't understand. He tells her that her beauty is a fate she can't escape. Apollo pursues her; she flees him and just as he's about to catch and ravish her she prays to her father, the river god, to transform her into something impervious to Apollo's advances. So her father turns her into a tree. See, just as Apollo touches her, her skin turns to bark, her hair to leaves, her arms to branches."

Miranda walks around, wanting to see all sides of the sculpture, the beautiful foot of the young god, the girl's hair turning to leaves, her lovely limbs becoming branches. What has been captured is the rush of motion. Impossible to tell if she is turning toward him or away from him. Can he see her? Does his hand on her stomach sense the agitated beating of her heart?

"They're so young," Miranda says. "They're hardly even grown-ups. And he doesn't even seem to notice that she's turning into a tree beneath his hand. It's there again, that male unconsciousness, a slightly different brand from Pluto's but basically the same thing. He looks like he's going to keep right on, even though her skin is bark. Just as Pluto is going to keep right on, although Proserpina is in despair."

"But they seem very different to me.

Apollo and Daphne are both so young, so Apollo doesn't seem in the slightest bit brutal to me. And it isn't completely Apollo's fault: he's been shot by Cupid with that poisoned arrow. But what I don't understand — first, from the perspective of someone who wants to stay alive as long as possible — is why turning into a tree is preferable to being violated? And as a father, why turning your daughter into a tree is a better move than helping her back to life after something horrible has happened to her. He's lost his daughter to the forest."

She wonders if he's being purposely, aggressively obtuse.

"You just need to be quiet now," she says. It has taken all the will she has to say only these seven words, to keep back the words she wanted to say. *Blindness. Ignorance. Malign ignorant blindness.*

She understands that it wouldn't be a good idea to pour on his head the years of boiling rage at the uncomprehendingness of men. And she's exhausted by the fight, the fight she feels she's been in for so long, tired of hearing herself say, "You'll never understand." Worn out by the erosion of the belief that any of this can be resolved by talk, and by the effort to put into words what she knows on her skin, that of course rape isn't worse than death, but it is a loss of self no man can fall victim to.

But he isn't understanding that he should be quiet. He's determined that the greatness of the statue not be diminished by a reflex of collective outrage. She has asked him to be quiet, but her asking him only increases his determination to make her see his point.

"The consolation is, of course, that she's turned into the laurel. Sacred tree of the poets. All poetry derives from her."

She is walking very fast; she no longer considers that the stents in his heart should cause her to accommodate to him. Can he really be saying that? Worse, can he really believe in that idea of consolation?

"I have no patience with the idea that the sacrifice of a woman is worth it in the cause of art. I don't think any of Bernini's art is worth one drop of his mistress's blood."

"So you will refuse to look at Bernini?"

"I will never be able to look at him again in the same way. Not without a sense of unease at my pleasure."

"And if my pleasure is unmixed with unease, then I'm some sort of brute who doesn't care about the shedding of a woman's blood."

"I didn't say that."

"But you thought it. I know you, Miranda, I know that's what you thought."

"You don't know me at all."

"But you think you know me."

She doesn't want to pour the scalding brew of a rage against male power onto Adam's head. He is a good man. She understands this. He has suffered a terrible loss of one wife. He loves his second wife; above all things he loves his daughter. He has not hurt women. Except, perhaps, herself. And she was not destroyed. She is, after all, the wife of another good man, the mother of two good sons. As the mother of sons, she abhors the wholesale criticism of the male gender. She doesn't spend her days collecting grievances, demanding redress. Today, she feels unhinged: all these representations of female violation and male power. It has brought her to a place that isn't properly hers at all. An old place she has long since ceased to visit.

"Can we just go somewhere and sit and not talk?" she says.

"Of course."

Silent, unhappy, disliking each other, they walk toward the lake. He points to a bench. She would like to lose all potential for language to the sound of the water in the fountains. She thinks of all the anger that has been so much part of the engine of her life. She has said it was anger against injustice. She used to feel it was the fuel without which there could be no movement of the machinery of change. Now she is no longer sure.

Perhaps, she thinks, it is impossible, this business of being man and woman. We will never understand each other.

He wishes he were with Clare and not Miranda. Clare, almost incapable of anger, puzzled by it; causing her to blink in that way she has, as if the light were suddenly too bright. Clare, incapable of generalized resentment. Incapable of even forming in her mind a sentence beginning with the words "all men." Perhaps it's simply that she's younger, not part of that angry, pioneering generation. But no, he thinks, it's that she always takes the larger view. Or perhaps in this kind of case, the more modulated one.

Miranda sits and mourns the days given over to anger. Wasted days. She wishes Yonatan were here. It is possible that she and Yonatan would be having the same argument as she is having now with Adam. They might even be angry with each other, as she is angry with Adam. But the anger would have a different flavor, a different color. Clearer, without residue. And held in the vessel of a complex and satisfying life. She has no life with Adam: only these days. She wants to let go of this clogged mess she's holding on to with such fierce determination.

She has an idea of what might help. If she observes something, with no pressure for understanding, something in the natural world, she will regain herself. This is her father's gift: the taste for observation. Her father's curse: the taste for anger. She takes out of her purse a turquoise pad for which she paid too much. She waits till her eye falls on what it needs. A bush that a week ago, when she bought the pad, might have been splendid, now holding on to its last brilliant red leaves. Tomorrow, in a few days, even these will be gone. Floating in the water of this thing called a lake, too small really to be what she thinks of as a proper lake, this smallish pool of gray-green water, surrounded by a temple and a goddess, worshipped once, now headless and anonymous.

Red leaves turning purple, or perhaps blue-brown, are scooped up by a boy in a black T-shirt, skimming leaves from the surface of the water with his net, the handle silver, the netting white.

On the shore: three overturned rowboats, dark green.

Beside them: six white ducks.

Four gray waterbirds, whose name she doesn't know, but will, before the night is out, discover. Her evening's project: find an Internet site for Italian waterbirds.

It would be good if one of them could say something to create a place where they could meet: a bridge over their differences, the differences that thirty-six years have muted but not bleached away. But neither of them can say a word.

"I'm going to ask that you do me the favor of leaving me here," she says.

"Of course," he says. "I'll do as you like."

"If I can stay here quietly sitting in the sun and resting like this and just looking at these things, I'll be better than I was, I promise."

"You don't need to be better, you know."

"Everyone needs to be better."

"And if they can't be?"

"Then they should be left alone."

SEPTEMBER 1970

It has struck Adam over the years, as he has thought and rethought that time, that, in the memory, months blur. The quality of one's life in October might have been radically different from its September counterpart, but unless some natural disaster occurred or some personal disaster happened, so that the day on the calendar was markable and separable, we are vague and imprecise about the route of change through our past.

But he is sure that between September and November 1970, he and Miranda were growing apart. He couldn't say: it began on September 1 and by the seventh the slope was steeper, and by October 1 they had reached a critical mass of separateness. No, he couldn't say that. But what he could say in remembering that time was that when Fatima telegraphed Miranda in late November and said, "We need you here," it was less difficult for them both to contemplate being apart than it had been a year before, or even than it would have been in August, when they were swimming in the Long Island Sound, eating a picnic lunch provided by his mother.

The rhythms of their lives had grown radically different. She'd been hired full-time by Planned Parenthood; she was working from nine to five; her commute was half an hour. He was a student and could make his own schedule; if he stayed practicing till midnight, he could make up the debit of fatigue the next day by sleeping late. She could not. They had played at this rhythmic unevenness in Rome, but it wasn't the same; he was always home when she was; they relaxed every evening and all weekend, exploring, wandering, eating, happily making love. Her job was unpaid; she was a volunteer, therefore still a child.

But now she is an office worker. A paid employee. She had hoped she'd be making policy in the area of reproductive rights, but most of the time she's making appointments for clients who, hobbled by shame or a lifetime habit of not keeping appointments, too often fail to show up.

She was told that clients would be sensitive and easily abashed. Particularly if they weren't married. Contraception has only been legal in the state of Massachusetts for ten years.

It is noticed by the people in charge of the clinic that Miranda's demeanor of unruffled calm is a great asset. It's easy for her to conceal her impatience, because she is most often sympathetic. She has an almost endless sympathy, an admiration, for the women who do show up, who are taking their lives and their futures in their own hands. She tells herself it would be better if she could muster sympathy without admiration, but she can't.

But often she's bored, and boredom is fatiguing, and in Miranda's case, fatigue fuels her impatience, which she can't express at work. Adam bears the brunt. His pleasure in ordinary things, which used to charm her, now seems irritating. She wants to say: *So what if there are new McIntosh apples in the store, so what if the color of the sky turns from pink to blue to gray in ten minutes' time, so what if Madame Rostavska is pleased with your phrasing of the first movement of Mozart's K 271?* She wants to rub his face in the sorrow of the world, in the difficult lives of her clients. She can't remember when issues of phrasing and tempi that she had once found so pressing began to seem more than irrelevant: a bore. And what is worse: she doesn't like the Messiaen. She'd grown used to his playing the record of whatever piece he was preparing, over and over again, lifting the needle up, putting it down again and again at the same place. She'd grown used to his doing whatever it was she was doing — reading, talking to friends, performing household chores — while he was doing this with Schubert or Beethoven, but she finds the Messiaen disturbing. It steals her peace. He tries to make her appreciate the approximation of birdsong, of bells — the great range of mood: from terror to contemplation. But she just says, "I'll be happy when this is over and you're back to Schubert."

He knows that she's tired, that she doesn't like her job; he knows that she's staying in Boston to be with him so he can finish the work he'd missed when he'd had to take a semester off because of mono. He's grateful to her, delighted and aroused by the mix of lightness and solidity that make up her physical presence; his desire for her is as ardent and as constant as it has always been: there's no need even to acknowledge it. She doesn't seem to notice that he isn't talking to her about the music he's playing; he never mentions the intense conversations he's having with Beverly about the Messiaen.

Beverly copies Messiaen's comments on the piece they are playing, *Visions de l'Amen.* On a piece of thick ivory paper, she copies in a calligraphic hand what Messiaen has said about the role of the two pianos. "*Visions de l'Amen* was conceived and written for two pianos, demanding from these instruments their maximum force and diversity of sounds. I have entrusted the rhythmic difficulty, clusters of chords, all that is velocity, character, and tone quality to the first piano. I have entrusted the principal melody, thematic elements and all that expresses emotion and power, to the second piano." In blue ink, she made delicate drawings of two birds and underneath wrote, in a finer script, "From the second piano to the first."

He doesn't bring this home; he leaves it in his locker; it's the first thing he's ever concealed from Miranda. And he's even more determined to keep from her the card, light blue, the words written in brown ink, which she took from Messiaen's comments on the "Amen of Desire," one of the seven "Amens" that make up the piece. "There are two themes of desire. The first, slow, ecstatic, and yearning with deep tenderness, already the peaceful perfume of Paradise. The second is extremely passionate; here the soul is torn by the terrible love that appears carnal (see the Song of Songs) but there is nothing carnal about it, only paroxysm of the thirst of love. The two principal voices seem to merge into each other and nothing remains but the harmonious silence of heaven."

Below the words, she had drawn two angels, invisible beneath their conjoined wings. He tells himself that this is only her expression of their connection as musicians; that, like Messiaen, what she meant by "desire" was spiritual: certainly not a threat. But he understands that Miranda might not see it that way.

And he doesn't share with Miranda his extensive worries about Beverly, who has tried to kill herself again and given the emergency room his number as the number of the person to be called. She's twenty-one; she no longer needs to give her parents' number. Mutt and Jeff, she called her parents, full of contempt for them: a stockbroker and an interior decorator from Greenwich, Connecticut. She says Adam is the only person in her whole life with whom she has ever felt entirely safe.

385

Adam understands Miranda's impatience with, if not Beverly (whom she'd hardly met: he was careful of that), then the kind of girl Beverly is. Miranda has said he must stop saying "girl" for someone their age now and use the word "woman," but Beverly doesn't seem anywhere near being a woman to him. He knows what Miranda would say if he told her about Beverly: *She needs to go out and see people in the world with real problems. I'd like to take her to Bangladesh for one day.*

Somehow, in the chaos of her life, Beverly keeps very good track of Miranda's schedule and never phones except when Miranda is at work. She seems always to know the nights Miranda works, the mornings she doesn't go in till eleven. Each morning when he arrives at his practice room, he finds a small card from her, a witty drawing, a musical joke. He keeps them in his locker, wondering what he'll do with them when he graduates.

Physically, Beverly is almost comically opposite to Miranda. She is dark eyed; Miranda's eyes are grayish green; Beverly's hair is black and thick and always in a tangle; she pins it to the top of her head, but it is always falling down, and it's almost a tic with her (he finds this charming) to be continually pinning it up. Sometimes, she sticks pencils in the bun she makes of her hair as if she were a Chinese woman using hair sticks. Her legs are long and almost worryingly slender; she is vain about them and wears the shortest skirts she can. He loves Miranda's thick straight legs, to him like the trunks of beautiful trees, but he knows she is distressed by them and covers them in jeans or long peasant skirts. Miranda's breasts are small; they sit neatly on her rib cage: innocent, tender. He will not allow himself to think of Beverly's breasts, even when he knows she is purposely brushing against him so that he'll have to. But though he's tried to banish the thought, he knows Beverly's bosom is fuller than Miranda's, particularly in relation to her bird-like frame.

Adam believes that if only Beverly could spend time with his mother she'd be much better. Rose would feed her and give her advice, and that would lead to her greater happiness. But then Beverly might say: *What's happiness? I don't believe in happiness.* He doesn't know if she would say it in her bitter voice, or her wounded one: he can never predict which Beverly he is going to encounter: the hissing snake, the trembling rabbit, the soaring bird of brilliant song. Adam understands that his mother is incapable of offering comfort without offering food, and that if Rose offered Beverly food she might not eat it. Beverly has a long list of foods that are "too, too sick making." So of course he wouldn't try to introduce them, particularly since he knows how much Miranda would dislike Beverly, and it would be wrong to try to place her under Rose's wing, where Miranda has pride of place.

Miranda sees that the kind of conversation she and Adam always had is stalled now, as if some dam, whose construction she had failed to notice, has cut off the stream of their shared life. But she doesn't want to think about it because then she would have to understand her part in it, the depths of her own boredom. She agrees to go for a drink with Jeremy Sussman, a medical student who is organizing a storefront clinic, and allows him to kiss her, but she runs away (he laughs nastily at her escape down the street), and she is ashamed that she allowed herself to get this close once again to the danger of betrayal. This time, though, she goes right back to Adam, and her silence, her evasion — "Where were you?" "Oh, just having a drink with Valerie"

— is the first time she has directly lied to him, as opposed to keeping something back, and so the stream is befouled now, clogged yet more.

And when Fatima's telegram arrives, "We need you here," both Adam and Miranda understand that it is right for her to go. She will be away for his recital, and she expresses her regret, but both of them understand that they are secretly relieved. She will, she assures him, be back home for his solo recital: the last three Beethoven sonatas. She is particularly fond, she tells him, of Opus 110; Think of me when you're practicing it, she tells him.

"As if I don't always think of you," he says, wondering, just a bit, if that's still true.

Realizing that he can't make Beverly's life better through contact with his mother, he makes what he thinks is the second-best choice. He's listened to Miranda for years when she says how important it is to have girl- (now women) friends. So he convinces Valerie it would be an act of kindness to spend time with Beverly, and to his surprise Valerie, too, becomes fond of her. He knows what Miranda would say, *That doesn't mean anything, Valerie likes everybody.* Beverly invites Valerie to go on what she calls "a thrift shop crawl." They come back with bags of clothing that could have been costumes from thirties screwball comedies, or later Betty Grable films: a big-shouldered beaver coat, a beaded handbag, a cinch-waist polka-dot dress with a white patent-leather belt.

"All for five dollars, it's unbelievable fun," Valerie says, and soon she has included some of Miranda's other friends on her expeditions with Beverly. Only the more law abiding, less adventurous of the friends had stayed on in Boston after graduation; Renee is in Morocco with a Moroccan boyfriend, Lydia has gone out to San Francisco to an art scene she found more "open." So those who are left are serious, purposeful, con-cerned with doing good, still with the residue of pleasing their teachers clinging to them, although they are officially, now, not students. They feel in Beverly's company steered into a more adventurous and less safe world. A world that simultaneously harks back to their mothers' youths (the choice of Manhattans over hashish, stiletto heels over cowboy boots, velvet capes over Aztec ponchos) and skates close to a world of danger their mothers wouldn't even have the name for. Do they believe that Adam and Miranda are inviolable, as safe as Fort

Knox, so there's no need to be concerned about his spending time with Beverly? Is that why they don't mention her in their letters to Miranda? Or are they keeping something from her, something that might disturb her in her new difficult life? Or have they secretly come under Beverly's sway, because they're tired of Miranda's certainty, her calm, silent judgments?

And Adam feels in having introduced Beverly into this female society that he takes a new place among them. No longer is he the pampered, gifted boy whom they must instruct about the world while protecting him from it. In knowing Beverly, he showed himself, in a larger sense, more knowing. On Beverly's advice, he grows a beard. Beverly's voice, the cigaretty undertone, her diction, at once sharp-edged and louche, challenge him in a new way. She talks passionately about artistic growth. She says he must break out of the comfortable cocoon of the eighteenth and nineteenth centuries where he feels so easily at rest and listen to the music of John Cage and Varèse and Schoenberg. Particularly of Messiaen, whose synesthesia fascinates her. She talks about Messiaen's idea that each chord represents a specific color. She says that unless he lets the dark bitter tones enter in he will remain a competent pianist, but one among many, and if he wants to break out of that circle and enter the circle of the great, "I don't believe in words like 'great,' not for myself anyway," he says and she replies with impatience, flicking the ash of her cigarette on the floor, "Oh, nonsense, Adam, you must dream big and your dreams must include chaos and darkness."

And in her filthy room, listening to music he has only just learned to like, he feels the lure of her challenge. He does want to grow as an artist; he doesn't want to rest in safety. Miranda is safety; she is certainty, and rest and perhaps . . . he will not finish that sentence. He takes another drink of gin and Campari, which he actually doesn't like, but knows to be the right thing to be drinking when listening to John Cage and taking Beverly up on her offer to run his fingers up and down the multiple scars on her arm, marking her suicide attempts. She takes the twenty bottles of pills from her medicine chest and puts them on her coffee table, burned by cigarettes, and says, "I'm a mess, Adam, don't you think I'm a mess?" He thinks of her passionate, inspired playing of the Messiaen. And he says, "No, Beverly, I think you're a kind of genius."

And she says, "Adam, you are my fortunate island. You are my island of the blest. So often I feel that I am a small, unseaworthy boat, rocked back and forth by tumultuous waves, and then the glimpse of you, reachable, makes me know that I'm all right. That I will be all right."

The words she uses, "a small unseaworthy boat, rocked back and forth by tumultuous waves," strike him as false. He suspects that she's said this before, to other people. But then, suppose she never has, suppose he really is the only person who makes her feel safe? Is it that he's had too much to drink, is it that he fears Miranda no longer loves him in the way he loves her, unquestioningly, uncritically, that she no longer believes he's enough for her, that he fears she's not enough for him, that she has not written in three weeks, and what she writes is dry, perfunctory, as if she can't take her mind away from the compelling horrors to bring it back to him. The man she says she loves.

Beverly is weeping. She has drunk too much. She's talking about her "bitch mother, the refrigerator." And her father, "the drunken bully holding the purse strings like a whip." And her brother, banished from the house for being homosexual (she thinks he's in France somewhere, no one knows exactly where he is, they haven't heard from him for five years). This pileup of loss and deprivation (he thinks of his mother, his grandparents) breaks his heart, and there she is, her frame so frail, her legs looking as though they can barely support her, and she is saying, "Hold me, Adam, I just need you to hold me. It's hard for me to ask for things so simply, but I must." He can't refuse; he is holding her; her dark hair comes loose from its pins, smoky, hypnotic, her full breasts, unhampered by a bra, press up against his chest, and how does it happen, they are kissing, then they are lovers, and he is a betrayer, and in the morning he only wants to be away from her and she knows it and weeps again and says, "I knew it. I knew you'd be just like everyone else. Everyone who comes near me finds me loathsome in the end." And he says, "You're not loathsome, you're beautiful, but this is a mistake. I shouldn't have done this. Miranda and I . . . well, we belong to each other."

"Nobody belongs to anyone," she says, and for the first time she looks ugly to him. "That's a disgusting way to talk. My bicycle belongs to me. My jade ring. People are free, and if they aren't, well, that's less than human. Or they're just slaves."

He kisses her good-bye, miserable. She

has used the word "loathsome" about herself, but he knows it rightly applies only to him, and he can't wait to shower in his own bathroom, but it isn't only his. Miranda's shampoo, Breck, is in the shower, and he opens it, smells it, uses it to wash his own hair, as if then he could be with her, could become her, pure as she is pure, and the water falls on the flesh that he can only loathe and the smell of her shampoo pierces his heart. The words he uses for himself he never imagined he would have to use. "Profligate." "Betrayer." He is unworthy of Miranda, unworthy of her love.

Miranda, in Pakistan, is exhausted, overwhelmed, in despair, thinking there is nothing she can understand. She can hold back for an hour, a day, the tidal wave of horror, the psychological correlate to the tidal wave, the typhoon that is the natural disaster that is the reason for her being where she is. If she is not absolutely engaged in an activity, the images return: the bloated bodies floating like black dolls, the swollen cattle, drowned, the wandering children, their mouths open, silently abashed. And even when she feels that something is being done to feed and clothe the victims and provide medicine, she has to come to terms with the corruption and cruelty of people to their own people. Her romance of poverty, the solidarity of the poor, is blasted through, as if a cannonball had breached the solid ramparts of her understanding. She sees a young man stealing a blanket from a shivering old woman. Then she observes some small act, some gesture — two boys share a piece of bread, a woman tears her shawl in half and gives half to another mother — and she thinks: people are good, they can love each other.

Too tired at night to write more than a few lines, and unwilling to worry Adam or her parents, she provides only telegraphic news assuring them she is all right. She is working with Fatima and her father, on a team set up by the WHO. Fatima's father asked her to contact Miranda because he remembers that what she is good at is organization, and he sets her the task of keeping track of people and supplies, and she understands that, although she isn't relieving suffering directly, she is making marks on paper, creating files, telling people to go here or go there, making something a little better, doing something to cut into the chaos of this world of death. Half a million dead, mostly women and children, a world into which she wakes each morning and from which she retreats gratefully into sleep.

At night as she lies on her cot she questions for the first time in her life the goodness of life, the desirability of living. For the first time she thinks it would not be the worst thing to be dead. She begins to understand that she is getting sick. She knows she is really sick when, trying and failing to straighten a stack of files, her eyes fall on her own hands, and they become her father's hands, and miraculously (she was her father so she did not succumb) she gets herself to her desk and sits shaking, realizing she is really ill. She slips into a delirium in which she is herself, her father, her father's hands, Adam's hands, of which they had to be so careful touching the white keys, but the music she produces is dangerous, unsoothing, and she says to someone (but she is alone in the office, there is no one there), If I die please let me die as myself.

In her fevers, she dreams of the safe, clean, sweet-smelling solid world. Her place beside Adam's body in the bed whose sheets she'd chosen, washed, made up for the comfort of their sleeping. At night hearing the sounds of weeping and screaming and trucks backing up and misfiring sounding more like guns than she can bear, she hears him playing a Bach partita, one of the preludes of

Debussy, and she realizes that she had moved herself away from his music, thinking it irrelevant to the suffering of the world. Now and newly she sees it as essential, an alternative to chaos, a sign of the goodness that is the counterpoint of the dread conditions she is living in.

And when she is diagnosed with hepatitis and sent home, she is, to her shame, not entirely sorry.

Her mother wants her home in Hastings, but she doesn't want to be in the house with her father, who had warned her of precisely what has been the case: disease, disorder, a horror nothing in her life has prepared her for. Ever since she began arguing with her father, since Rob left for Canada, she had a secret fear that all along he was right: that violence was endemic to human nature, that inequality of wealth was also part of the human condition and to deny basic inequalities was to deny nature, that men and women were made different and to deny that, to insist that they could inhabit the same realms, do the same work, was another denial of nature. His certainty, his hard conviction that the old ways were right, was a stone wall she had to butt her head against. Everything she saw about the injustice of privilege, the disproportionate grabbing of wealth by the West, everything that had made Bhola inevitable, made her know that he was wrong. But then he stood like a fort, impervious to wind or storm, willing himself to imperviousness, to the loss of his son's love. And that very steadfastness, while it turned her heart to stone, was capable at the same time of making her doubt herself. Sometimes in her fever he became the calm place in her imaginings. She thought of how cool he was in emergencies: when she had fallen off her bike and her head was bleeding, when Rob broke his leg in football, when her mother lay on the floor hemorrhaging (later she would understand it was a miscarriage) and five-year-old Miranda ran screaming to the garage where her father was working on the car. She hoped she did not cry out what in her dreams she cried: *Daddy, you're the one who should be here, not me. Everything you are is what they need. What I am is at this moment of much less value.*

She wants her mother. In her fever dreams, she yearns for her mother's cool hands on the pillow, on the white sheets of her childhood bed, the pink room, the wallpaper pink flowers, the lampshades pink, the pink of her mother's nail polish, and she hopes that she didn't cry out for her mother.

But she will not go home to her father's house; she makes her mother come to her. She wants to be with Adam. To the spare clean rooms she has paid for with the salary she has earned for work her father would not approve of, thinking of it as another fool's errand, the money she has earned fool's gold.

Her mother agrees to come to the Somerville apartment to care for her. Her father will not, as he says, "cross the threshold" of the apartment where his daughter lives with a man she isn't married to, and Harriet says, "Oh Bill, they're as good as married," and her husband says, "There's many a slip twixt the cup and the lip," and for the first time since he banished their son, Harriet tastes hatred for her husband. She will not allow it to settle in her mouth. She will spit out the bitter taste of hatred as quickly as she tastes it, slake it with the sweet taste of gratitude for a life made safe by this man and everything he stands for. But having tasted hatred, and for the second time, so she knows it could arrive again, she is newly frightened, of herself and of the world, a world her daughter has entered in a way she never could.

Harriet admits only to herself that she is happy taking care of her daughter. And Miranda allows herself to be cared for. But Harriet sees: Adam's attention is not entirely with her daughter. Not as it was. He loves her now as a weak thing, but he doesn't love her as a tree loves the sun, which is how he loved her when they sat in her living room holding hands watching Leonard Bernstein on the television, or when they sat in the back of the car holding hands. She knew they were doing other things besides holding hands, she knew everything they did . . . did they really think she didn't know what happened in Miranda's pink room when she wasn't there? She knew even before she opened the door that time . . . was it to let them know she knew that she made that mistake . . . she will never admit that to herself, will never speak of the incident to anyone.

Miranda has taken her last step out of childhood. Her skin is no longer a girl's, no longer untouched. Her residency in the country of the sick has guaranteed that she will never be the child she was. Harriet's child, untouched. No longer what Harriet understands as an American girl.

She is ashamed at how happy she is that, sick, her daughter is more beautiful to her than ever, more lovable than she has been in all the years since she has ceased, literally, being a child. She is thinner, and so the bones in her face are sharper, the lines clearer. She has always looked charming, Harriet thought. Now she is heartbreakingly beautiful. She has gone from being Vermeer's sensible housewife to a Filippo Lippi Madonna. The darkness of the world has wiped its brush across her face, and the effect, Harriet thinks, ashamed, is beautiful. How can it be good that her daughter has suffered. It has made her kinder, Harriet could see; it has also made her lovelier.

Harriet stays with her daughter and Adam for two weeks; she sleeps on the foldout sofa in the living room, shy at the idea of Miranda and Adam in the marital bed. And she knows, though she says nothing, that they are slipping away from each other and at night she weeps quietly because she sees too clearly the end of it. Was Bill right all along? These beautiful young people who loved each other, had loved each other, are perhaps not the people they were. Who are they, then? Adam with his beard. Miranda with the shadows underneath her eyes.

Her mother leaves, but Miranda can't go

back to work; she barely has the energy to shower and dress herself. She forces herself to shop and cook, but her only appetite is for bland food. Omelets. Potatoes slathered in butter. Occasionally, a hamburger. A vegetable overcooked and unadorned. She finds it difficult to make love to Adam. Her body seems an unhealthy thing; she has been, she thinks, literally diseased. She doesn't want to expose Adam to this disease, its traces, and its history. His forceful health seems more than she can bear, as if she'd been living in a cave and could only experience the noonday sun as an assault. When she wakes from fitful daytime sleep, she often dislikes the unfresh smell of her body, and the idea of another shower exhausts her. Her body feels heavy to her; it is making her move with difficulty, and she focuses on her hair, hanging down her back four inches above her waist or in a heavy braid; but the labor of braiding often strikes her as impossible. One day — it is cold and gray and at four the sun has stopped making even false gestures of illumination — she gets a scissors and standing in front of the bathroom mirror chops her hair off till it is nothing but a boyish cap.

The shushshush of the scissors, the hill of hair building around her feet, dry but soft, a delightful texture to walk in or through, give her the first energized pleasure she has known since she's been sick, or perhaps since the tornado and the people it struck replaced her energy with despair. Then she looks at her face. She likes the bare look of it, the light look. She sweeps the hair up and puts it in a paper sack.

She is proud; she sees herself a heroine.

She never thought of what it might mean to Adam. He comes home at ten. She anticipates the delight of putting her hot face up against the coldness of his beard; he is bringing her the outside, January, the liveliness of winter and its clarity. But she sees in his eyes, seeing her new hair, a look of horror. "What have you done," he says, and then, unpardonable: "What have you done to me."

"To you? I thought it was my hair. My body."

He can't unsay what he has said. Anything he says would be ridiculous: *Of course it's your body, of course I know that.* He says instead, "I can see that it would be more comfortable."

He goes into the bathroom to take a shower. What is it that he is trying to wash off? His own sense of having been betrayed?

He knows that he is wrong to feel betrayed. But how can she have done it? Her beautiful hair that he so loved, like honey on her shoulders, his grandfather had said, her tender hair, promising, abundant. Of course it wasn't his, and yet he knew that she did what she did *to* him, to take something from him. Because he thinks perhaps she knows about Beverly, and whatever she does, whatever she takes from or does to him, she's right, because he has squandered everything, he is unworthy of her love.

Is it sensible to say that everything that happened was because of Miranda's hair? Because she cut her hair? It needn't have proceeded as it did. She might have fallen into his arms weeping and said, *I don't know why I did it, I'll never have it again, my hair, my beautiful hair.* And he might have said, *No, no, you'll have it again, it will grow back and we can have it again.* Would he have used the word "we"? And would that have made her angry all over? Or could they have wept together, could he have kissed the ill-cut ends of her cropped hair and said, *Poor hair, poor head, poor darling, you were tired, your body was too heavy for you, everything was too heavy, everything was too hard.*

But this wasn't possible because she could

not admit regret. To say nothing of a joint mourning for something she insisted had happened through her choice, an act of freedom. As she would have said in those days, in those years, an act of liberation.

Instead of weeping in his arms, she goes down to New York, to visit Valerie, who is working in her uncle's real estate office and has "an adorable apartment in the Village. Come down," she said. "We'll see Merce Cunningham. He's bald. Or we could see *Hair.*"

And that weekend in the practice rooms Beverly tells Adam she's thinking of suicide again, that she'd tried heroin and she really really liked it, it was a sense of well-being greater than any other. He knows this is a false bravado, but he allows himself to interpret it as a kind of strength, a strength that enables him to tell her about Miranda's hair. She is tender, maternal, sympathetic. Poor boy, poor sweet boy, she says. She tries to distract him, telling him about seeing Peter Serkin play Mozart, Webern, Schoenberg, and their very own Messiaen against a background of black and red psychedelic lights. She tells him how handsome Peter Serkin is, but that he's married and has a baby. She suggests that otherwise she would have offered herself to him. He finds himself, to his incomprehension, jealous. In her tenderest voice, she asks him if he's thought about the Freudian implications of Miranda's cutting her hair. "Maybe I've had too much analysis . . . but I don't think I'm too far off the mark to bring up symbols of castration."

Later he will regularly associate Beverly with snakes, but this is the first time the association rises up in his mind. The serpent in the garden. He feels the strike of her words. He feels the poison in his blood, but relishes it, hungers for it. He wants her now; he wants to take her, not pretending, like the last time, that it's accidental, comforting, but because he wants her bitterness, her jagged understanding of the world. And she says, "Well, well, punishing the golden girl with the dark lady." She laughs her bitter laugh, and then she cries, "You think I'm defiled and you want to defile yourself with me," and he says, No, no, of course not, of course not. But he cannot say he loves her.

For the first time he makes love, or has sex, without the slightest tenderness, pounding at something, wanting to get to something to tear it down. And he is pleased with himself because this is being the kind of man he has never allowed himself to be. The wildness that he had felt in his frustrated fantasies before Miranda, when twelve, thirteen, fourteen, the irresistible forcefulness of this thing that was him but could not be him, inexorable, unloving, something he knew must be erased: for the first time it is of use. And now with Beverly he thinks, I can be what I thought I could not. I can use this power. Isn't this the Dionysiac? Isn't this the source of art? I can approach this darkness. I need no longer be my mother's son. Any mother's son."

Miranda comes home after the weekend in New York. He sees it's done her good. Valerie took her to a fancy hairdresser who made something stylish of her butchery. She's wearing large gold hoop earrings; she has bought a black turtleneck which suits her boyish torso, and she throws her arms around him and, half horrified at his own defilement (perhaps Beverly was right to use that word), half exhilarated, he enters Miranda's body which is different to him now, not the only female body he has known, and he knows more than she, he is older than she will ever be, and she is, in her innocence, a child, and he, uninnocent, a man.

She goes back to work; she is praised for her heroic months in Pakistan and for her abiding competence. The music Adam now seems interested in playing is moving in a direction she can't follow. Neither will acknowledge that both are guilty of violence (her hair, his infidelity) and they are newly kind to each other, as if they had traveled a great distance and are now, tentatively, home.

April comes, the days are warm, the sun is stronger, and the evening falls later. They eat sandwiches for supper by the river, and they walk hand in hand. He is finishing his time as a regular university student. Next year he will enter the New England conservatory and be nothing but a musician, not studying history or languages or philosophy or art. Only a musician: chosen above many others, for this purpose, this gift. They will stay in their apartment; Miranda will keep her job.

And two days before graduation, Beverly comes into the practice rooms, and says, "Guess what, you knocked me up."

Later he understood that a cliché became literal in his body. People say, "My blood ran cold," and they don't mean it, but he felt a freezing liquid travel in his veins, without a sense of warmth and no connection to his heart.

"But you told me you were on the pill."

"But I'm not that good about being regular with something you have to take every day. And you know, I take so many pills, you can't really blame me for forgetting one every once in a while."

What he cannot say, because he will not be that brutal (this is a way that men are brutal that he will not allow himself to be): *How do you know it's mine?*

His first thought is: She needs to talk to Miranda about getting an abortion. Abortion is illegal, but Miranda has been involved for years with finding doctors who get around the law. One of the most common ways around the law, he knows, is psychiatrists going on record to say that an abortion is necessary because of the precarious state of the mother's mental health. Surely this would apply to Beverly. But instantly he understands: Miranda is the last person in the world he can go to for help. He mentions, nevertheless, the possibility of abortion.

"The bad news is, it's too late to get rid of it. I never know when my periods are. I

410

often miss a month or two, and I just went to the doctor because I thought I had the flu and guess what, voilà, five months gone."

He thinks it is somewhat better that it happened the first time they made love, which at least had something of tenderness, than the second time, which was a dark time, where tenderness was not anywhere in sight.

In his mind he hears the word "better," but soon it turns to "bitter," and he feels this is a bitter outcome, a bitter fate. And he remembers that he had craved her bitterness and now he will drown in it.

When he thinks of those days later, it is not the events or words he calls up, but tastes and tones. The taste of bitterness. A tone like a gong, a dark unmelodic sound: the end of something. No turning back. Or the sound of buzzing wires, a downed wire on the road, signaling the approach of danger, death.

Beverly regularly becomes hysterical, moving from tears to howls of laughter that seem inhuman. *You're laughing like a hyena,* he wants to say to her, *you've become a beast.* Then scalding, torrential tears. I want to kill myself, I'll kill myself and take the baby with me.

He thinks of the word "baby" and then

"mine." He must think of himself now using the word "father," which he believed he would not be doing for a very long time, until much more of his life had been lived. Until words like "career," "future," "livelihood" would be things he had a clear sense of, things possibly under his control.

"I'll take care of everything," he says, and she looks at him with that murderous sharp bitterness that will never leave her eyes again when she looks at him. Never, even when she is looking at her child, will her eyes be drained of bitterness, and certainly never when she looks at him. Only sometimes she is entirely desperate, and then her eyes are drained of everything: eyes empty as the blank eyes of a ruined statue: an empty blankness that nothing could ever fill.

He doesn't know what to do. He does something he's ashamed of doing, even as he does it, but it's the only thing he can think of. He goes home to his parents. Runs home to his parents: what could be a more humiliating cliché. For someone's father. A man.

Rose asks practical questions: how far along.

Five months.

Her beautiful generous lips disappear into an unfamiliar line.

"I see, then, it's too late."

Too late for her son to have a happy life.

Too late for her to have Miranda for her daughter.

"She could go away somewhere to have it, then put it up for adoption."

And even as she says it, some old instinct of blood forbids, for all of them, the prospect of a child brought up by strangers. A child with their features living in the world unknown to them, unreared by its own.

"I'll have to marry her."

"Yes," his mother says. "You will."

His father says, "A child is always a blessing."

His mother says, "Unfortunately that's not true."

And his father, sterner than Adam has ever heard him, says, "Rose, you must not say that. You must not say that ever again."

Adam breaks down. "How will I tell Miranda?"

"There is no good way," his mother says.

"It must be done, though, son, and soon," says Sal.

He hates himself for thinking, when Beverly threatens to kill herself, that he sometimes

413

wishes that she would. She says she's thought of adoption, of course, but she wants "the kid," and if he doesn't want to be "in on it," she'll do it by herself. She'll go on welfare. "Possibly I have hidden depths. Hidden resources." Then she laughs her hyena laugh.

At least she was never a woman he thought he loved.

The hour of dread. The moment that must be lived. The leaden day. Heavy as lead, as lightless.

"Miranda, there is something I must tell you. It's a terrible thing."

And says the words.

"Yes, well, I see you have no choice," she says.

She doesn't know who is saying those words, or where they are coming from. Some mouth not hers. Someone with a body; she is outside her body. She is watching herself, her bloodless face, her freezing hands, but she is seeing these things from a distance, a cold height, unsheltered, incalculably far away. She is not standing on this place, this promontory, but hovering above it, weightless. Gravity, the law of cause, have been taken from her. This is a thing that cannot have happened. She does know

414

whom it has happened to. Herself, but someone she has never known. She will know this person now; from now on, when she says "myself," it will be the person to whom this thing has happened. She thinks she is going to be sick, and she doesn't want him to see or know that. Above all, she doesn't want to be in the place he is.

She goes into the bathroom where he can hear that she has washed her face. He cannot see that she is sitting on the floor rocking herself like a mad child, tears coming down her face like sweat. She can't stop them, but she can stop herself from making the accompanying sounds. The only thing to be done is to act. To act quickly. To become the new person she now is. To end that other life.

And she comes out, blank-faced, the tears pouring out, wetting her face, but soundlessly, and when she speaks her voice is not choking with tears, but flat and slack, like the expression of her eyes. She is hearing a phrase in her mind, over and over the words, *I am not the beloved's and the beloved is not mine.*

"You have to leave here now," she says. "You have to be with her. Your place is with her now, not with me. I'll go away. I'll go to

Valerie's for a week. When I come back, I want all of your things gone."

He sees that saying this has made her lose her slackness. Her fists are clenched; she has dug her nails into the palms of her hands and they are bleeding. Her tears have not stopped. She hasn't raised her voice.

"Good-bye, Adam," she says.

"When will I see you? When will I see you again?"

"I don't know, Adam," she says, in a dead voice. "Probably, I think, never."

MONDAY, OCTOBER 29

THE PIAZZA DEL POPOLO,
THE VILLA BORGHESE
"In Order to Have Had the Children
We Have,
We Had to Lead Our Lives Exactly As
We Did.
Therefore, There Can Be No Regrets"

She lifts the phone and wonders whether there will ever come a time in her life when she won't have to make this kind of call. The call that says forgive me: my bad temper, my irritability, my rudeness. Does it matter that she wasn't so bad as she might have been, that she kept back many of the vile things she wanted to say? No, she thinks, a coin of acid settling at the back of her tongue, you can't be forgiven for the thing you've spared someone from knowing. Or what would be the point of sparing them?

417

"I'll take you for a drink at Rosati's," she says. "I know it's noisy, smack in the middle of the Popolo, but I like the waiters' uniforms. Like out of a forties movie."

"I'd enjoy that, but then I hope that we can walk a bit. It's nearly our last day, and we have the weather."

"Yes," she says, "I'd like that, too."

They meet at four, drink *prosecco* in the crowded amiable outdoors, the café that seems part of the street, only just not a victim of the traffic. She pays the check, not even looking at the amount, aware that she's paying for the location, not what they have eaten and drunk. Then amiability vanishes; they try to cross the street; cars careen around the corner, making a wide circle; Vespas stop inches from their toes; buses belch smoke and show no signs of slowing down. She closes her eyes and takes his hand to cross. "I'm not used to this kind of traffic," she says. "I don't spend much time in cities anymore."

She lets go of his hand at the bottom of the staircase. Then they walk, with a deliberate slowness on her part, up the steps to the park.

"This light is strange for Rome," he says. "Rome without full sun seems somehow not itself. But I love it; it's like another place. Melancholy."

"I very much like the word 'melancholy.' It's much better than 'depression.' " She is grateful to him for forestalling any further gesture of apology.

They walk more deeply into the tree-filled avenue.

"It's almost too appropriate for one of our last walks," he says. "The weather of regret."

"Regret for what?" she says sharply. "Our lives have been our lives."

"A regret for the life we didn't have together."

She is grateful to him for saying it out loud, but she will not let him rest in what she knows to be untrue. She does not regret not having had a life with him, because having had a life with him would have meant not having had the life she has. These days have taught her that: what happened was all right. Was right.

"What I think of often is the mystery that if we hadn't lived our lives exactly as we have, but I mean exactly, we wouldn't have the children we have. There would be no Benjamin, no Jeremy. No Lucy. And the world without them is unthinkable. In order to have had the children we have, we had to lead our lives exactly as we did. Therefore, there can be no regrets."

He sits on a stone bench. He puts his head in his hands, a gesture that he knows is almost too symbolic, almost a parody. Yet he can't resist it: the symbolic seems the only possible posture for the impossible things that he feels now must be said.

"That's not the whole of my life as the father of children. There is Lucy. But then there is Raphael, my son by Beverly. My son who doesn't want to know me, my son who lives a life I find so foreign, so horrifying. A life that has brought harm to the world. My son and I are, to each other, entirely unknowable."

"I don't know anything about your son."

"You know the circumstances of his birth."

There is nothing for her to say: of course it is a thing she knows.

"From the moment of his birth, his life was swaddled in unhappiness. Unhappiness seeped into the cracks of every place we lived. The months in the apartment in Beacon Hill. And then, almost immediately, Henry Levi found me the job teaching music at Grenham. Which I have never left. But every house we lived in there . . . the air was poisoned with unhappiness. The houses were never ours and never had what Beverly believed was the only kind of light that could make her happy. It was in one of those faculty houses that she killed herself. Her note said, 'Sorry, it's too dark for me. Here.' "

Miranda doesn't know what to do with her eyes or her hands. Touch him? Not touch him? Meet his eyes or look away?

"So the school moved Raphael and me to another house, but Raphael had breathed in all that sadness. Sadness and loss. And I saw him grow into a boy who enjoyed doing harm. I had to know that my son was a bully. He enjoyed humiliation. He enjoyed humiliating me. He thought I was weak. He despised music. He left home as soon as he could. Enlisted in the army at eighteen. He didn't tell me; the only one he told was my father. Somehow he responded to my father's kindness . . . perhaps he understood that my father was sympathetic to Beverly. But my father was sympathetic to everyone, and I think that endless unquestioning kindness was important to Raphael. Certainly, he didn't get it from me. He must have known that his aggressiveness was something I judged, and judged harshly. I don't know why my father didn't; he was the least aggressive man I've ever known.

"Anyway, Raphael joined the army, and he was very successful: he was always good at languages, and during the first Gulf War they sent him to school to learn Arabic; he was soon fluent, and apparently that led to a series of rapid promotions. I don't know quite what his rank is, I don't know even what he does, but it's something important. We rarely speak. Now he's become involved in an Evangelical church, and he doesn't want to have anything to do with me or Clare or Lucy. His wife wrote me a letter to say that they thought our 'permissive lifestyle was a danger to their children.' When I asked what she meant — our lifestyle couldn't be more circumscribed — she said it was that we had a lot of homosexual friends. I have grandchildren I have never seen. I know their names and ages, but Raphael has never even sent a picture. The last time he called, he mentioned that he was 'involved in some things in Iraq.' He said, 'I bet you have a problem with Abu Ghraib.'

"I said I did. I asked if he had anything to do with it.

"He went silent, then he laughed. His laugh was terrible to me. 'Maybe,' he said. 'Call me up, Dad, when you have any idea how the world really works.'

"And so it is impossible for me to be spared regret. Every time I see films of Abu Ghraib I ask the question: *Would it have been better if my son had not been born?"*

"But you don't know that he was involved in torture."

"But I can't say with any certainty that he wasn't. It was part of his desire to humiliate me not to tell me either way. I had to understand that his saying that one word 'maybe' was a special kind of sadism. So that if I imagine he was involved, I have the guilt of thinking the worst about my son. And if I refuse to imagine that he might be, I bear the burden of not having the courage to imagine the worst, and I have to know that his contempt for me is earned."

She walks a bit away from him, stands in the middle of the road. She thinks that it is possible that she has never heard anything so disturbing. What could be a worse sentence: *It would have been better if my child had not been born.*

And most disturbing to her is her own reaction. Her stripe of satisfaction: that what he and Beverly did ended not in beauty or in consolation, did not justify the thing they did. Did to her. But what can that possibly mean: "did to her." What was done was done to a young girl. Twenty-two years old. She is now nearly sixty. What was done marked her, but if she is truthful, she must ask herself: did it mark her as much as hav-

423

ing a talent for statistics, or having met Yonatan and lived with him for nearly thirty years, being married to an Israeli, having two sons, sons instead of daughters, being chosen for the grant that has shaped her work for a decade or more. Of course what happened, happened to her. She thinks of the word "her," and it buzzes around her head, turning meaningless. Her is me. But her is not me. Her is not this woman, standing here in this dim light on an afternoon in Rome, looking at a man whose life has, far more than hers, been marked by suffering.

She sees him sitting, his head in his hand, as the light thickens around him. And she cannot feel anything but sorrow.

"We're close to November now," she says, "the early end of light."

She sits beside him and the streetlamps, art nouveau, that flank the road turn gradually pink, then yellow, then a yellow-white.

"Time to go," he says. "My daughter."

"Yes. And so you see it is the right thing to have no regrets."

"Tomorrow I would like to bring you to the one place I can mourn my wife."

His voice is strange to her; it is not his own. He is speaking and not speaking to her. What he has said about his son has emptied him of something. The flatness of his tone is, she understands, a substitute for weeping. Tears, though, would have brought relief; the emptying would be a kind of cleansing. The dryness in his voice alarms her; it can lead to nothing.

They are terrible words, those words "the one place I can mourn my wife," and she can only guess the effort it has taken him over the years to say them. To say them in a tone that comes close to the ordinary. To say them in a way that has anything at all to do with the way he said, "We'll go see the paintings of Caravaggio, the view of Rome from the orange garden."

They agree to meet in the morning at the top of the Capitoline Hill.

TUESDAY, OCTOBER 30

THE CAPITOLINE,
THE MEDUSA
"The One Place I Can Mourn My
Wife"

She climbs the many shallow steps, her eye
on a huge equestrian statue, Marcus Aurelius, colossally astride the universe as he is
colossally astride his horse. The horse, free
of the responsibility of rule, seems far more
eager than his rider. At the far end of the
piazza, two reclining gods, meant to indicate
the Tiber and the Nile, hold what she tells
herself can't be gigantic penises: they must
be some fertility symbol, she tells herself.
On the other hand, they do seem quite
relaxed, much more relaxed than the emperor or the stone twins, the Dioscuri, flanking the staircase: the emperor, the twins, so
tense with the responsibilities of empire.

  She worries that the steps were difficult

for Adam and wonders if he arrived before her so she wouldn't have to observe his effort. She tells herself that the steps are shallow, the climb gradual. He stands between the stone twins, his hand shielding his eyes from the pure Roman sun, which, unlike yesterday, is now doing its good work of plain illumination. It bleaches the stones pure white; it nourishes the pinks and yellows of the neighboring walls. All possibility of cloudiness has long ago been burned away.

He nods to her, and even this greeting, she sees, is difficult for him to give. She doesn't know what he wants to show her.

Taking her hand, he nearly pulls her along, and in the pressure on her wrist she hears, *Not this, not that, don't stop don't look at that, it isn't what we're here for.*

She is swept past rooms painted from floor to ceiling with the story of the Roman victory over the Etruscans. As they pass through the room devoted to the statue of the she wolf who suckled Romulus and Remus, he tightens his grip, annoyed at the knot of schoolchildren and their earnest teacher who explains the origins of the city of their birth.

"Just here," he says, a moment after. They

427

stop before a marble head. Bernini's *Medusa.*

He drops her hand and moves apart from her. She is uneasy being even this close to him. She feels like an intruder.

Her eye falls on the statue's parted lips. Open — in anguish, or exhaustion? The blank eyes finished, overwhelmed. The snakes that are her hair are by contrast lively and amused. Their mouths are making hissing jokes. They are where they belong.

Miranda is afraid to say a word.

"She looks so miserable," he says. "In the stories of the Medusa, the focus is never on her, what she might be suffering with a headful of snakes, her own horror at what becomes of people at the sight of her, at the sight of what she can't help but be. I look at the snakes now as a kind of excess of vitality. Too much life for her, and there's not a thing she can do about it. So I stand here and say to Beverly: I'm sorry. I feared you. I resented you. I couldn't love you. I was turned to stone."

She knows that what she says will not be of the slightest use, and yet she feels that she must say it.

"You know, of course, that it wasn't your fault. It was an illness."

She looks up at the suffering face. The

face of marble. And Adam's face, a suffering face of flesh and bone and blood. She thinks: For years that woman whose name I have not even been able to pronounce, this woman, Adam's wife, whom I could think of only as the one for whom I was betrayed, the one who stole my hopefulness, my innocence, that woman was someone I felt free to hate. Felt free to say I hated. And so I felt free to be a person who says the words "I hate." This woman whose death I did not mourn. Whose suicide meant nothing to me but a kind of bitter satisfaction. Grim, the satisfaction, nevertheless satisfaction is what it must be called. This woman whose suffering I would not credit, called manipulation, a thief's sleight of hand.

And looking at the statue's empty ruined eyes, the desperate mouth, and Adam's posture, hands at his sides, spine rigid, she weeps as he cannot for the poor destroyed creature who brought in her wake such damage, such harm.

"You know this is Costanza, of the ruined face," he says.

Is he expecting her to say something? Some reiteration of her earlier outrage, a rekindling of the Galleria Borghese coals? Some reassertion that all Bernini's art was not worth one drop of her blood? She can't bring her mind to such considerations now. She is thinking of something else. Something terrible she did. Or didn't do. The harm inflicted on a woman dead three hundred years ago now seems, in comparison, a distant, an invisible horizon.

"I need to tell you something I should have told you long ago," she says. "Can we go somewhere we can talk?"

"There's a nice café here, it's usually quiet."

They pass the original Marcus Aurelius on his horse (the one in the piazza, it turns out, is a copy: this one is kept indoors out of the weather), gentler somehow in the modern room newly designed for it. The emperor is domesticated here, made kinder by his place among the disembodied heads, each ten feet high, surrounding him. They pass Etruscans, calm, reclining on their tombs. Peaceful. Connubial.

At the end of a series of corridors, flanked by showcases they ignore, they come to the café. The room itself is full of light, and it opens onto a terrace bordered by dwarf trees in terra-cotta pots, and a balustrade upon which one can lean to see the whole of Rome.

"Shall I get two coffees?" he says.

She nods, although she doesn't at all want

a coffee.

She walks inside and sits at a table below a blown-up black-and-white photo of a fragment of a sculpture. The high small breasts of a young girl, her torso, the beginnings of her sex. The girl cups one breast, coyly half concealing a ripe nipple, and with the other half hides her crotch. Miranda feels, to her distress, aroused. Crawling, or climbing up the surface of her skin: a moving heat. She hopes that she shows nothing. She thinks of the term "hectic flush." She doesn't want to be sitting with Adam feeling these sensations, which she tells herself are no more meaningful than sweat. You can't, she tells herself, be responsible for your arousal. You can be responsible for what you do afterward. But she cannot convince herself.

How can this be happening at this moment, when she must confess one of the worst things she has ever done, and why is the sight of a teasing adolescent girl the cause of something she would do anything rather than experience right now? She has just listened to a man speak of the failure of love, of madness, of self-inflicted death. She must reveal her own transgression. And now she is aroused. She knows that if Yonatan were here, they could turn her surprising arousal into a sexy joke, a kind of foreplay.

They could walk out of this bright morning light into the perpetual twilight of the Via Margutta flat, pull back the heavy coverlet, and make joyful easygoing love between the cool expensive sheets. But she is not with Yonatan now, not with her husband, but with Adam, her first love. With whom sex could never have anything about it of a joke.

They had given each other their virginity at a time when the word had weight. A solemn word, an ancient concept. For them, being lovers stood for leaving home. Too young, too inexpert, they couldn't make a place for play. There were no words for what they did but "making love." They said "making," but they believed they had invented something.

She must pull herself out of this. She must stand in a cold place, an open place, the space of penitence, atonement.

"As I said, I have to tell you something."

He meets her eye for the first time that day.

"Probably you don't really have to tell me at all."

"I do, Adam, because for years I have allowed you to think of yourself in relation to me as the betrayer. But in fact I betrayed you first. I slept with Toby Winthrop long before you slept with Beverly. During the

Cambodian demonstrations, when you were home sick. He made me feel it was a kind of cowardice not to do it. Right afterward, I was hard on myself. But I convinced myself that telling you would only make things worse. I felt I'd be asking your forgiveness for something I knew was unforgivable."

"I have no place in my thoughts anymore for the category 'unforgivable.' "

"And yet I feel you must forgive me."

"Me? I forgive you? It is I who need forgiveness."

"Oh, Adam, we were both so young. And it seems, as we are here, living as we've lived, entirely beside the point."

"The point?"

"The point is: we have had our lives. The point is: we are here."

They take each other's hands.

And then it enters, thickening itself against the background of the old trees and the domes and campaniles. Desire. They could once again be lovers. It would not be difficult. It would, in some way, be the most natural thing.

Something happens to the both of them. They are taken up, taken out, taken away. They are in their bodies, they are in this café, they are in this moment in late October in the year 2007, and yet they are somewhere else entirely. In younger bodies, other places, walking on streets, dancing, swimming, freezing in winter, sweltering in summer, climbing stairs, sitting at desks or tables. Not these tables. And yet these tables, yes. They have both been taken up, they are both somewhere that is not in their present bodies, but they are experiencing it differently.

He is watching himself from a great distance, himself or not himself, it could be the corpse that was himself, or someone who had never been born who has his name, but the name has no meaning. He — and who is he — he knows it is himself, one to whom the word "I" would properly be applied, and he uses the word, for lack of any other, but it has no meaning. He hears a whirring; he senses a darkness. Then on a screen: images that change too quickly for interpretation. He is everything in the room. He is the room, the darkness, the hot light of the projector, the smoke that rises up before the light, the beam of light that makes the images, the screen. The images, of course, they are images of him and of Miranda. But they will not stand still. They are their present selves and their past selves. Impossible to say: which is the real one. On which should I depend.

Then he hears a snap. The film has broken. The lights are turned on; the darkness vanishes.

She hears not a whirring but a rushing. It is a sound she heard when she was the closest she has ever come to death.

She was with Yonatan on a holiday in New Mexico. They had been warned by the owner of their bed-and-breakfast to pay attention if they saw a sign on the highway that said WARNING: DIP. The warning was about what could happen in the arroyos, which, he said, pedantically, you may or may not know is the Spanish word for ditch.

Perhaps it was his pedantry, perhaps it was the fact that Yonatan, who had come of age in the Israeli army, was constitutionally unable to take seriously the warnings of people he did not think of as "experts." He was always sure that people were "overreacting," "paranoid," "afraid of their own shadows." She, too, was suspicious of what she perceived as the excessive timidity of many of their friends, particularly in relation to their children. They talked about the American obsession to create for children what Yonatan called "a shockproof world." When she relived that day, though, she was always grateful that the children had not been with them.

They'd been told that if they saw even a cupful of water in an arroyo near the sign WARNING: DIP, they should turn back immediately. You think there's no problem because the sky is blue, no sign of rain, but it's not about the rain you can see, it's about the rain in the mountains. "Terrifying things can happen in a matter of seconds. I mean seconds," the annoying bed-and-breakfast host had said. "So, you take my word you see even a cupful of water in one of those suckers, you turn back."

It was a sunny day, and they saw the water. "Do you think it's a cupful or half a cup?" Yonatan said. "No more than three-quarters," Miranda responded. But suddenly, the arroyo was filling, and they couldn't stop fast enough. They put on their brakes and skidded right into the middle of the dip. They were only there a few seconds when the wall of water hit them. They rolled up the windows. Just as they did, the car was picked up, turned around, carried down the arroyo for a quarter mile; they could hear large boulders bouncing in the water close to them; they thought they were going to be dumped into the Rio Grande, which was only another quarter of a mile away.

But somehow the car got stopped by a rock too large to have been moved by the water. And they sat in the car, pressed up against the boulder, the water going over the top of the roof. Then as always happens in an arroyo, the wave lasted only a moment or so. The water dropped; they were able to open the window. They sat there until the water was down to almost nothing, which it was in a few minutes, and they walked away. Trembling, they held each other and then laughed; they said they shouldn't be allowed out in the world unsupervised, that they'd never tell the host that he'd been right, they should have listened.

As Adam was everything in the dark room, Miranda is everything in the arroyo: the dry ditch suddenly filling up, the car picked up and carried, her terror, her husband's terror, her relief. She remembers something else about the water in an arroyo. What quickly becomes a gushing stream began by only little fingerlings of water. They collected and became something enormous, something dangerous and powerful. But if she had listened to the conventional wisdom, she would have been quite safe.

Had she known all along that seeing Adam was putting herself at risk? The risk, she had thought, was reliving her sorrow. It had never occurred to her that the risk might be to her fidelity, the hard-won peace of a shared life. But she had not been honest with herself: the flirty conversations, the accidental or only tender brushing of hands or arms. Had she always known what she was doing? Had she wanted this all along?

And what, she asks herself, now, does she want?

Whatever has taken them up has, at the same moment, released them. They are back in their bodies, back in the present moment of their present lives.

What do I want? Adam asks himself. He remembers a therapist asking him once, "When you say you want sex, what is it that you really want?"

His eye falls on Miranda, the sprinkling of freckles on her downy forearm, the airy sharpness of her scent — expensive, probably, no longer the innocent demotic scent of Breck shampoo, the lightness she has never lost. She is a lovely woman, he thinks. This is a woman I would like to take in my arms. He castigates himself for not allowing himself to say what he really means: into my bed.

What do you want, what do you want? Miranda sees the words, black letters against a white sky. Should I? Should we? The

438

words form a question, and the question mark shimmers beside them, glimmering like a hook.

She is exactly where she is: in the body of a woman nearing sixty, at high noon in a public place where people who seem to value the great art of the past are paying much too much for what they eat and drink. The noise is not the noise of the flood in the arroyo; it's the cappuccino machine, providing milky comfort for the well-, or relatively well-, to-do. The boulder that stopped the car in the arroyo has placed itself squarely in her path. She won't do it. She won't put herself, her long complicated marriage, in danger. She won't do it simply because there is a question of her doing it or not doing it. Because the grammatical mood of her desire came to her in the interrogative. Should I? What do I want? Or the subjunctive: what if.

The answer to the question is no for the precise reason that the question came to her in the form of a question. It came to her in the form of a question. It came to her as a question because she is, she knows, no longer young. She is able to form a question because she is far from the inexorability of young desire. What came to her, what took her up, took her away, was certainly desire. But desire without urgency. Desire that could be refused, cast aside, ignored.

Able to calculate in this way, able to imagine these terms, she knows the act would lose its innocence. It would be an act of the mind. Cold. Without the warm lovely freshness that makes of desire a desirable thing. She thinks of the couple on the bench at the Villa Borghese of whom Adam said contemptuously, "They were practically fucking in front of everybody." But they, she thinks, were innocent. We would not be. She looks at Adam's forearms, and the beautiful dark hair that covers them. She looks at his hands, the same hands she first loved at sixteen. She remembers that he was the first male person of whom she used the word "beautiful." She finds him beautiful still. But she will not make this cut into the crust of the firm earth she walks on. She will build a bridge over the arroyo. A construction for safe conduct. They will not be swallowed up.

He is no longer in the dark room. The light has been switched on; at once a relief and a sadness to him. He will not do it; he will not hurt Clare; he will not have to face the dreadful encounter with Lucy, cooking her supper, having just betrayed her mother. Something has been lost, and yet, he thinks he has been saved. At least from an error in category. He's been saved from the unseemly error, made by so many men, even great men, of a certain age: the error of confusing desire with a fear of death. She is a lovely woman. But did he want to make love to her because she is a lovely woman, or as a way of denying the loop of time? And whom would he be making love to, who would be the real object of his desire? The lovely woman, nearly sixty now, the girl she was, whom he had wounded? Or his own young self, his youth, forever in the past? The past is past, and it is not recoverable. In the present, as they are, pledged to other people, it is right that they no longer know themselves as lovers.

She is a lovely woman and he doesn't want to say to her, *I do desire you, but not enough to warrant the complications it would create for my life.* This is, he knows, a brutal sentence. He sends up a prayer to the impervious Roman gods: *Please make her understand that we must not speak of this. Please ensure her silence.*

His prayer is heard. They walk outside, into the bright air. They unclasp their hands, and then, arm in arm, they circle the terrace, taking it all in: Rome, about which everything important certainly has already been said. She puts her head, companion-

441

ably, on his shoulder.

Between them, there are no words.

WEDNESDAY, OCTOBER 31

THE VILLA BORGHESE
"Any Minute Now That Man Will Insist
That
You Buy Me a Rose"

Her plane will leave at 6:00 p.m., the flight will be long, twelve hours, and she knows that it is a good thing for her to take a real walk before; she has learned this helps with jet lag. So she suggests that on their last day they arrive at the park early and walk from one end to the other: from the Pincio to the Galleria and then back.

They approach the fountain of the Cavalli Marini, cheerful horses, lounging, supporting on their heads the bowl of the fountain, their manes sluiced by its streaming jets. She dips her hands in the water; the early morning chill pleases and saddens her: it is the end of something.

And as she is staring at the cheerful

marble horses, a truck approaches. She can see horses' heads pushing their way out of the truck's opening. Three policemen jump out, let down the back, and push a lever that releases a metal ramp. And like a joke in a dream, a joke that the dreamer can't quite comprehend, they lead to the horse fountain five real horses. Elegantly, extravagantly uniformed, their knee-high boots gleaming like the horses' hides, their brass buttons, professionally brushed and polished, the handsome young policemen lead the horses to the water. Their shining flanks, black, gray, and chestnut, shine in the sun. Hard to believe, she thinks, this brilliance can be natural. And the horses drink from the fountain of the horses, and she takes Adam's hand and says, "Isn't this wonderful? Isn't this just a lovely piece of luck."

The policemen mount their horses and trot or canter away. It is as if they had never been there, as if they had dreamed it all.

She can see that he is too downcast to enjoy it. But despite himself, the horses' cantering, their insistence on their own liveliness, engage him, and she can feel his spirits lift. They walk into a little bower where they can hear a smaller fountain. The light falls through the trees, blurred shafts of whiteness that transform, when they reach the water in the fountain's bowl, into dazzling lozenges that blink and shimmer.

Adam and Miranda sit down on a bench and listen to the water.

A man with copper-colored skin and a mustache like a dirty toothbrush and a comical hat, like an organ-grinder's, the kind of hat no one wears anymore, saunters toward them, as if he had no real purpose in his walk.

He is holding roses wrapped in white paper. The leafy light falls on the paper, revealing the roses as he walks unsteadily, crabwise, only partially in their direction.

"Any minute now that man will insist that you buy me a rose," Miranda says.

"And what shall I do about it? What should I do?"

"I think you should buy one."

"I think I should not, that I should tell him to go away."

"Why?"

"For so many reasons."

"Which reasons."

"It's a ridiculous way to make a living. It shouldn't be encouraged."

"Make a living. Why is a living something we should have to make?"

445

"The flowers aren't fresh. They're wilting."

"If you tell him to go away, he won't decide to change his life. He will only be a little more unhappy. If you tell him to go away, where will he go?"

"That probably can't be imagined by the likes of us. We don't even know where he's from."

"East Africa. Some part of India. One of the new Russian republics."

"We can't begin to understand where he comes from. Or what he hopes for."

"Doesn't everybody hope for the same thing?"

"Perhaps he hopes more than anything for a very large car. Or to play on a soccer team, or in a band. Perhaps he dances beautifully, a dance no one here knows the steps of or the name for. Or perhaps he wakes up every night screaming because of the horrors he's seen."

"Then shouldn't you give him a few euros for a rose?"

"No, it would be giving a false sign."

"Of what? To whom?"

"To everyone here who'd see us. And on our last day, it would be, well, another kind of wrong sign. A sign that we are something we are not."

"And what are we? Who are we?"

"I am Adam. You are Miranda."

"And we have always been. Doesn't that rate a flower?"

"We aren't who we were," he says.

"Who are we, then?"

"People who haven't seen each other for more than half our lives. People who walk in a park together, eat meals together, enjoy the streets or the art, for an hour at a time, for a week or two, then go back to being who we were."

"And how will we think of this? Of who we were in these days, which are as real as any other days, after all, any other days that we have lived. We haven't made them up," Miranda says.

"Except, in a way, we have. Here we're not in the world."

"Where are we, then?"

"Some dream, someplace, I don't know what to call it."

"Flower, mister, buy a flower. Very pretty. And the lady, very pretty. Nice."

"Take this," Adam says, handing the man a five-euro note. "But no flower."

The man nods his head conveying nothing, everything. He lays a flower on the bench. He runs away, as if he's afraid they'll chase him.

"Just leave it here, then," Miranda says. "Someone will find it and take it as a good sign. A sign of good luck. For our part, we have both been lucky."

She takes his hand. "It's time to go," she says.

They walk out to the road. "Stand here, Adam, just stand here. It will be easier for me to remember if I can remember other things. You against this pale sky, the red, or is it purple, of these leaves. And the silly palms, and the yellow of the plane trees. And the building, and the heads of all those poets, or whoever they are that made someone think they deserved to be remembered. By the likes of us."

"I can't leave the flower back there on that bench. It seems a heartless gesture."

"And if you give it to me, if I take it, what kind of gesture would that be?"

"I'm afraid it might be obvious. And sentimental."

"We say 'obvious' and 'sentimental' because many people have done it before us. But perhaps that's a good thing. So let's say it's an obvious gesture, a sentimental gesture. Something that many people have already done. Couldn't we say it's another kind of gesture as well. Perhaps, a grateful one."

"Grateful? To whom?"

"This light," she says, spreading her arms. "These trees."

"Oh, yes, I see," he says. "These trees. This light."

ABOUT THE AUTHOR

Mary Gordon is the author of six previous novels, including *Final Payments, Spending,* and *Pearl;* the memoirs *The Shadow Man* and *Circling My Mother; The Stories of Mary Gordon* (winner of the Story Prize); and the recent nonfiction work *Reading Jesus.* She has received many honors, among them a Lila Wallace–Reader's Digest Writers' Award, a Guggenheim Fellowship, the 1997 O. Henry Award for Best Story, and an Academy Award for Literature from the American Academy of Arts and Letters. She teaches at Barnard College and lives in New York City.

The employees of Thorndike Press hope you have enjoyed this Large Print book. All our Thorndike, Wheeler, and Kennebec Large Print titles are designed for easy reading, and all our books are made to last. Other Thorndike Press Large Print books are available at your library, through selected bookstores, or directly from us.

For information about titles, please call:
(800) 223-1244

or visit our Web site at:
http://gale.cengage.com/thorndike

To share your comments, please write:
Publisher
Thorndike Press
10 Water St., Suite 310
Waterville, ME 04901